All Creatures Dark and Dangerous

All Creatures Dark and Dangerous

DOUG ALLYN

Crippen & Landru Publishers
Norfolk, Virginia
1999

For James Allen
Agent Extraordinaire, who has sold everything
I've ever written, an accomplishment that says
more about his talents than mine.

Contents

Introduction

The first thing people ask writers at conferences or cocktail parties is, "where do your ideas come from?" It's not always an easy question. But if we're talking about the David Westbrook stories, it's a snap. You see, I was raised by dogs.

I'm only half-kidding. My family always had dogs about, mostly German Shorthaired Pointers, a quirky breed. Perhaps you recall a dog taking a dump on national television during a Westminster Kennel Club show? A German Shorthair, naturally. No doubt expressing her opinion of the proceedings.

The summer I was sixteen, Donda, my mom's Shorthair bitch, had a litter of ten pups, a rare occurrence. Four to six is normal. Ten were far too many.

The first pups came easily, but by the fifth or sixth the dog was so exhausted she couldn't push anymore. A pup lodged in the birth canal and we were very close to losing both the mother and her pups.

Fortunately, my stepfather was a doctor. After laving his hands in a bowl of warm, soapy water he knelt by Donda, murmuring in low tones, then gently probed inside to help ease that sixth pup into the light.

The birthing continued for hours, until midnight or so. I watched from the steps. My dad's specialty was cardiology. Needless to say, I'd never actually watched him ply his trade before. It was a revelation.

He was so patient, so caring. It was my first glimpse of his soul. He was a WWII vet and men of his generation didn't talk much. Watching him help with Donda's birthing told me more about him than years of conversation could have.

Over the next weeks, the pups took over our lives. Donda couldn't nurse all ten, so we fed them by hand with little baby bottles, tiny, rat-sized beings with closed eyes.

They suckled voraciously, then fell back to sleep in our hands. And they dreamed. In their sleep, they ran. Little legs pumping, their blind eyes twitching, seeking . . . what?

They were not wholly in our world yet. Their eyes were still closed and they'd never taken a step. So what were they chasing in those dreams? They had no images from our world to populate their visions. Their memories could only be of the place they came from.

My mother joked that they were still seeing Puppyland, a faraway place of green hills and lush plains where they could run free. The hereafter? No. The herebefore.

By midsummer the pups weighed fifty pounds apiece, speckled, bundles of energy, bright-eyed and eager. They needed room to run.

And so, with my new driver's license warm in my wallet, I would load them in my mom's station wagon and drive them to the old family farm.

Where something very odd occurred. When the pups were released into this new territory, they didn't frolic about the way they did at home. Instead, they intuitively formed a hunting pack. With their mother and an old Labrador Retriever named Smoky Joe at its center, our lovable, impetuous puppies became a feral army.

Scouts took the lead as they ran, crisscrossing each other in front of the main body, noses down, effectively covering every inch of ground, seeking scent.

As the scouts tired, they would rejoin the pack and others would range out, never more than three. And God help any critter they spotted in the open.

With no training of any kind, they instinctively hunted with near Prussian precision. They'd never known hunger so the hunt wasn't really about food. Something much older and stronger was at work. They were clearly enjoying themselves, doing what they were put on this earth to do. And they arrived here knowing how to do it.

Dogs have complex instincts and intuitions we're scarcely aware of, and they're the open books of the pet kingdom. Cats don't even pretend to share their secrets. All Creatures have their Dark and Dangerous side. Humans most of all.

I learned much from our hounds that summer, about loyalty, and tenacity and enjoying life and living it to the limit. So in a sense, I was raised by dogs.

As many of us are. Most of us learned from animals as kids and if we're lucky we never stop learning. Gary Larson of *The Far Side* fame admits he judges people by the way they react to his dog. Haven't you done the same?

Naive? Not at all. A person who's uncivil to animals . . . Need I say more?

Of the sixty short stories and novels I've published to date, the *All Creatures Dark and Dangerous* stories are among my favorites. And with readers as well. Two of them have won Ellery Queen Readers Awards and others have fared very well in that competition.

I especially want to thank one of my best friends, Dr. David Lavigne, DVM who generously helped to keep the medical details accurate, as well as Dr. Thomas Hanzek who also consulted.

If you have half as much fun reading these tales as I had writing them, you're in for a treat.

Doug Allyn
Montrose, Michigan
February 1999

Franken Kat

There wasn't much blood. As David sliced open the hound's hip, a thin red line trickled down the incision into the drain of the stainless steel surgery table, but the gush of crimson that should have pulsed out of an eight inch wound didn't occur. Edema was already restricting the circulation to the leg.

"Damn," he said softly.

Bettina glanced up at him, her pale blue eyes unreadable above the surgical mask. "It's worse than we thought, isn't it?"

"Welcome to the wide world of surgery," David said, nodding.

"On the x-ray, it looked like the femur was in three pieces, a serious break, but repairable. What we've actually got is a shattered bone, twenty little pieces, maybe more."

"Will you have to amputate?"

"Maybe," David said grimly, "but not today. The hip socket seems to be in good shape. I'm going to start removing the chips. I want you to scrape them and recover every bit of cancellous bone, the spongy stuff inside of the marrow cavity. I think I can shift the larger bone fragments around and reduce the pieces into a usable femur. Then we'll use cancellous bone to fill the gaps, like putty."

"Will she be crippled?"

"Hard to say. This leg will be shorter than the others, but she's slightly built, only forty-five pounds and a year old with a lot of growing to do. With luck, she'll make a good recovery and her gait might not be affected all that much. But we've got to—"

The telephone gurgled. Bettina quickly lifted it off its cradle and switched it to speaker. "Westbrook Veterinary Clinic."

"Bettina? Is David available?"

"I'm busy, Yvonne," David yelled at the phone as he lifted a bone chip out of the incision with his forceps. "What is it?"

"There's a man here, asking about a handyman's job. He said George Coontz sent him."

"I told George you wanted somebody for the summer," David

acknowledged, "but I'm in surgery now. You'll have to handle it."

"What am I supposed to do, look him over?"

"You can see well enough to count his arms and legs," David snapped. "If he's got two of each and wants to work, hire him. I really can't talk now."

The bang of the phone being slammed down came clearly over the speaker. "Sorry," Bettina said, "I should have switched the machine on."

"You're fired," David said. "Never darken my clinic doormat again."

"Yeah, right," Bettina said. "Would you like some music while you operate?"

"Better make it Mozart," David sighed. "We're going to have a long afternoon."

∗ ∗ ∗

It was nearly dusk when David eased his Jeep to a halt in the brick-topped parking area at the rear of the estate. He sat there a moment, drinking in the scent of the ancient lilac trees that shaded the rambling Tudor house, letting the tension of the day roll away. He shook his head to clear it, then climbed out and started toward the back door. A figure stepped out of the shadow of the garage, blocking his path.

"Somethin' I can help you with, buddy?"

"That depends," David said. "Who are you?"

"I'm Greg Malley. I work here."

"Good for you. I'm Dr. Westbrook. I live here."

"You're the doctor?" Malley said doubtfully, eyeing David's battered Jeep, scuffed jeans and faded flannel shirt.

"I'm afraid so," David said, offering his hand. "Don't look so surprised. Not all vets wear hospital whites or drive Cadillacs."

"Sorry, I guess I thought you'd be a little older," Malley said. His grip was firm, but not pushy. He was half a head taller than David, with broad shoulders and blond, close cropped hair. He was wearing a fitted chambray shirt and pressed khaki slacks with a knife-edge crease. His face was lean and chiseled, with wide set gray eyes. Not male-model handsome, but not far from it.

"You're looking for yard work?" David asked curiously. "Keeping the stables clean, feeding the horses, whatever?"

"I'm looking for steady work that keeps me outside. This job suits me fine, if it's okay with you."

"It's my wife's house, it's her decision," David said with a shrug. "As long as the work gets done, we'll get along fine."

"There is one thing, Doc," Malley said. "I've, ah, been away from Algoma for awhile and I don't have a place to stay. Your missus said it'd be okay if I moved into the servant's quarters over the garage till I can get a place of my own. She said I should check with you first."

"It's fine by me," David said. "The rent'll be a hundred and fifty a week, though."

"A hundred—?"

"I'm kidding, Greg," David said dryly. "I kid a lot. Sorry about that. Crash as long as you like. You'll find blankets in the cedar chest at the foot of the bed. Oh, one friendly word of advice? Don't tell Yvonne you expected me to be Marcus Welby M.D. She's a few years older than I am and she's a tad touchy about it."

"No problem," Malley said, glancing around, noting the contrast between David's battered Jeep and the immaculate Tudor home and three car garage. "I understand."

"I doubt that," David said. "But it doesn't matter. Make yourself at home. See you around."

He trotted up the back steps, pulled off his dusty wellington boots inside the kitchen door, then padded through the house in his socks. "Yvonne?"

"Out here," she called. He followed the sound of her voice through the kitchen to the dining room. And stopped. The table was draped in white linen and with place settings for four. Damn. He continued on through the french doors that opened onto the elaborate redwood deck that overlooked the grounds. Yvonne was dressed for dinner, white slacks, heels, a turquoise Armani blouse, and pearls, her dark hair coifed to perfection. And she wasn't alone. Vernon and Louise Beck, old family friends of Yvonne's with the accent on old were seated at a canopied table on the deck.

Double damn.

"You're late," Yvonne said brightly, offering her cheek for his kiss, "but you're forgiven. By the time you've changed I'll have delmonico steaks on the grill, a salad awaiting your delicate touch, and Vernon's ordered a spectacular sunset to go with dinner. Now hurry up."

"Actually, I'm going to have to pass on dinner," he said, waving hello at Vernon and Louise over her shoulder. "Can I see you in the dining room a second?" Her smile was fading as she followed him in. It was gone when he turned to face her.

"Honey, I'm sorry as hell, but I've got to get back to the clinic. I've got a shorthaired pointer bitch with a smashed hind leg. I'll have to spend the night."

"But, David, we have guests."

"All the better. At least you won't be lonely. Besides, listening to Vern drone on about the bond market's the conversational equivalent of a Thorazine overdose for me. I'd just nod out, topple into the salad and embarrass you anyway. Make my apologies, okay? I just came home to shower and grab a sandwich. Is there any coffee?"

"No," she said, "but I'll make—dammit, David, you could have called."

"I know, but the break was a lot worse than I expected and the surgery ran long. I don't want to lose the dog."

"Can't Bettina stay with her and call you here if anything goes wrong?"

"Bettina's a good assistant, but she's only a veterinary tech. If anything serious developed the dog could die in the twenty minutes it'd take me to get there. Sorry, but I'm elected."

"David, this must be the fourth or fifth time in the past couple of weeks."

"Is it? Great, business must finally be picking up. Look, I've really gotta go. Coffee?"

"It'll be ready. But, David, we need to talk about this."

"Honey, we have talked about it. I know we've had a rough few years but as soon as the clinic gets a little better established I can take on a partner, and—"

"You can take on a partner now, and you know it. We can afford it."

"You mean you can afford it," David said coolly. "I can't, and the clinic can't. Not yet, anyway."

"And if it never can?"

"Thanks for the vote of confidence."

"This isn't about confidence, it's about reality. The reality is,

Algoma may be too small to support a full time veterinary clinic. I don't think it's fair to put our lives on hold while we wait for business to pick up. It's been nearly four years."

"You're kidding. My, but time flies when you're having fun. Or aren't you having fun?"

"Of course I am, when we're together. But lately you're at the clinic at all hours—"

"Yvonne, I'm sorry but I don't have time for this now. Let's leave it until the weekend."

"You're attending an orthopedics seminar in Chicago this weekend."

"Then we'll talk when I get back, okay?" he snapped. "Look, I'm not putting you off, but I really have to go."

"David, I want to have a child."

That stopped him. "Then I guess we really do have to talk," he said, turning to face her. "This is kind of sudden, isn't it?"

"It wouldn't be if we'd had more than a ten minute conversation in the past few weeks."

"Touché. But I thought you wanted to wait awhile."

"I did. I was hoping my vision might improve, but . . . Dammit, David, I'm thirty-seven. I want to get on with the rest of our life. If we're going to have one together."

"Whoa, that sounds ominous. What does that mean, exactly?"

"That sometimes I have the feeling that you're just passing time here, waiting to go. We're living in my home, and everything you own could still fit into a cardboard box you could toss in the back of your Jeep."

"So I'm not into owning things. I was broke in college. I guess I never got out of the mindset. Nor do I want to, particularly. Look, I know that makes me a square peg in your social circle, but . . . Ah hell, to be continued, okay? Make my apologies to Vern and Louise. I'm outa here."

He tried to kiss her cheek but she turned away. "I'll call you from the clinic."

"Don't bother," she said. "I think I'll retire early."

"Suit yourself. But call me if you want to talk. And babe, if you do decide to have a kid, don't start without me, okay? I've seen your new handyman. I admit he's a major hunk, but he's also a blond. I'd recognize his offspring in a heartbeat."

"You know, there are some things you shouldn't joke about."

"Who's joking?" he said.

He loped upstairs, changed into clean faded jeans and a scruffy Michigan State sweatshirt, then trotted back out to his Jeep. Malley was coming down the outside stairway of the garage apartment. David noted that his spotless shirt and slacks looked like they'd been tailor made. He gunned the jeep across the drive and pulled up at the foot of the stairs.

"Did you find everything all right?"

"All set, Doc." Malley nodded. "I was just gonna start cleaning the stables, unless there was somethin' else you wanted me to do."

"Nope. Whatever Yvonne tells you is job one. I'll be working late tonight, so keep an eye on things, okay? By the way, are you a light sleeper, Greg?"

"Not really, why?"

"Good. My wife is. And as you probably noticed, her vision's slightly impaired. And the thing is, when I'm gone, she sleeps with a gun under her pillow."

"You don't say? But if she doesn't see very well, how does she know what to shoot at?"

"It's a nine millimeter automatic. Fourteen rounds. She doesn't have to see very well."

"Point taken," Greg said, with a easy grin. "Don't worry, Doc, I don't sleepwalk. And anybody who does is gonna have to go through me. Which isn't so easy to do."

"Glad to hear it. I'll see you tomorrow."

"Oh, Doc, there is one thing. I saw a kind of . . . weird animal back of the garage."

"Weird? You mean like a three legged cat with an eye and an ear missing?"

"Coulda been, I guess. I chucked a rock at it."

David's knuckles went white on the steering wheel. "Did you hit it?"

"No, just spooked it off, is all."

"Good," David said, relaxing slightly. "Look, Mr. Malley, we'd better get on the same page on one thing. I'm a veterinarian. Simply put, I fix broken critters. So I'd really appreciate it if you don't toss any more rocks at any more animals around here. Understood?"

"Sure, Doc, whatever you say. Sorry, I just didn't know what it was."

"Next time, just ask. That was Franken Kat."

"It was what?"

"Not it; she. Her name's Franken Kat, you know, like the movie monster, cat version. She's an old patient of mine. And if you think she looks bad now, you should have seen her before."

"What happened to her?"

"I don't know, she was a stray I found by the side of the road all ripped up. Probably got run over. Took me months, off and on, to put her back together."

"You spent all that time workin' on a stray?" Greg asked curiously. "Why? I mean, nobody's payin' you, right? And what good's a three-legged cat anyway?"

"Hey, she's a terrific mouser. She can't catch anybody but she spooks the hell out of 'em and they change neighborhoods. Be nice to her, Greg, she's had a tough life."

"So who hasn't?" Malley said.

✳ ✳ ✳

Bettina was sprawled across the cheap vinyl couch in the waiting room reading a back issue of *Veterinary Forum* when David walked in. She'd unpinned her hair, and it hung tawny and loose about her shoulders.

"Hi, how's our patient?"

"Stable," Bettina said, swinging her long legs off the couch and stretching. "Her temperature's slightly elevated, a hundred and three. Her eyes are open, but she hasn't tried to move yet."

"The atropine and acepromazine won't wear off completely for a few hours. I expect she'll have a pretty subdued night. You can take off. Thanks for waiting."

"I'm in no hurry. I thought I'd send out for a pizza and eat dinner here. In case our patient acts up."

"Ummm, that's probably not a good idea. I'll be gone all weekend at that seminar and you have to pull extra duty then. Escape while you can."

"I don't mind spending extra time here, as long as you're here, David. What do you want on your pizza?"

"I'll pass, thanks. Have to watch my waistline. Especially now that my wife just hired a handyman who could do ads for Jockey shorts. His name's Greg Malley. Do you know him?"

"Greg? Sure. He was a couple of years ahead of me in high school. Hot stuff, or at least he was then. As nearsighted as Yvonne is, I wonder how she checked his qualifications? By touch?"

"I presume he gave references."

"From whom? His parole officer? As I recall, Greg was a pretty wild child."

"Are you serious? You think he might be an ex-convict?"

"No, not really. He always was a bit of a hardcase, though. Drank too much, ran with a rough crowd. I doubt he ever went to jail for anything. Too smart for that. Cadillac eyes, you know?"

"What kind of eyes?"

"Cadillac eyes. It's an old local saying, Indian, I think. Cadillac eyes, pony money? It means a guy who has big ideas but not much else."

"It's not a compliment, then?"

"Hardly. I'm surprised you haven't heard it. People used to say it about you, sometimes."

"About me?"

"Sometimes. It's just small town talk."

"Well, they're wrong about the pony money part. I couldn't afford a pony if it came in a box of Crackerjacks. And I don't see what's so ambitious about being a small town vet."

"A small town vet whose business is so slow he patches up stray cats and dogs? So he marries a rich old maid? While she was still recovering from a nasty traffic accident? You have to admit, it looks . . . opportunistic. Maybe even suspicious."

"I don't give a damn what it looks like. I've never taken a dime from Yvonne."

"Whoa, lighten up. I know that, I do your books, remember? But she is a bit older than you are."

"Six years. It doesn't mean a thing. I'm that much older than you are."

"Actually, you're only five years older, and anyway, it's different with men and women."

"The hell it is. Or if it is, it shouldn't be."

"Look, I'm sorry. I didn't mean to upset you."

"Sure you did," David said dryly, "but it's okay. We've always been straight with each other and it's nice to know what the neighbors are saying. Even when they're dead ass wrong."

"I'm not so sure they are. I mean, just for the sake of argument, let's say you did marry Yvonne for her money. You were fresh out of school so you must have been awfully broke, right? But it's been four years now. And since you apparently aren't collecting on your investment, maybe you ought to rethink things."

"Thinking was never my strong point, let alone rethinking. What are you getting at?"

She took a deep breath, then squared her shoulders and met his eyes. "What I'm saying is, that maybe Yvonne isn't the only one with a vision problem, David. You two have very little in common, and you can't feel very comfortable with her stuffed shirt country club friends. I suppose she's attractive enough if you like the prim type, but I'm not exactly chopped liver myself. Some people even think I'm pretty. And since you and I share the same professional interests, I think we'd make a great team."

"Yvonne said earlier that there are things we shouldn't joke about. I'm beginning to see what she meant."

"I'm absolutely serious, David."

"No, you just think you are. But I'll admit you're at least partly right. You're a lovely girl, Bett, a stunner, in fact. And we already make a terrific team, professionally speaking. As for the rest, I'm afraid I'm a lost cause. Maybe marriage is the one thing I do take seriously. Marriage and sick animals, that is."

"Bad marriages break up every day, David. Can you look me in the eye and tell me you're happily married?"

"If I can't, it wouldn't matter," he said, his tone cooling a bit. "Not all of our passions make us happy. And we're going to drop this subject now, okay? Permanently."

"Whatever you say, Doctor. I think I'll go, then. If you need me for anything, I'll be at home."

"You don't have to wait up. I've got a hunch this hound's gonna come along fine. And Bett? Just for the record, maybe the town's right. Maybe I did have Cadillac eyes for Yvonne when I came here. But you're wrong about her. She wasn't an old maid. She was the most . . . formidable woman I'd ever met. She still is. And I would have married her if she'd been broke, barefoot, and wearing burlap. Sometimes I wish she had been. It would've made things a whole lot simpler."

"My God, you're really serious, aren't you? I wonder if Yvonne realizes how lucky she is?"

"I sure as hell hope not," he said. And for once Bettina couldn't tell if he was kidding.

* * *

David was right about the hound's recovery. She was up and limping gamely around the next day and her temperature gradually returned to normal. Yvonne's temperature, though, remained decidedly chilly. She was civil but withdrawn, her eyes unreadable behind her smoked glasses. David tried to josh her out of her mood, but for once his warped sense of humor fell flat. He decided to play it cool, walk soft and back off. This too shall pass. Maybe. Greg Malley seemed to be working out all right, though David noticed that he seemed busiest when he sensed someone watching. The third day, he stopped David as he walked out to the Jeep in the morning. Greg was wearing gloves. And carrying a dead rat by the tail.

"Hey, Doc, I guess you were right about weird cat. It must've scared this guy clean to death."

"I doubt that," David said, frowning. "It's a barn rat. I think he'd be a little out of Franken Kat's league. Is that blood on its butt?"

"Looks like it," Greg said. "Mostly dried. What would cause that?"

"Usually a rat poison called warfarin. It's a powerful anti-coagulant. If rodents eat enough of it they bleed to death internally. Where'd you find this guy?"

"In the barn, why?"

"Odd. We don't use warfarin here. Never have. Too many other animals around."

"Maybe this one wandered over from another farm."

"Maybe," David said doubtfully. "But rats don't usually range very far, especially when they're as sick as this one must have been."

"Maybe he heard a doctor lives here. One who fixes strays for free."

"Cats and dogs only. The rats are on their own. Keep an eye

open for any more. If their numbers start to build up, we'll have to trap 'em out. These guys could eat Franken Kat for lunch. See ya." He climbed into his battered Jeep.

"Hey, Doc? I found the rat in a horse stall near a grain bucket. Would that make any difference?"

David hesitated. "Why should it?"

"I dunno. Just thought it might. See you later." He turned and walked confidently away, carrying his grim trophy. David watched him go, frowning. Then he fired up the Jeep and headed into the village. Algoma was small enough that a kid with a fair pitching arm could chuck a rock from end to end. Glen's supermarket anchored one end of the main street, a Forward gas station held down the other. A pharmacy, an Ace hardware store, a doc-in-a-box emergency clinic, a few small shops and Tubby's restaurant filled the block in between. A black and white patrol car was parked in front of the restaurant. David pulled in behind it.

Sheriff Stan Wolinski was alone in his usual spot, a scarred, antique pine table near the front window with a view of the street. He was a big man with a thinning G.I. butch haircut, a square face, square silhouette, and an outlook to match. David slid into one of the heavy captain's chairs facing him.

"Mornin', Doc. What can I do for you?"

"Help me out with a little background information, I hope. My wife hired a handyman a few days ago, a young guy named Greg Malley? Do you know him?"

"I know who he is. He played football for Algoma High some years back. Defensive tackle, and a pretty good one. He has no local police record, if that's what you're asking."

"That's part of it. Would you give him a character reference, then?"

Wolinski picked up his coffee mug and took a thoughtful sip, then carefully replaced it. "Probably not," he said carefully. "Greg was a wild kid. He got into a couple scrapes but nothing stuck, you know? Heard he got busted for d.u.i. up at Traverse City last summer. Don't know what came of it."

"Just kid stuff, then? Nothing serious?"

"I didn't say that. I said nothing that stuck. Which actually makes his record cleaner than yours."

"Mine?" David echoed, surprised.

"Sure. I checked you out, Doc, way back when. Some of Yvonne's society friends were worried you were taking advantage of her while she was laid up, you know? Tryin' to sweep her off her feet. So I made a few inquiries, nothing official, you understand. You were arrested once, as I recall. For petty theft. When you were in college at Michigan State."

"Shoplifting," David said evenly. "My roommate and I tried to steal some food from a supermarket. We were broke and hungry and very stupid, in that order."

"I've never worried much about motives, Doc. Everybody I bust has a sad story. I did mention your record to Yvonne once, when I visited her in the hospital. I thought she had a right to know. She said you'd already told her. Somehow I didn't quite believe that."

"You could have," David said, rising to go. "It was true. Thanks for the information, sheriff. All of it."

"No charge, Doc. And for what it's worth I've got nothing personal against you. But I've known Yvonne most of her life. Maybe I hoped she'd do a little better when she married."

"Somebody like you, for instance?"

"Not at all. Yvonne's out of my league, Doc. And, no offense, but from where I sit, she was out of yours, too."

"Well, at least we agree on something," David said. "See you around, Stan."

"Count on it," the sheriff said.

✳ ✳ ✳

David had to leave for the seminar late Friday afternoon. He asked Greg to ferry him to the airport to save parking fees. And to have time to talk to him. Alone. The talking part was easy. Greg liked to talk. Or, at least, to listen.

"Does it take a lot of school to be a vet, Doc?"

"At least seven years. Took me ten. I had to drop out a couple of times to earn enough money to finish. Why?"

"Just wondered. I figured you had to be pretty smart to fix up animals like you do. Even if some of 'em turn out lookin' like that Franken Kat."

"The eye of the beholder, Greg. She's beautiful to me."

"Your wife doesn't seem to like her much."

"Yvonne's vision is pretty limited, so when Franken Kat lurches out of whatever corner she's in, they spook each other sometimes, that's all."

"What happened to your wife's eyes? I noticed she's got a couple little scars. Some kind of accident?"

"She rolled a car in the rain four or five years ago."

"That was before you got married, then?"

"That's right. Why?"

"Oh, I don't mean to be nosy, I'm just passin' the time, you know?"

"Fine. So pass some about yourself. You grew up in Algoma, right? But since you didn't know about my wife's accident, you must have been away for awhile. Where, exactly?"

"Just driftin' here and there."

"I said exactly," David said. With an edge in his tone.

"Hey, you sound serious. Okay, I traveled with a carnival awhile, then worked oil rigs in Oklahoma. Got tired of driftin' and came back to Michigan last year. Worked in a hospital for a few months over at Traverse City."

"Funny, you don't strike me as the hospital type. Do you have medical training of some kind?"

"Naw, I was just helping out, like a volunteer, you know?"

"Or like community service? The kind they give you instead of jail time?"

Greg glanced at him sharply, then smiled that lazy grin. "That's exactly the kind. I spent two hundred hours working in the detox ward there, where they dry out drunks. Very educational."

"In what way?"

"I quit drinkin' for one thing. Looked at some of those ol' boys and saw my future. Didn't much care for the view."

"And you see shoveling horseshit as a career advancement?"

"Bein' a handyman suits me for now. Gives me time to think. I've been thinkin' I might like to be a writer. Write the story of my life, maybe. Or maybe yours. That English guy, Herriot? He made a lotta money writin' about bein' a veterinarian. Maybe we could do the same thing."

"We?"

"Sure. You tell me some great vet stories, I'll write 'em down, we'll both get rich."

"I don't think so."

"Why not? No offense, but I can't help noticin' the way you live; this Jeep, your clothes. Your missus keep the purse strings tied pretty tight, does she?"

David glanced at him. "I wouldn't know. I've never asked her for money. Not that it's any of your business."

"Sure it is, Doc. If I'm gonna write the story of your life I need to know all the details. But if you're touchy about money, maybe we oughta stick to the vet stuff. Like, what's the fastest diagnosis you ever made?"

"The fastest? It doesn't work that way. Some things are easy to see, like a broken leg, but most aren't. And animals can't tell you where it hurts."

"So if you're a vet, bein' a fast worker isn't necessarily a good thing?"

"No, why?"

"Oh, I just heard a story once from one of the winos at Traverse, about a vet that cured five horses in just a couple minutes. Never even examined 'em. Just ran into the barn, gave 'em each a shot and ran out. Fastest vet in the west."

"Or the most incompetent. What was wrong with the horses?"

"Dunno. I'm not sure the wino told me. And maybe he was lyin'. Does the story sound likely to you?"

"No."

"I didn't think so either. Still, the old guy told me other things that were true, so I thought this story might be, too."

"Like what?"

"Just local gossip about doin's in Algoma. Stuff that happened while I was gone."

"He was from Algoma?"

"Didn't I mention that? Yeah, that's why we hit it off so good. Big hospital like that, two homeboys runnin' into each other in the detox ward. Spent a lotta time talkin', you know? In fact, he was the reason I decided to try bein' a handyman for awhile. That's what he'd worked at, before the bottle got him. Even worked at your place for awhile. Well, not your place, your wife's, I mean. It was before the accident, before you two got married. Guy's name was Carl

Willis. Remember him?"

"I'm . . . not sure."

"Funny, he remembered you pretty clearly. But I guess he'd be easy enough to forget. He was just a handyman, and a drunk to boot. Your wife's uncle fired him. Fact is, he kinda blamed ol' Willis for her accident. Said if he'd cared for the horses better they wouldn't have gotten sick. And your wife wouldn't have gone tearin' into town to fetch a vet and cracked up her car. Well, here we are."

He swung the Jeep into the airport entrance drive and parked in front of the terminal. David climbed out and lifted his suitcase out of the back. "See you in four days, Doc. Don't worry about a thing. Sure wish you'd think about us writin' a book together, though. Between the two of us, I'll bet we could make a killing."

David watched him drive off, all the way out to the highway. Then he turned and trudged into the terminal, lost in thought. He was going to have to do something about Greg. He just didn't know what.

But the following Tuesday, Greg didn't meet him at the airport. Instead, Bettina was waiting at the gate when his flight disembarked. She was dressed in a Michigan State teeshirt and jeans, casual, but they set off her figure well, as though she'd chosen them with care.

"Hi," she said brightly. "I hope you don't mind the change in plan. Greg's driving your missus to Traverse City for a shopping trip. She asked me to pick you up."

"What kind of a shopping trip?"

"Clothes, I think. Greg's quite a dresser when he wants to be, maybe she wanted a man's opinion. Which is just as well. I wanted to talk to you alone anyway."

"Why alone?" he asked, after he'd tossed his suitcase into the trunk and folded himself into the front seat of her tiny, bottle green Geo Metro.

"Discretion," she said, skillfully piloting the car through the crush at the airport gate and heading south. "You have a problem, maybe two, and if you're going to blow your stack, I'd rather you did it privately, with me."

"Why should I blow up?"

"Because you're not going to like what I have to say. It's about your wife, and Greg. And the office."

"What about my wife?"

"Maybe nothing. But Greg's been squiring her out and about quite a bit the past few days."

"So she hasn't had anyone to drive her around for awhile and she's making up for lost time. I admit Greg Malley's a hunk by some standards, but Yvonne's not the sort to flip over some muscle-bound clown she's only known a few days."

"Why would you think they've only known each other a few days? They both grew up here and he was a local football hero. She must have known who he was when she hired him."

"Somehow I doubt that they moved in the same circles."

"Why? You mean because she's older and richer than he is? That didn't bother her where you were concerned."

"Look, Bettina, I'm willing to cut you some slack because we're friends and colleagues, but you're out of line. Drop it."

"No problem," she said archly. "If I offended you, I apologize. I only mentioned it because of the other problem. I think you mentioned once that Yvonne isn't computer literate, right?"

"She has difficulty reading the screen," he acknowledged. "Why?"

"Because someone got into the office computer over the weekend."

"What do you mean someone got into it?"

"Used it. I'm a fastidious housekeeper, David. I remember where I leave things. When I opened the clinic Monday morning, I could tell someone had been there."

"You mean they broke into the building?"

"No, that's what made it seem all the more odd. There was no sign of a break-in, and nothing seemed to be missing. I checked the drug supply first thing and it was okay. But someone had definitely been at the computer."

"Are you sure about this?"

"Absolutely. Whoever the burglar was, he wasn't all that careful about it. He left a three and a half inch floppy in the slot and put the others back in the wrong order. It was almost as if he wanted me to notice."

"What was on the disks?"

"The office financial statements. Records, purchase orders,

billing, the works. Even your income tax returns. It's possible he looked at other things, too, patient records or whatever, but the financial statements were the only things that were obviously disturbed."

"That makes no sense at all."

"Not to me," Bettina said carefully. "I thought it might to you. Is there something going on you haven't told me about?"

"Like what?"

"You tell me. Since the burglar didn't have to break into the office, he must have used a key. And the only keys I know of are yours and mine. And I presume your wife has one."

"There are spare keys at home, sure, but if Yvonne wanted to know about the office records, she could just ask me."

"Unless there's a reason she didn't want to ask you, or didn't want to rely on your word for it."

"What are you getting at?"

"Maybe it's just wishful thinking on my part, but it occurred to me that a smart wife, one like Yvonne, for example, might want to know exactly what her husband's finances were. If she was considering a divorce, for instance. I don't suppose anything like that's in the wind?"

"Not . . . that I'm aware of, and I think I'd know. And you've got a very devious mind."

"Thank you. What are you going to do?"

"I don't know. Have you told anyone else about this?"

"No. Since it wasn't a break-in, exactly, I thought I'd better talk to you first."

"Good. You did the right thing, Bett. I'll handle it."

"Handle what? Aren't you going to tell me what's going on?"

He started to reply, hesitated, then shook his head. "No," he said. "I guess not. But ah, look, there's no easy way to say this. I think you'd better start looking for another job."

"What? You mean . . . you're firing me? Why? Look, I really didn't mean to offend you, I was only trying to help."

"It's nothing like that. You've been a terrific assistant and you'll probably make a fine vet someday. But I've got some problems here that I don't think I can solve, without . . . Anyway, however things turn out, I'll probably be leaving, maybe quite soon. I'll give you a glowing recommendation and severance pay, of course. I'll mail it to you."

"David, I don't understand."

"Maybe not, but you will. I need one last favor, Bettina." He took an envelope from inside his jacket and handed to her. "Give this to my wife tomorrow. Please."

"Of course. But . . ."

"No buts. Just see that she gets it. Thanks for the lift, and the friendship and . . . Well, you know. Good luck, Bettina."

She left him at his front door and drove off slowly, watching him in the rear view mirror all the way out the gate.

He waited until she was gone before entering the house. It was silent and empty. Good. It didn't take him long to pack the odds and ends of clothing that weren't already in his flight bag. Yvonne had been right. He tossed a few books into a cardboard box, added a couple of photographs, and it was as though he'd never been there.

He loaded them into the back of the Jeep, then, on a whim, went back into the house and trotted up to his wife's bedroom and checked the top drawer of her nightstand. The gun was there, the nine millimeter Glock automatic. He stared down at it for a long time, lost in thought, but in the end he left it where it was.

Then he walked over to the servant's quarters and used his pass key to let himself into Greg's room. He searched it quickly but thoroughly. He didn't find anything useful. Hadn't really expected to. He left the room in mild disarray, the door ajar.

He walked to the barn and whistled, long and low. And after a moment, an ungainly, three-legged figure lurched out of the shadows and made its way to him. He knelt and scooped Franken Kat into his arms and carried her to the Jeep. Then he climbed in, took a long last look at the house, and drove into the village to his office.

He opened a can of cat food he found in the fridge and set it out for Frank, but she was more interested in exploring the office, sniffing for scents, peering into nooks and crannies with her one good eye.

He left her to it. He unlocked the drug cabinet and got a five cc syringe with a short 22 gauge needle. He filled it with tincture of iodine, then emptied it into the sink and washed away the stain. He attached a short piece of adhesive tape to the barrel of the empty syringe and placed it on his desk next to the computer.

He spent the next few hours at the office computer settling up his bills. The office phone rang twice. He didn't bother to answer it. He was halfway through Bettina's letter of recommendation when a car pulled up in the lot out front. He paused long enough to slide the used syringe up his sleeve and tape it to his wrist. And then he was out of time.

Greg Malley stepped into the office and glanced warily around. He was wearing a sport jacket over his usual tee shirt and jeans. The cut of the coat accented his broad shoulders and narrow waist.

"Hey, Doc, good to see you back. How come you ain't been answerin' the phone? Your missus hit panic city when she saw the Jeep was gone, and your clothes with it. Was all I could do to talk her outa comin' down here. Said I'd check you out first, in case you and Bettina maybe had somethin' goin'. But that's not the deal, is it?"

"No. Actually, I've been waiting for you."

"I figured that. What were you lookin' for in my room?"

"Weight. Anything to counterbalance the dirt you think you're holding on me."

"Sorry, Doc, there's nothing to find. I'm clean. But so are you, in a way. I mean, I don't know anything that could send you to jail. All I got's a story I heard from an ol' drunk in detox about some rich lady's horses that suddenly turned sick, started bleedin' from the nose and mouth, and a vet who cured 'em without even lookin' at 'em. Because he already knew what was wrong with 'em since he'd mixed some warfarin in with their feed a week or so before. How am I doin' so far?"

"It sounds like a fairy tale a drunk might tell."

"Except fairy tales have happy endings and this one doesn't. Because when the lady sees how bad off the horses are, she naturally calls the vet. Only she can't get through. Why was that, Doc? I mean, you set this thing up to get her business, right? So why didn't you answer the phone?"

"I was in surgery," David sighed. "Operating on a cat that I found in the road."

"You're kiddin'?" Greg said, grinning widely. "You mean that one-eyed abortion, whatchacallit?"

"Franken Kat," David said. Greg shook his head in wry amusement. "So the lady panics, drives into town like a bat out of hell, rolls her car and gets banged up pretty good. And you're so nice to her she ends up marryin' you. Sounds like a happy ending, for you. Only it didn't work out like you figured. She doesn't give you a nickel, does she? Don't look so surprised. I took a look at your books."

"Then you know you can't hold me up. I don't have any money of my own, Greg. Not enough to bother stealing, anyway."

"Oh, I figure your wife might be willin' to lay out some semi-serious cash to hear my little story, but that'd only be a one time thing, and I've gone to too much trouble to settle for that. Especially since I've figured a way to make this deal pay off big, Doc. We can make a lot of money together, you and me."

"Can we? What have you got in mind?"

"Drugs, Doc, what else? I almost flipped when I read your inventory. Man, you've got a legal drugstore here, and most of it's just as good for people as animals. PCP, half a dozen kinds of steroids, even nitrous oxide. You got any idea how much this stuff is worth on the street? With the right connections, we can both cash in bigtime."

"And you can supply the connections, is that it?"

"I definitely know the right people, sure. And it's not like you've got a lot of choice."

"At least we agree on that," David said. "My options are definitely limited. But so are yours."

"What do you mean?"

"I'm leaving, Mr. Malley. I'm already packed and ready to go. I always knew it would come down to this. I've been waiting for it since the day I got married. It's almost a relief."

"Wrong. You're not going anywhere."

"Or what? You'll tell your story to Yvonne? You're a little late. I left a letter for her. It's probably not as colorful as you could make it, but it covers all the details."

"I don't believe you."

"Believe what you want. You can try to sell her your fairy tale tomorrow but it'll be yesterday's news. I doubt she'll give you a plugged nickel for it. And as for us going into the drug trade together, not a chance. None. Give it up, Greg. It's over. We've both lost."

Greg stared at him, blinking, trying to compute what he'd just heard. Then he reached under his jacket and came up with an ugly little revolver. "No," he said, "I'm not losing anything. I've put too much time into this. Ever since Willis told me about you, I knew this was my big chance. One way or another."

"You're making a mistake, Greg."

"No more talk! Just get your ass over here and unlock the drug cabinet. I'm damned if I'll come out of this deal empty-handed."

"No," David said, folding his arms across his chest. "I don't think so."

"Yo, Doc, it's not like you got a lotta choice," Greg said, easing back the hammer of the pistol. "I don't figure on shovelin' horseshit for the rest of my life. Or endin' up like Willis, dyin' broke in some detox ward."

"It beats prison, which is where we'll both end up if I open that cabinet. I just won't do it. I've made enough mistakes for this lifetime."

"Damn it, Doc, I'm not—"

Greg flinched as a figure suddenly lurched out of the shadows. Franken Kat. He eyed her a moment, then turned to David. "Okay, Doc, you won't do it for yourself? How about your buddy there. You went to a lotta trouble over her, right? So how about I just stomp her some, see if you change your mind?" He lashed out at Franken Kat with his boot. She stumbled aside, barely avoiding the kick. Greg shifted his stance, backing her into a corner. She hissed at him, teeth bared. He raised his foot, but the blow never landed.

With a roar, David launched himself over the desk. His rush caught Greg shoulder-high, carrying them both across the lab table to crash into the counter beyond. David grappled for the gun, but Greg pulled his wrist free and slashed David across the face with the weapon, spinning him around, slamming him into the computer console. David went down hard, dragging the monitor down with him. It exploded on the floor, in a shower of sparks and tangled cables. David frantically thrust himself away from the flames and staggered to his feet. To look straight down the barrel of the pistol in Greg's fist.

"Still feelin' frisky, you stupid bastard?" Greg panted, dabbing at a trickle of blood from the corner of his mouth. "Hell, I don't need a gun to handle you. I've busted up guys bigger'n you for laughs. C'mon, Doc," he said, shoving the gun into his hip pocket. "You don't look like the fightin' type to me. Let's see what you got."

David lunged at him, swinging wildly, but Greg slipped the blows easily, and countered with two hard body shots that folded David in half, dropping him to his knees. David knelt there a moment, head down, panting, then stumbled painfully to his feet. And raised his fists again.

"You want more, Doc, I'll be happy to oblige. We got all night." He lashed out with a quick jab that caught David solidly in the ribs, then followed with a hard right cross, flush on the jaw, knocking him across the desk. He grabbed David by the lapels, pulling him upright for another blow. Then winced as David slid the hypodermic from beneath his sleeve and stabbed Greg lightly in the shoulder with it.

"Gotcha," David gasped.

"What the hell?" Greg staggered back, pulled his pistol again and aimed it at David's head.

"Hold on, now" David said, raising his hands. "Don't do anything stupid. I just gave you a half cc of Xylazine. We use it to knock cattle down and you weigh a helluva lot less than a cow. You've got roughly fifteen minutes to get an antidote. Or you're dead."

"What?"

"You'll die, Greg. Cardiac arrest. You've got to get to an emergency room. Right now."

"You bastard!" Greg snarled. "I'm gonna—"

"Die," David interrupted. "If you don't get moving. I'll call the emergency room and tell them you're coming and what antidote to get ready. But I won't do it until you're on the road. If you want to shoot, be my guest. But we'll both die. The clock's running, Greg. You've got to go. Now, damn it! Move!"

With a sob, Greg whirled and stumbled out the door. David heard Greg's car roar to life then burn rubber out of the lot, howling away into the dark. He dropped the empty syringe on his desk, then scanned the wreckage of his clinic. "Frank?" he said softly. "You okay?"

The misshapen cat peered cautiously out with her lone eye from beneath the desk. Then she emerged warily and limped off into the waiting room, on business of her own.

"Smart cat," David said. He gingerly touched his cheek where the gun had caught him. His fingertips came away bloody. He opened the medicine cabinet, found some gauze and alcohol, then walked carefully to the bathroom to clean himself up. He'd bandaged his face, but had barely made a dent in the shambles of his office, when a prowl car roared up outside, flashers spinning.

Sheriff Stan Wolinski stepped cautiously through the door, his hand on his weapon. "Holy shit," he growled. "What the hell happened here?"

"Greg Malley and I had a disagreement over his severance pay," David said.

"Is that a fact," Wolinski said, glancing around, taking in the wreckage. "Greg showed up at the emergency clinic, half out of his tree, wavin' a gun around. The night security guard clipped him upside the head, got the gun. He's in an observation room now. Thing is, he was raving about being poisoned. Said you'd given him some kind of shot and he was gonna die. Xylophone or something? Said it really burned. Is he in any danger, Doc?"

"No. He got pricked with a hypo in the scuffle, and it may have stung a little because there was iodine residue on the needle. I told him it was Xylazine. It wasn't, but a small dose wouldn't have hurt him anyway. It's only effective on ruminants."

"On what?"

"Ruminants. Like cattle or elk."

"I see. Well, Greg may be a horse's ass, but you'd never mistake him for a cow. He, ah, he also ran a crazy story by me about you. Said you'd poisoned some horses once."

"Really?"

"That's what he said. 'Course he claimed he'd been poisoned, too, and he was wrong about that, wasn't he?"

"Yes," David said, "he was definitely wrong about that."

"You wanna file any charges against Greg, Doc?"

"No."

"I thought not. He won't be filin' any against you either. I already asked. Pity. A mess like this, seems like somebody oughta pay for it somehow."

"Don't worry, it'll be paid for," David said.

"Well, I'll leave you to your busywork," Wolinski said. "By the way, your phone's not working."

"I know. It got stepped on."

"Looks like your whole damned office got stepped on. And you with it," Wolinski said. "Your wife should be along shortly. I called the house when I couldn't raise you here. She was gonna catch a cab. I noticed suitcases in your Jeep. You leavin' town, Doc?"

"It looks like it."

"Sorry to hear it," Wolinski said. "Folks tell me you're a good vet. And anybody with guts enough to mix it up with Greg Malley can't be all bad. See ya around, Doc." He walked out without a backward glance.

David sighed and went back to straightening up the carnage in the office. And somewhere in the middle of the job he realized that he wasn't alone. Yvonne was sitting on the waiting room sofa, knees together, hands clasped on her lap. Waiting. She was wearing a simple black blouse and slacks and her hair was tousled. And somehow she still looked elegant.

"I'm sorry," David said. "I didn't hear you come in."

"I . . . wasn't sure you'd be alone. I didn't want a scene. My God, what happened to your face?"

"Your new handyman used it to demonstrate the fine art of fisticuffs. I think I cut that class in college. Kinda wish I hadn't, now."

"You look awful. Shouldn't you see a doctor?"

"I am a doctor. A dog doctor, which is kind of appropriate under the circumstances."

"You mean because you're running out on me?"

"I'm . . . going away, yes. It's best. I left a letter with Bettina that explains—"

"It's all right. I've been expecting it. I've always known you'd go eventually. My God, it couldn't have taken you more than twenty minutes to pack everything you own."

"More like fifteen," David said. "When you read the letter you'll understand."

"I think I understand now. It's about the horses, isn't it? You poisoned some of them."

"That's right." David released a long ragged breath he hadn't realized he'd been holding. "Look, I don't know what Greg told you—"

"Greg didn't tell me anything," she interrupted. "Carl Willis told me about it nearly four years ago. While I was still in the hospital."

David stared at her blankly, trying to make sense of what she'd said. "Are you saying that you knew?"

"I'm not a fool, David. Neither was Willis. He saw you treat the animals without examining them, though the symptoms could have been for any one of a half dozen ailments. So when he heard we were engaged, he told me what he suspected. He thought I'd be willing to pay for the information. I told my uncle to fire him."

"I don't understand."

"It's not complicated, David. I was a woman of a certain age at a very low point in my life. I'd partially lost my vision in the accident. But while I was recovering, you were so . . . attentive. I hoped you really did care for me. And that no matter what had gone before, that we might have a chance together. But we didn't. You lived in my house like a lodger and spent most of your time working. And then one day I noticed that deformed cat of yours. And realized how you really felt."

"You've lost me. What's Franken Kat got to do with anything?"

Hearing her name, Frank poked her head out from beneath the sofa and warily cased the room with her good eye. David scooped her up and cradled her in his arms.

"I guess she is a bit of a monstrosity," he admitted, scratching the scar of her missing ear. "You've never liked her, have you?"

"It's not that I don't like her. She's quite a character, in her odd way. But sometimes I can't help resenting her. You were operating on her the day of my accident, and you've done surgery on her several times since and you've patched together God knows how many other strays. You have a rare gift for . . . compassion. For things that are broken and need care. Like Franken Kat. And me. In a way, Franken Kat and I are sisters."

"You're wrong. It's not the same thing at all."

"Of course it is. I don't see all that well, but it's clear to me. If I'd had more pride, I wouldn't have let it drag on as long as it has. But it's over now, and maybe it's best. But you really should leave the cat with me, David. She won't be happy living in the back of a Jeep."

"No, I suppose not," he said, gently passing Franken Kat to Yvonne. Frank squirmed for a moment, then settled down, accepting Yvonne's stroking as her just due.

"Look, I know it won't mean much to you now," David said

quietly, "but I'm sorry. About the accident. About everything. I never meant to hurt you."

"The accident wasn't your fault. It was raining and I was driving too fast. It could have happened anytime. I would like to know one thing, though. Willis was sure you poisoned the horses. Is it true?"

"I dropped a fistful of warfarin in their grain." He nodded grimly, avoiding her eyes. "The symptoms are ugly but the horses were never in any real danger. Still, it was a lousy thing to do."

"Yes it was. I'd have you thrashed within an inch of your life if somebody hadn't beaten me to it. Even now it's hard for me to believe you actually did it, knowing how you are with animals. You must have needed the money desperately."

"Money?" he echoed, blinking. "You think I did it for money?"

"What else? Some of my friends told me to my face that you were a fortune hunter."

"Ah, the man with Cadillac eyes, you mean?"

"That phrase came up, yes."

"And you believed it? Look at this place, for godsake! Do you think anyone who gave a damn about money would choose to be a small town vet? I never even thought about it until I met you, and only then because your money and class put you out of my league. But you had horses you loved, and I thought if I could pull off a miracle cure . . . Ah, hell. And then it all went wrong. But while we're clearing the books between us, there's something else you may as well know. When you were in the hospital, I deliberately took advantage of the situation to con you into marrying me. And that was probably a lousy thing to do, too. But I'm not sorry I did it. I'm only sorry you got hurt. And that it's over." She stared at him for what seemed like a very long time, then shook her head slowly.

"My God, we've been together nearly four years, and the truth is, I don't really know you at all, do I?"

"I'm not sure anyone truly knows anyone, no matter how long they've been together."

"Then maybe it's not so important. Maybe what matters is fitting the pieces together into something that works. Like you did with Franken Kat, here," she added, stroking the feline's scarred brow. "We don't understand cats. We don't know their thoughts, and they couldn't care less about ours. And yet we live together.

Quite happily, sometimes. How many times did you operate on her?"

"Three," he said. "Most people don't think the results are very pretty."

"And does it matter so much what people think?"

"Not to me. And certainly not to her. But then we're strays, she and I. We have no family or old friends here. You have."

"If you think their opinions matter all that much to me, then you don't know me very well either," Yvonne said. "But one thing I don't understand is how you could go to so much trouble over . . . Franken Kat, and then decide to leave her."

"It's not that I want to leave. It just seemed like the right thing to do. Don't you think it is?"

"I honestly don't know. So much has happened . . ." Her voice trailed away.

A deep, bass rumbling from Franken Kat broke the silence, startling them both.

"What on earth is that noise?" Yvonne asked.

"Her vocal cords were damaged. I've never been able to tell whether she's purring or growling when she does that. Maybe you'd better put her down."

"No," Yvonne said, rocking the disfigured cat gently in her arms. "I'll take that chance."

Roadkill

The dead dog on the shoulder of the road twitched. Only a reflex, David thought, even as he touched his Jeep's brakes and switched on its flashers. He pulled off onto the shoulder of the highway and slowed to a halt a few yards from the dog's body. Big dog, brindle fur. Boxer, maybe? Or a Staff? It was so battered and bloody he couldn't even be sure of the breed. Or whether it was one of his patients. He considered getting a hypo of Socomb, sodium phenobarbital, out of his bag on the off chance the animal was still suffering, but decided against it. The movement he'd noticed was probably windblast from a passing car. The dog certainly wasn't moving now.

Some moron leaned on his horn as he blew past at eighty per. Traffic on the State Road four-lane was always fast and furious. Commuters from Algoma or points north hurrying to or from factory jobs in Saginaw. He waited for a break in traffic before climbing out of the Jeep and trudging up to the dog, automatically cataloguing its injuries. A godawful mess. Belly ripped open, purplish tangle of entrails oozing out onto the gravel, shoulder battered, possibly broken, and blood flowing freely from a dozen different lacerations. Not quite dead yet, there was still some faint, feathery spasms of respiration. But it would only be a matter of minutes now. Maybe less. It looked like it had been hit and run over by some hotshot who probably hadn't even checked his rear view mirror to see what it was.

What it was, was a Pit Bull, female, four to six years old. David didn't recognize the dog, and he was fairly sure he would have remembered. The breed wasn't common in this part of the state and they were remarkably hardy. He seldom saw them in his veterinary practice.

The dog was wearing an ordinary leather collar, not one of the spiked monstrosities some of the macho clowns who favor this breed seem to prefer. David knelt beside the dog, slid his fingers along the collar, feeling for a name tag or license so he could inform its owner what happened—

She bit him! Her jaws clamped onto his forearm like a vise, holding him immobile. Sweet Jesus! He froze, unable to move, even if he'd wanted to. He could already feel his right hand chilling, going numb, and so far she was only maintaining her hold. She hadn't savaged the arm, or even clamped down on it full force, yet. She was just holding him, to keep from being hurt. But Pits have jaws like metal shears. Dying or not, if she bit down much harder, she could break his wrist. Or sever it.

He shifted his position slightly, trying to read her eyes. They were clouded with pain, but not glazed. She was conscious, or at least partly so. He could feel the faint whisper of her breath on his upper arm. She was terribly injured. Not quite dead, though. But his arm was going to be, and soon, if she didn't let it go. If he'd brought the damned hypo, he'd have put her down on the spot. Death would've been nearly instantaneous, especially for a dog in her condition. But without it, trying to pull free or struggle with her was risky business. Any movement that caused her pain might well cost him his arm.

And so he knelt and began talking to her. Quietly, he tried to explain the situation. That he hadn't meant to hurt her; he'd only stopped to help. That he was the only veterinarian in thirty miles and wouldn't be nearly as useful with only one arm. She didn't seem impressed. He tried stroking her head with his free hand but she growled, or seemed to. It was hard to be sure considering she had a mouthful of his wrist.

He talked nonstop for nearly five minutes, to no effect. Her jaws remained tightly clamped. Maybe she'd forgotten she was holding him, or why. His right hand was totally numb now, and his lower back was on fire from crouching over her. The stench of blood and offal and road dust in his nostrils was beginning to make his stomach churn . . . And then she released him.

Just like that. She relaxed her hold on his wrist, and let him go. And lowered her head to the dirt. To die. He rose stiffly, massaging his bruised wrist, staring down at her. She hadn't broken the skin, but his fingers were sizzling with the fiery pinpricks of returning circulation. And his eyes were stinging, too, for no particular reason he could fathom. God knows, he'd seen animals die before. It came with the territory. Some of them, he'd known quite well. Still . . .

A car rocketed past at maximum speed, shaking him with its windblast, horn blaring.

"Asshole!" he yelled, shaking his fist at the driver. And the universe. The hell with this! He stripped off his leather jacket, then his shirt. He made a loop out of the shirtsleeve, slipped it over the dog's muzzle and tied her jaws closed, apologizing all the while. Then he slid her onto his jacket, picked her up and sprinted for his Jeep.

At the clinic, he barreled through the front door, yelling for his assistant, Bettina, as he charged past the startled patrons in the waiting room, blood streaming from the maimed animal cradled in his arms. In his surgery, he gently lowered the dog to the stainless steel operating table. Still alive. Barely.

"Give her atropine intramuscular, skip the Acepromazine," he barked as Bettina, his veterinary tech, trailed him into the small operating room. "She's already in shock. Give her a light dose of sodium pentothal and get a tracheal tube in her. Oxygen, nitrous oxide, and halothane."

"Respiratory monitor?"

"Not now. Her breathing's the least of our problems. I'll check her intestines for lacerations. You start cleaning up the gashes on her torso and throat so we can see what the hell we're into here."

"You'd better scrub," she said. He almost bit her head off. But she was right, of course. No point in suturing the body cavity closed only to have the dog die of infection later. Hell, she was probably going to die on the table anyway.

But she didn't. Bettina anesthetized her without incident. The dog was too weak now to offer even token resistance. The intestines protruding from the gash in her belly looked grim, but they weren't damaged. David cleaned off the road dirt, rinsed the wound with tetracycline in saline, then gently prodded the bowels back into the abdominal cavity and began suturing the gash closed.

"What happened to her?" Bettina asked.

"She got run over," David snapped. "What does it look like?"

"That's my point," Bettina said calmly, unruffled. "Look at these lesions. No car did this."

David glanced up from his stitching for a moment, and paused. She was right. The Pit Bull's shoulders and throat were crisscrossed with puncture wounds, dozens of them.

"How deep?" he asked.

"Two to three centimeters. They're obviously bites, David, but look at the span between the canines. Something very big did this. And why so many? I've seen dogs that have been torn up in fights. I've never seen anything like this."

"I've seen it once," David said grimly. "In my last year of vet school at Michigan State. The state police busted a dog fighting ring south of Saginaw. Arrested over a hundred people, seized three dozen dogs, picked up nearly sixty grand in illegal bets. Most of the dogs were Pits or Staffordshires, a few Rottweilers. Some of the ones who'd fought in the ring looked like this one. Or worse. We had to destroy most of them."

"Destroy them? Why?"

"It wouldn't have been safe to place them with families. Pit Bulls as a breed aren't much more aggressive than any other, but dogs that have been blooded in the arena are like loaded guns afterward. They may seem docile, even friendly. Until some kid accidentally pokes Fido in the eye or something else trips his trigger. And then they're instant fighting machines, all reflexes and fangs and jaws and no compunctions about chewing people up. They've been bred for battle, and they're pretty damned good at it. Personally, I think people ought to be licensed to own them, the same way you need a license for pistols or a powerboat."

"Hey!" somebody yelled from the waiting room.

"Be with you in a minute," Bettina called. "We've had an emergency."

"How many people are waiting?" David asked.

"Not as many as there were when you came charging in with this godawful piece of meat. There's still a trail of blood——"

"Hey!"

"Go ahead, pacify the natives," David said. "I'll be finished here in a few minutes."

David was neatly tying off the final stitch in a shallow gash in the Pit's shoulder when the dog's eyes blinked open. He knew she was still unconscious, the anesthetic machine was still pumping a mix of nitrous oxide and halothane into her lungs, but somehow her eyes seemed alert, as though she was aware of what was happening.

David gently touched her bloodied brow a moment, and her eyes closed again.

"David?" Bettina said, sticking her head around the corner of the door, "I think you'd better step out here. A gentleman, and I use the term loosely, claims we have his dog here. A Pit Bull bitch? I suggested he come back later, but he's quite insistent."

"No problem. Why don't you take over here. Give her oxygen for a few minutes, then room air. I'd like to meet the gentleman who owns this particular lady, anyway. What's he look like?"

"Tall. You'll have no trouble spotting him," Bettina said dryly. "Trust me."

David stepped through to the waiting room counter. And stopped. Dead. The man at the counter towered over him. David was five eleven, but the Viking type facing him was nearly a foot taller, maybe more, dressed in faded work clothes. He was fortyish, thinning sandy hair, and gray eyes. His long narrow face had been permanently reddened by the wind, but even more striking were his scars. His face was marked with three deep vertical gashes, livid as warpaint. Love bites. From having a chainsaw blade buck back into your face. A savage, ugly mark. And not all that uncommon in this part of the state.

"You the doc?" His voice was gravel, and David could smell whiskey from across the counter.

"I'm Dr. Westbrook," David acknowledged. "And you are. . . ?"

"Kaipainen," he grunted. "People call me Ox. Somebody seen you pickin' up my dog. A brindle Pit Bull bitch? You got her?"

"I found a dog by the side of the road. She's in pretty bad shape."

"So you just brung her in, fixed her up, and now I suppose I owe you a whole lotta money, right? Pretty slick. You had no right to take my dog."

"Maybe not," David admitted. "But right now I'm more interested in how she got into the condition she's in."

"What condition? I thought she got hit by a car."

"She was hit, all right. But she's also been thoroughly chewed up. As bad as I've ever seen. What do you use this dog for, Mr. . . . Ox?"

"Use her for? She's my dog, that's all. She tracks some, looks out for my place when I'm workin'. What the hell business is that of yours?"

"I'm making it my business. She's been badly mauled. I think she's been fighting."

"Yah, well, she runs loose a lot, in the swamp. Maybe she tangled with a boar coon or somethin'. Or when she got hit—"

"No. Her injuries weren't caused by a car, or any animal she'd likely meet in the swamp. What happened to her?"

"How the hell do I know? She got loose, is all. Look, it won't do you no good to try to hold me up, Doc, I ain't got no money. So just gimme my dog and I'll get outa here."

"I'm afraid not. Not today. She can't be moved yet."

"Dammit, she's my dog and I'm takin' her."

"You try to move her now and she'll be dead before you get her to your car."

"Ain't got no car. I'll carry her careful—"

"Forget it," David said flatly. "You're not taking her. For one thing, I don't know that she actually is your dog."

"I just told you she was."

"Sorry, but that's not good enough. I'll have to see some proof. Why don't you come back when you're sober and we'll talk about whose dog she is. And what happened to her."

"Look, you little wimp, I don't wanna hurt you, but I ain't lettin' nobody steal my dog. You'd best step aside . . ."

A police car roared into the clinic parking lot, lights flashing, and pulled up in front. The effect on Kaipainen was instantaneous. He seemed to shrink before David's eyes. The drunken rage faded like mist, and he was blinking and swallowing like a child who knows he's going to be beaten. He backed away from the counter, looked around the waiting room, then carefully sat down in one of the plastic chairs. And folded his huge hands in his lap.

Sheriff Stan Wolinski sauntered in, square as a block of concrete in his gray summer uniform. He glanced at Kaipainen, then nodded to the only patron who hadn't already fled, a tiny, silver haired sparrow of a woman in a flowered dress, holding her cat.

"Miz Hitchworth," Wolinski nodded, touching the brim of his uniform cap. "You causin' trouble again?"

"I certainly am not!" she snapped. "Mr. Kaipainen came stomping in here yelling, and he's been drinking—"

"Yes, ma'am," Wolinski said, cutting her off with a smile. "I imagine he has. Doc, you and Ox got some kind of problem here?"

"I'm . . . not sure," David said, eyeing the subdued giant, who was all but cowering in the chair. "I, ah, picked up an injured dog by the road this morning and did surgery on her. Mr. Kaipainen here claims the dog is his—"

"She is my dog," Ox interjected. "Ask anybody."

"Okay, Ox," Wolinski said mildly. "Chill out, I'll take care of things. So Ox owes you a big bill, does he, Doc?"

"I'd like to be paid, of course," David said evenly, "but that's not the point. The dog will die if she's moved now."

"But if she's his dog, that's his lookout, isn't it?"

"I don't know that she's his dog. And under the circumstances, I'm not going to release her today. To Mr. Kaipainen or anyone else."

Wolinski eyed him a moment, then shrugged and turned to face Kaipainen. "How you been, Ox? Haven't seen you around lately."

"I been workin' over to Oscoda at the pallet plant there. Stackin' and cleanin' up."

"Kind of a long walk, isn't it?"

"I hitch. Most days I get rides. I never hitchhike on ten, though. I know that ain't legal."

"That's right," Wolinski said. "It's not. Tell you what, Ox, why don't you go home now, let me sort this thing out for you."

"But he's got my dog—"

"I know, and I promise you'll get her back. When she's better, I'll have the doc here deliver her personally so you won't have to walk back to town. That sound fair?"

"I don't know, Stan," Kaipainen said, swallowing. "She's all I got—"

"Look, Ox," Wolinski said, kneeling beside the Viking's chair, "do you remember Yvonne LeClair, the girl I used to go with back in high school?"

"Yeah, I remember Yvonne."

"Well, the doc here, he moved up here from Lansing a few years back, and, ah, he and Yvonne got married. So you see, I'm not a big fan of his, you understand? And I won't let him do you wrong, Ox. You just trust me, okay? You go on home now." He rose and dusted off his knee. Kaipainen rose too, towering over Wolinski. And then stalked out without a word.

"My God, Stan," David marveled. "He's absolutely terrified of you. What on earth did you ever do to him?"

"Put him in jail once," Wolinski said simply. "Picked him up drunk, tossed him in the tank. He about went crazy in there. Tore the place up, tore himself up. I should have known better than to lock him in. So now he's afraid of me. And it's not something I'm proud of. Which is why you really are going to deliver his dog to him as soon as possible."

"No," David said. "It's not that simple."

"Look, Doc, if you're worried about your bill, Ox hasn't got doodley squat anyway. There's no point in trying to hold him up."

"It's not about the money. His dog's been ripped from one end to the other. I think she's been fighting. In a ring."

"Dogfighting, you mean? Are you sure?"

"The only time I've ever seen dogs chewed up the way this one was, they'd been fought."

"I don't know," Wolinski said doubtfully. "Ox lives out in the middle of no place and I know that dog runs loose. Maybe she tangled with a 'coon or a bobcat—"

"No, from the bite patterns it was definitely another dog. A big one. You see, when dogs mix it up, they don't normally fight to the death. They battle long enough to decide who's stronger and then the loser lights out, end of story. Pit bulls are different, of course, because they were bred for fighting, but if they're losing, and believe me, this dog lost bigtime, they'll still run as a last resort. Unless they're somewhere where they can't get away. Like in a ring, for instance."

"I can't see it, Doc. For one thing, I haven't heard a thing about a dog ring. I'm not saying we've got a crime-free county. Two bikers from Pontiac are runnin' a crank lab over on the west end somewhere, some locals grow reefer in the state forest and a few cars have disappeared from the village. Hell, some kids even broke into my tool shed. But it's all small stuff. A dogfighting ring would involve a lot of people and a lot of money. There's no way I wouldn't hear about it. But even if there was one, Ox wouldn't be involved."

"Why not?"

"Hell, you met him. He's not your average social butterfly. He didn't mix with folks much before he bounced that saw off his face, avoids 'em altogether now. Doesn't drive. Can't read, for that matter. Lives alone out on Elkhart Road, traps some, probably poaches, works when he needs money for things he can't barter pelts for. He's just not the organized crime type, you know? Now, if you told me Ox was fightin' people for money, I might buy that. But his dog? Nah. Not likely."

"Then why does he have a Pit Bull?"

"As I recall, he found her runnin' loose a few years back. She was just a stray. Like him. Tell you what; I'll make a deal with you. I promise I'll keep a sharp lookout for any sign of your dogfighting ring, okay? But meanwhile, since a man's still innocent until proven guilty in this county, you give Ox his dog back as soon as she's fit to travel. Fair enough?"

"I guess," David said.

"Good. Oh, and Doc? The next time you see a roadkilled dog? Do me a favor and just let it be, okay? Ox Kaipainen thinks the world of that dog and he's nobody to mess with. For your sake, I surely do hope she makes a good recovery. And a quick one."

"Yeah." David nodded. "So do I."

✳ ✳ ✳

And she did. Incredibly, when David checked on the dog a few hours after the anesthetic wore off, the bowlegged little bruiser was on her feet in the cage. She was weaving, and swathed in enough bandages to pass for a mummy's pup, but she was up. And from the fire in her eyes, she was game for a rematch with any and all comers. Bring 'em on. David pulled a chair up beside her cage and talked to her for a full ten minutes before he even considered opening the cage door to check her wounds. No point in pushing his luck. The lady was no more sociable than her master and David's arm still ached where she'd latched onto him. Over the next few days, she gentled down enough to tolerate his attentions, though she never really warmed to him. Still, they achieved an acceptable level of co-existence, civil, if not friendly. The only problem was, Kaipainen hadn't mentioned the dog's name, and it wasn't on her collar. So David called her Roadkill.

✳ ✳ ✳

By the end of the following week, he could no longer justify keeping the dog on any medical grounds. She was still moving stiffly due to the contusions on her shoulder where she was struck, but the gashes in her back and belly were closed with no sign of infection.

So he swallowed his misgivings, loaded Roadkill into a travel cage in the back of his Jeep, and followed the crude map Bettina jotted for him. Elkart Road trailed off into the bottomlands east of Algoma, low swampy ground, not good for much but ducks, frogs and muskrats.

And poachers. When David pulled into the overgrown yard near Kaipainen's small cabin, Ox was dressing out a dead deer. The buck was hanging from a branch of a large pine, spreadeagled and eviscerated. Ox was peeling off its hide, rolling the skin down from an incision in the animal's throat. He straightened slowly, still holding the bloody skinning knife, as David climbed out of the Jeep.

"Doc," Ox said, nodding. "Wasn't expecting you."

"I can see that," David said. "That buck's out of season, Mr. Kaipainen. Suppose I'd been the law?"

"What if you was? I found this one dead in the road. Musta been kilt by a truck."

"Not unless the truck shot it behind the ear with a small calibre weapon. I can see the bullet hole from here."

Ox glanced at the deer, then back at David. "Maybe you can. Look, Stan don't care much if a man takes meat illegal, if it's just to feed himself or his own. Long as he don't get to sellin' it, you know? You gonna rat me out to the D.N.R.?"

"What you eat and how you get it is your business, Mr. Kaipainen, I just came to bring your dog back."

"She okay?"

"She's doing very well, considering," David said, opening the cage door and carefully lifting Roadkill out. The dog limped directly to Ox, then sat obediently at his feet. The giant knelt slowly beside her and let her lick the blood off his hands. When he glanced up at David his eyes were swimming.

"She looks good," he rasped, swallowing. "I she thought might be, you know, scarred." He gestured toward his own face with the skinning knife.

"No," David said. "She's got a remarkable constitution. I doubt the scars will show at all in a year or so. Maybe a line on her belly where her fur is thin. No more than that. You'll need to change her bandages. I'll show you how to do that and give you some antibiotic ointment for her."

"No," Ox said, "I don't think I can do that."

"Do what? Change her bandages? Why not? You obviously don't go woozy at the sight of blood."

"It ain't that. Look, when I seen you that day in your office, I thought you was . . ."

"Trying to rip you off?"

"Somethin' like that, I guess. But I've talked to a few guys around town about you. They say you're okay, pretty much straight up. That you pick up stray animals sometimes, just to help 'em if you can. Somebody told me you even got a three-legged cat with one eye."

"That's right. Her name's Franken Kat."

"What the hell good is a three-legged cat?"

"She's a fair mouser. Can't catch anything but they take one look at her and decide to change area codes."

"But why do you still have her? Didn't her owner want her back lookin' like she does?"

"Actually, we never found her owner, so I kept her. Why?"

"See, that's the thing. I ain't sure I can take Pekka back."

"What did you call her?"

Kaipainen repeated the name, but David still couldn't make sense of it. "Are you saying that in English?"

"Nah, it's Finn. Like me. So how much do I owe you for fixin' her up?"

"I'm not sure you owe me anything, Mr. Kaipainen."

"Ox. My front name's Osmo, but people just call me Ox. Kinda fits me, you know?"

"Okay, Ox, the way I see it, you didn't bring your dog to me and you didn't authorize any treatment. I did it on my own. So, technically speaking, you don't owe me a dime."

"That ain't right. Hell, look at her. If you hadn't sewed her up she woulda died. But . . . see, I ain't got much. I don't own this place, don't even know who does. I'm on my own, you know? Free. Always have been. But I don't take no charity. And if I take her back without payin' you nothin,' that's what it'd be."

"Wait a minute, are you saying you don't want her back?"

"It ain't that I don't want her. I just can't take her like this."

"Fine, then I'll take her," David said. "She's mine, right?"

Ox nodded, frowning.

"Good. I like this dog a lot. Unfortunately, I've got a three legged cat, and strange animals coming in and out of the clinic all day. I think she'd be better off with room to run. Someplace in the country, maybe. Like . . . here. Mr. Kaipainen, I wonder if you could help me out by taking a stray dog off my hands. Not charity, you understand. You'd be doing me a big favor. She needs care, though. Maybe you ought to think about it."

Ox eyed him a moment, reading him. He shook his massive head slowly. "That's the other thing people said about you. That you're more'n a little crazy. Okay, Doc, you put it that way, I guess I can make room for a stray dog around here. Why don't you show me about her bandages?"

David knelt beside Roadkill and untaped the corners of the oily gauze draped over her shoulders. Ox winced at the savage tapestry of bite marks.

"Whoa," he said softly, "no wonder you thought I mighta been fightin' her. This is real ugly."

"The sheriff thought she might have tangled with a raccoon," David offered.

"Naw, no 'coon did this. Dogs. Big 'uns. Wolf size, I'd say."

"You think it might have been a wolf?"

"Ain't been no wolves in this part of the state for sixty years, Doc. 'Sides, the space between the front teeth . . . Where did you find her?"

"On State Road, just east of town. There are no farms nearby that have big dogs that I know of."

"Ain't nothin' around there," Ox acknowledged, massaging Roadkill's brow with his massive thumb. "Nothin' but state land around there, mostly swamp . . ." His voice trailed off.

"What is it?"

"Nothin', " Ox said. "Just thinkin'. How often do I change the bandages?"

"Actually, she's healing so quickly I think you can leave her shoulders uncovered now. Just apply the ointment once a day, and don't let her get too active. She's still stitched together like a rag doll. I'll stop by in a week or so to take her stitches out."

"Naw, no need for you to come all the way out here. You've gone to trouble enough. I'll bring her by your office," Ox said absently. "Tell you what, why don't you give me a bill. Write down how much I owe you."

"There's no need for that, I've already—"

"Just do it, okay? It don't have to be official, you know, with everything listed. Make it like a IOU. Use that little pad you got in your pocket there. And one other thing. Can you tell me where you found her? Exactly, I mean?"

David hesitated. There was an odd light in Kaipainen's eyes, an angry intensity. "Yes," he said at last, "I think so."

* * *

But Ox didn't bring Roadkill back. Two days later, as David was closing his office, Stan Wolinski stalked into the waiting room carrying a small plastic bag. He laid it carefully on the counter. "You recognize this, Doc?"

David swivelled the bag to read the single scrap of paper it held. "It's a bill," he said. "I gave it to Ox Kaipainen a few days ago."

"When, exactly?"

"Wednesday afternoon. Why?"

"Five hundred and seventy bucks? A little steep, isn't it?"

"Actually, it's low, but it doesn't matter. I never expected to see a dime of it anyway. How did you get it?"

"If you didn't expect to collect, why did you give it to him?"

"He asked me to. Look, what's—?"

"He asked you?" Wolinski echoed, not bothering to conceal his disbelief. "For a bill? Why would he do that?"

"How the hell do I know? In case you haven't noticed, the gentleman's a couple of sandwiches shy of a picnic. I took the dog out to him but he said he couldn't take her back. Didn't want to be obligated."

"So you gave him a bill?"

"No, I gave him the dog. She was his, and just looking around that place I knew he couldn't afford fifty bucks, to say nothing of five hundred. But as I was leaving, he asked me to write him a bill, so I did."

"A bill he couldn't pay."

"Lots of my clients can't pay their bills, especially the ones I pick up by the side of the road. It's no big deal. So what's the problem? Is Ox in some kind of trouble over this bill?"

"I don't know," Wolinski said. "Did you make any threats when you gave it to him? Like maybe you'd take his dog back if he didn't pay? Anything like that?"

"Threaten Ox? Are you nuts? He had a . . ." David hesitated.

"Had what? What were you going to say?"

"Nothing. Not until you tell me what this is all about."

"Look, Doc, you don't make the rules, I do. And I'm telling you to finish what you were going to say."

"Sorry. Not without a lawyer present."

"A lawyer? Why would you think you need a lawyer?"

"I don't know, but it always works on TV when people don't want to answer questions. So how about it? What's going on?"

"Nothing," Wolinski sighed. "It's over. Ox Kaipainen's dead. Suicide, looks like."

"Suicide? But . . . I don't understand. Why?"

"Who knows why anybody does a thing like that. He didn't leave a note; couldn't write. God knows Ox wasn't wrapped any too tight."

"How did it happen?"

"Buddy of his found him in his cabin. Looks like he shot himself in the head. Weapon was in his hand, a .22 Colt Woodsman pistol, long barrel. Poachers favor 'em. Real accurate. Especially when you're shooting at yourself. So what were you going to say about Ox?"

"It doesn't matter now. He was skinning out a deer when I dropped off his dog and he had a bloody knife in his hand. Under the circumstances, I didn't make any heavy threats about a bill I didn't expect him to pay anyway."

"Maybe you didn't expect him to pay it, but I wonder how he felt about it? He'd always been on his own, you know? Maybe he shouldn't have been. When he drank, he could be a real handful. I've scuffled with him more'n once over the years. But he wasn't mean, really. Mostly he kept to himself, livin' off the land like a . . . natural man, I guess. Maybe the idea of owing an unpayable debt was more than he could handle."

Wolinski picked up the plastic evidence bag. "Who knows what a guy like that was thinking? Growin' up around here I knew a lot of guys like Ox. Woodsmen. Cedar savages, we called 'em. Not many left, anymore. And now, one less and it's a damned shame. I've got his dog in the car. Do you want her or should I take her to the pound?"

"No, I'll take her, for now anyway. She still needs some care."

"You sure?" Wolinski said sourly. "There's nobody to bill anymore, you know."

"She was roadkill when I found her, remember? I guess she definitely is now."

After Wolinski left, David led Roadkill into the clinic, put her up on the table, and removed most of her sutures. She offered no resistance. Twitched a time or two when a stitch pulled coming out, but didn't growl at him or even glare. The dog seemed as numbed by what had happened as David felt. Or perhaps generations of fighting to the death in Pits as a diversion for subhumans unfit to share the same planet with her had made her skin less sensitive. If not her heart.

As he worked on the dog, snipping the Braunamid sutures and carefully threading them out of the wounds with tweezers, his thoughts kept returning to Ox, and their last conversation. Had the big man given him some hint of what he felt or what he'd planned? Or had he just missed it? Overlooked it because Ox didn't seem much brighter than some of the animals David treated . . .

No. It just wouldn't compute. Kaipainen hadn't seemed at all depressed. Quite the opposite, in fact. It wasn't so much what he said, as the look in his eyes.

After Ox had examined the bite wounds on Roadkill's shoulders, he'd said . . . that they were wolf size. But there weren't any wolves in this part of the state. Hadn't been for sixty years. And then he'd asked David for a bill . . . But, damn it, he hadn't seemed upset about it. It was almost as though he'd thought of a way to pay it. But that made no sense either. He'd only looked at the bite marks, then insisted on getting a bill. And then he'd asked David exactly where he'd found Roadkill. It made no sense at all.

David applied fresh ointment to the wounds and decided to leave the stitches in the deep gash in her belly for a few more days. He set the dog on the floor, then fumbled through his office junk drawer and came up with a county map. He traced State Road east of Algoma with his fingertip. He'd found her right about . . . there. Roughly six miles from the village. Kaipainen's cabin was probably a mile or so south of the spot where Roadkill was struck, with a farm and some small holdings in between.

David knew the farm, a small dairy operation owned by an old-timer named Jase Papineau. He'd inoculated his cows, and once he'd handled a difficult calving there. Jase had a pair of Border Collies, but they couldn't have caused the wounds on Roadkill. She'd have eaten them for lunch. Besides, Jase was salt of the earth. No reason to think anything was out of line there.

The small holdings were forty and sixty acre patches of unimproved hunting land. No one lived on them and since they bordered Kaipainen's place, he would have been familiar with them. Hell, he probably poached on them. So why would he think he could pay his bill if he knew where Roadkill had been struck? David frowned at the map. State Road was a four lane highway and the dog was hit on the side farthest from Kaipainen's place. The north side. So perhaps she'd been crossing it coming back from somewhere. But there was nothing north of the road. Sixty thousand acres of state forest. Had Roadkill been ranging in there? And tangled with . . . What?

It didn't add up. David decided to call it a night. He locked up the clinic, lifted Roadkill into the Jeep's passenger seat, and headed home. It was after six, but thanks to the wonders of daylight savings time, the sun was still well above the hills west of Algoma, painting the farm buildings and forested bluffs of the rural countryside with purple shadows.

State Road was a river of steel, jammed with commuters. David settled into the right lane, musing as he drove.

Roughly halfway home he passed the spot where he'd rescued Roadkill. He pulled off the road, waited for a break in the traffic, then gunned the Jeep across the four lane in an illegal U-turn, and parked on the shoulder of the road as close to the spot as he could guess-timate.

He scanned the area. There was nothing unusual about it. To the north, rolling, timbered bottomlands, mostly swamp. You'd need a tank to get through it. But Ox had definitely been curious about this spot, so . . . As David climbed out of the Jeep, Roadkill vaulted across the seat past him, and took off, trotting in her lame, herky jerky gait directly into the swamp.

"Roadkill!" She didn't even slow. Hell, why should she? It wasn't her name. Damn! He sprinted after her but she disappeared into the woods before he could run her down.

The brush at the edge of the wooded tangle was literally a wall of poplars and jack pines interspersed with tag alders, a trash tree that thrived in the sodden ground. David thrashed through the tangle of brush and ground cover into a more open area. He glimpsed Road-kill off to his right, moving at a steady, uneven trot. He slogged after her. His shoes were already soaked but at least the water was down this time of year, no more than ankle deep most places. The tricky part was just staying on his feet over the uneven ground.

And in keeping the dog in sight. She was setting a good pace, but he was sure she'd fade quickly. The only question was whether her stamina would give out before she'd torn open her stitches. Damn it! What the hell did she think— He tripped over a hummock, and went down hard, face first into a stand of alders.

He rose to his knees, slightly dazed, and looked around. He was all right, a scrape along his cheek. No problem. Lucky he'd fallen where he had. There was a sharpened stake only inches . . . No, it wasn't a stake, just a sapling, severed near the base by a machete or an ax. As he glanced around he noticed other signs that someone had been through here before, carving a rude, barely visible path. Or at least one barely visible to people. To a dog, it probably looked like a forest freeway.

There was a familiar rusty stain on a clump of grass beside him. He tested it with his fingertips and they came away with a powdery residue. Dried blood. There were dribs and drabs of it on the grass all along the path. Roadkill must have come out this way after she'd been chewed up. And now she was following her own blood trail back, to . . . whatever.

But she hadn't cut this crude path out. Someone else had. Ox? Maybe. A woodsman who could kill a deer with a .22 pistol could certainly follow a blood trail as well marked as this one.

David glanced at his watch as he rose stiffly to his feet. Nearly seven. Two hours of daylight, less than that in the deep woods where the sunlight dies early. He had to find the dog and soon, or they'd both be lost in here, and the idea of a night in the swamps with something that could chew up a full grown Pit Bull like an hors d'oeuvre had no appeal at all.

He plunged after the dog, moving more cautiously now, wary of his footing. He couldn't hope to outrun her in here, but her strength would have to fade soon.

Or maybe not. He'd plodded on a good half hour without catching sight of Roadkill again. At least the going was getting easier. The ground had been slowly rising as he marched, fewer holes and hummocks, higher and drier. And then he came to the reason why. A slow moving creek meandered out of the woods. It didn't look deep, probably no more than chest high on a man, but it was ten or twelve feet wide. Roadkill had apparently just plunged in and paddled across. He could see her muddy tracks on the far bank. David spotted a fallen tree roughly forty yards to the east. He detoured down to it, clambered across the stream on it, then worked his way back to the trail.

Walking was almost pleasant now. The trees were taller and more widely spaced. Mature poplars and spruce shaded out the sun and thinned the ground cover beneath their canopy. There were even clearings, or would have been if they hadn't been clogged with head high alders and ferns and reeds . . . And then he found Roadkill.

She was sitting on a hummock at the edge of a clearing, her sides heaving, tongue lolling, utterly exhausted. He talked to her gently as he approached her, but she made no move to run. She'd gone as far as she could, and then stopped, out of gas.

He knelt beside her, ran his hands over her flanks and checked her stitches. Still solid. She'd pulled a couple of gashes open on her shoulders, but not all the way. They'd probably close again on their own. No major damage done. Thank God for small favors.

He rose slowly and took stock of his situation. The sun was nearing treetop level on the horizon. They still had an hour or so of daylight to find their way back. The path was clear enough at this point, as though . . . it had been heavily used. As he scanned his surroundings, David realized that the grass around him had been trampled, ferns broken, in a rough circle. And the whole area was spattered with rust spots. Dried blood.

Sweet Jesus, this is where it happened. Roadkill hadn't stopped here because she was spent, she'd stopped because she'd arrived at her destination. She'd been here before, had fought here, and now her savage heart had brought her back for a rematch. She was resting, waiting for her opponent to show again.

But why here? There were no rocks or deadfalls in the area where a wolf could fort up; it was just a clearing, with tag alders and ferns and . . . reefer. In the mix of foliage ahead, every third plant was marijuana, mature plants with the telltale erose leaves and stalks as tall as a man. This was no whimsical patch seeded by some happy go lucky pothead; it was a serious growing operation, carefully camouflaged in the depths of the state forest. There were easily sixty to seventy plants in the clearing, possibly more, and God only knew how many more clearings like this one there were concealed back here. And for all David knew, they could have tigers guarding this place.

Time to go. He reached down for Roadkill, but she stiffened and growled. But the warning snarl wasn't for him. She was staring at something on the far side of the clearing. And then David saw it too. The ferns were moving. Something big was coming toward them. Moving fast.

Roadkill staggered to her feet to face the threat but David wasn't waiting. He scooped up the dog and ran, sprinting back down the path as fast as he could manage. Which wasn't very. Between Roadkill's sixty pounds and the brush snagging his clothes, the best he could manage was a reeling stagger. Still, he was covering ground. He could hear shouting behind him, and a raspy wasp-buzz as something whistled past his head and thwacked into a tree beside the trail. A bullet? No, there'd been no shot . . . Pellet gun. Like the one he used to inject aggressive bulls or elk. Not a boy's BB gun, a serious, high pressure air rifle. Lethal if they struck a man. And they fired .22 calibre pellets. The same size as the slug that had killed Ox.

The voices grew fainter, and for a minute David thought they might be giving up. But then Roadkill started growling and squirming in his arms, as though she sensed a danger he couldn't see. He risked a glance over his shoulder, and caught a glimpse of them. Rottweilers. Two of them, about sixty yards behind him, coming on hard and fast. A hundred and forty pounds apiece, hurtling through the brush like black and tan demons. Silently. No barking. They'd been well trained.

Seconds. That's all he had now. If they caught him, he was done. He had no illusions about fighting off a pair of trained attack dogs. If he dropped Roadkill, he might be able to make it up a tree in the confusion. Because she'd fight them, injured or not. She'd die fighting them. And he couldn't let that happen. He only had one ghost of a chance . . . So he kept on running, desperately wrestling with the fiery little Bull who wanted nothing more than to break free and give battle.

And then they hit it. David broke out of the brush at the creek. He didn't hesitate. He threw Roadkill in the general direction of the far bank and plunged in after her. He found his footing in the middle of the creek, then turned to face his attackers. And not a moment too soon. The first Rott hurtled out of the trees like a missile and leapt at David's head, all fangs and snarling fury.

As the dog pounced, David dropped to his knees below the surface of the water, clawing desperately for purchase as the dog came down on him. He grabbed a foreleg and pulled it under. The Rottweiler thrashed, snapping at him, but only for a second. It got a lungful of water and instantly forgot its attack, forgot everything but frantically trying to fight its way to the surface for air. He let it go, and burst out of the water himself, just in time to take the full force of the second Rott's attack.

The dog struck him shoulder high, knocking him off his feet. It whirled on him, churning the water to foam as it clawed furiously toward him. And then its eyes widened, and it spun back to its rear as Roadkill clamped onto its hindquarters with her iron jaws.

David grabbed a fistful of the Rott's pelt at the shoulder and thrust him under with Roadkill still clamped on his rear end. The water had the same effect on both dogs. They struggled to the surface gagging and gasping for air. David pushed the Rott away from him toward the opposite shore where its companion was still trying to claw its way up the bank. He grabbed Roadkill, clambered out of the water, and staggered off down the trail.

Behind him, he could hear the Rotts hacking and gagging as they coughed up a fair amount of creek water. Great dogs, Rottweilers. Loyal, intelligent, and no more aggressive than they're trained to be. But they can't hold their breath underwater. Only a very few retrievers can manage that particular trick. The two attack dogs were done, for the moment. And apparently their masters had counted on them to finish the job. David could hear no other sounds of pursuit.

The rest of the run was a nightmare, reeling through the woods in the gathering dusk, desperately trying to stay on the path and hold the dog struggling in his arms. Somewhere along the run, Roadkill settled down, panting with exhaustion. David knew exactly how she felt. He wasn't far from collapse himself. The sunlight was rapidly waning and he knew if they didn't get clear of the woods before dark, they'd never get out at all.

But, somehow, they did. As the light gradually faded into shadows, it took every ounce of his stamina and concentration to keep putting one foot ahead of the other and to stay on the crude trace of a path. So that when he suddenly broke through a tangle of brush and found himself standing on the edge of the highway, only a dozen yards from his Jeep and the steady stream of traffic beyond it, he was stunned.

He sank slowly to his knees, gasping, exhausted. Only Roadkill's squirming to get free kept him from passing out altogether. If he let her go, she could die in traffic in a heartbeat. So he struggled to hold onto her, and to his consciousness. And realized they were coming for him.

A pickup truck pulled out of a forest trail a half mile back down the road, and began rumbling toward him along the shoulder with its lights out.

Christ, no wonder they hadn't followed him. They didn't have to! They knew roughly where the damned path came out. They just took some back road out, found his Jeep and waited for him to show up!

David lunged to his feet and staggered toward the Jeep. The pickup was gaining speed now, the passenger window was down and he could see the muzzle of the pellet rifle centering on him.

He ducked around the Jeep and yanked open the driver's door. A slug ricocheted off the roll bar only inches from his head. He tossed Roadkill onto the passenger's seat, vaulted behind the wheel and fired up the Jeep. The truck was almost on him, veering up on the edge of the freeway to come alongside for a point blank shot. No time to run for it.

He jammed the gearshift into reverse and floored the accelerator. The Jeep backed into the pickup, striking it just ahead of the passenger door. The impact spun the Jeep around, nearly upending it. The pickup caromed off and skidded out onto the highway. David caught only a glimpse of a bearded face in the window before a flatbed truck loaded with steel beams slammed into the pickup cab at seventy miles an hour, and rolled over it, crushing the truck beneath it, and dragging it along in a maelstrom of sparks and rending metal that howled like the end of the world.

✻ ✻ ✻

David glanced up when the patrol car pulled into the clinic lot, but didn't bother to answer the door. The blinds were drawn and the "closed" sign was in place. Stan Wolinski came in anyway.

"Doc?"

"I'm back here."

Wolinski strolled through to the operating room. David had Roadkill up on the table, swabbing out the gashes that had reopened on her shoulders.

"How's she doin'?" Wolinski asked.

"Better than I am," David said, fingering the rubber neckbrace they'd given him in the emergency room. "This dog's got the damnedest constitution I've ever seen. I don't think you could kill her with an H-bomb."

"You look a little rough, though," Wolinski agreed. "The guy drivin' that flatbed got off with only bruises. The pair in the pickup are both dead. Real dead. It took the fire department nearly an hour just to cut their bodies out of the wreck. I've seen 'possums flattened in truck stop driveways that looked better."

"Who were they?"

"Couple of gang bangers from Detroit. Survivalist types. Figured they were gonna finance their new world order by growin' reefer up here in the great outdoors. You were right about that gun they were usin'. It was an air rifle, a Shamal, .22 calibre. I got a feeling when the medical examiner does the autopsy on Ox, he'll find the slug in him was from their gun, not his own."

"They fired at me without hesitating," David said. "They probably did the same thing when he showed up at their patch. Then hauled his body back to his place and arranged things to look like suicide. I feel partly responsible, though. If I hadn't given Ox that damned bill, he wouldn't have backtracked his dog—"

"You don't know that," Wolinski said, cutting him off. "Ox roamed all through that swamp, poaching. He probably would have come across them eventually. Or someone else would have. Those guys were ex-cons with a long record of violence. They were an accident waiting to happen. And, God bless him, maybe Ox was, too."

"Maybe he was," David conceded. "It still bothers me, though."

"A lot of things seem to bother you, Doc. So what are you going to do about the dog?"

"Actually, I was hoping you could help me out with her."

"Me?"

"Sure. Pit Bulls are terrific dogs, but they're not your average mom and pop house pet. They're more like . . . power tools, or even weapons. They're great to have around, as long as you treat 'em with respect. They've been bred for tenacity and fighting spirit for centuries, and that heritage doesn't evaporate just because you teach the dog to sit up or fetch your slippers."

"Granted, but what's that got to do with me?"

"For one thing, you're a man who's used to treating weapons with respect. And didn't you mention that you'd had trouble with vandals on your place? I guarantee this lady would put an end to that. Besides, if it wasn't for her, those two loonies would still be on the loose. I figure you owe her one."

The sheriff eyed the dog on the table doubtfully. She returned his stare, unintimidated. "What's her name?"

"I'm not sure," David admitted. "Ox mentioned it, but it was in Finnish and I didn't understand. I've been calling her Roadkill."

"What the hell kind of name is that?"

"An appropriate one," David said. "If you take her, you can name her anything you like."

"No, I don't think so," Stan said. "The name kind of suits her if you think about it. It'll do, I guess. Roadkill."

The dog cocked her head slightly, as though she was trying to understand what Stan was saying.

"Roadkill," Stan repeated. And this time her tail twitched. It was only a twitch, definitely not a wag. But it was a start.

Animal Rites

Hi, Dr. Westbrook. I'm Karen Cohen, TV 17 News. I'll be your moderator this evening. Could you take your seat at the table, please? We go live on the air in three minutes."

"We who are about to die, salute you," David said grimly.

"It won't be that bad," she said, with a plastic smile. She was shorter than she appeared to be on television, five two or so. Her sharply angular face was more forceful than attractive and her apparently casual hairdo was sprayed hard as a helmet. Navy blue suit, pearls, all business. David followed her to the interview set, wondering why he let himself be talked into this.

Two of the panelists were already seated: Helena Massey, the silver maned president of the local Humane Society. Tanned and taut, Helena was wearing a simple red and white print dress that probably cost more than David's veterinary practice earned in a month. He didn't recognize her companion, a younger man, pale and intense, wearing a green corduroy jacket, no tie. Their heads were close together, voices low, expressions earnest. They looked like they were plotting to overthrow the tsar.

Three chairs were still empty. David spotted Hutch Jaeger pacing at the back of the studio. The older man was wearing his usual rumpled khakis, an unlit briar pipe clamped firmly in the corner of his mouth. As chairman of the Algoma Sportsmen's Club, Hutch was a spokesman for local hunters. A reluctant one. He was soft-spoken by nature, and these debates usually turned into screaming matches. He looked pallid. Probably stage fright.

The television studio was a crude affair. Three small sets were positioned around a central camera island, a weather set complete with maps, the news desk and the personal interview set, which consisted of a round table in front of a faux bookcase wall. Beyond the backdrops, no effort had been made to disguise the concrete block walls. Welcome to small town broadcasting.

There was a bustle in the corner of the room as the last two panelists swept in. Randy Castle and his wife, Ilena, pop singers who owned a vacation home in Algoma. They'd only recently taken up the cause of hunter's rights but they were photogenic and even with their careers on the wane, their appearance would boost the local station ratings.

They were a striking couple. Randy was an All American Boy, Huck Finn grin, shaggy red hair and freckles. Ilena was the ultimate trophy wife, a green-eyed blonde with Vegas hair and a drop dead figure. Both of them were wearing full-length fur coats, mink for Ilena, wolf for Randy. The coats had the desired effect. Helena Massey and friend looked like they'd been jabbed with a cattle prod. Both of them were seething.

The Castles had a final word with a blue-suited bodyguard type who'd accompanied them, then took their places at the table.

"Good, everyone's here and we have one minute to airtime," Karen Cohen said as Hutch Jaeger reluctantly eased into his seat. "Here's a quick rundown of our format. The subject will be animal rights versus hunting. Dr. Westbrook, why don't you begin by outlining the situation here in Algoma and I'll pick it up from there."

First! Damn! Before David could protest, the theme music was already coming up, the floodlights brightened, and Karen was smiling into the camera.

"Good evening, ladies and gentlemen, and welcome to a News Channel 17 special edition of Open Forum. I'm Karen Cohen, your host. As most of you know, the annual deer season opens next week in northern Michigan. Nearly three quarters of a million hunters will participate, but not everyone agrees that hunting is a legitimate sport, and some feel it should banned altogether. What do you think?

"The members of our panel tonight are all Algoma residents, though Randy Castle and his lovely wife Ilena might be better known for their hit songs than their sportsmanship . . ."

She ran through the list quickly. Too quickly to suit David. Helena's pal in the corduroy jacket was an animal rights activist from Detroit named Jerry Feicke. He was chafing at the bit, as eager to debate as Hutch Jaeger was reluctant. The Castles' fur coats had obviously tripped his trigger . . .

David heard his name, Karen was smiling at him expectantly, and suddenly he was staring into the camera's unblinking eye.

"Um, actually I'm neutral in this debate," David said, swallowing. "As a veterinarian, I spend my time patching animals up, so I'm personally not a hunter. But from an ecological point of view, since we've all but eliminated the wolf and coyote populations in Michigan, there are no natural checks on the whitetail deer herds anymore, unless you count automobiles. Last year nearly forty thousand deer and five people died in collisions. So while I'm not a fan of hunting, when it comes to animal population control, it's the only game in town, no pun intended."

"And yet, many people feel that hunting is far more than a sport," Karen said smoothly, calling on Hutch Jaeger next. The older man began a halting, passionate paean to the history of the hunt. He was talking about the discovery of the five-thousand year old mummy of a prehistoric hunter in a Swiss glacier when he coughed and seemed to falter. Feicke seized the opening, launching into a tirade before Hutch could recover.

David listened to Feicke for a moment, then tuned him out. He sympathized with the animal rights cause, but urban zealots like Feicke left him cold. When David assisted at the birth of a calf, he knew that neither the cow nor her offspring were likely to die of old age, and the ways of the wild are harsher still. There are no retirement homes in the forest.

He sized Feicke up as a professional speaker imported to counter the Castles' stage presence. If so, he was a poor choice. He came across as a strident know-it-all. David met Hutch Jaeger's gaze. The older man rolled his eyes and David smiled.

Feicke made a crack about the Castles' fur coats. Ilena retorted that minks were first cousins to rats, and asked if Feicke believed in rights for rats, too?

Feicke began an "all living things are sacred" speech, but he'd barely begun when Ilena Castle stood up. And smiled at the camera. And uncoiled a snake from beneath her fur coat. A large snake. Nearly two meters of green boa constrictor writhing in her hands. David guessed it was either an Emerald Tree Boa or an Australian Green. Feicke froze, his eyes riveted on the snake.

"My friend Bobby the Boa eats rats for a living," Ilena said calmly, holding the squirming snake out towards Feicke, who'd gone absolutely ashen.

"Maybe you can explain to him why you want him to change his diet, Mr. Feicke? Because eating rats must violate their rights. Right?"

The room was silent as a painting. Ilena placed the snake on the table and he immediately wriggled into a defensive coil, nervously tasting the air with his flickering tongue.

"Is that snake dangerous, Dr. Westbrook?" Karen Cohen asked, through jaws that were nearly clamped shut.

"Any snake will strike if it's frightened," David began, but Feicke didn't wait for the rest. With a moan, he thrust himself back from the table, toppling over his chair in his haste to escape. He scrambed on his hands and knees across the studio. The camera followed him all the way.

"This snake seems calm enough, though," David continued. "Has he been fed recently?" No one was listening.

"We'll—ah, we'll take a station break now," Karen said, blinking, mesmerized by the snake. "This is Open Forum and we'll be back after these—"

There was a crash from behind the set and one of the overhead floods wobbled on its stand as Feicke apparently blundered into it. Karen Cohen quickly covered her mouth. Too late. She burst out with a strangled whinny of a giggle, as much a nervous release as anything else. Her laughter was contagious, and they all broke up, even the cameraman. Well, almost everyone.

"That was despicable," Helena Massey snapped, rising. "I should have expected this kind of cheap stunt from you, Castle. But for the rest of you to laugh, just because someone's afraid of a snake? You ought to be ashamed of yourselves."

She unclipped her lapel mike, tossed it on the table and stalked off.

"Mrs. Massey?" Karen called after her.

"Quit while you're ahead, lady," Randy Castle said. "That bit of theater will make every news show in the country. If you need to fill the air time, why don't we talk about my new tour?"

"I guess we'll have to," Karen said doubtfully. "We can't very well have a debate now. Will you all remain seated, please, while I introduce the next segment? And Ilena, please put that snake away. As far away as possible, preferably." Open Forum's producer buttonholed David after the show to ask advice about a vomiting cat. David listened sympathetically but the symptoms were too vague for a diagnosis.

"Sometimes cats get upset stomachs, just like people," he said. "She'll probably be fine in a day or two. If the vomiting persists, though, bring her by the clinic and I'll take a look at her."

The Castles and their companion were already halfway across the parking lot when David stepped out of the studio. The three of them were still laughing about the prank with the snake. Which is why they didn't notice Jerry Feicke half hidden behind a parked car at the far side of the lot. As they drew abreast of him, Feicke charged at them, full tilt.

"Hey! Look out!" David yelled, sprinting towards Feicke, trying to head him off.

Too late. "Bastaaard!" Feicke screamed, swinging wildly at Randy Castle. But before he could land a blow, David tackled Feicke from the side, grabbing his knees, pulling him down. The scuffle was over in seconds. David, Castle, and the bodyguard held Feicke down until a studio security guard showed up, took him firmly by the arm and ran Feicke off the lot.

"Whoa, that was more exciting than most TV debates," Randy Castle said, dusting himself off. "Are you okay, Doc?"

"No major damage," David said, more shaken than he cared to admit.

"Well, thanks for the help. What do you say we step into the pub across the parking lot for a quick pick-me-up? I'd like to talk to you anyway."

"I think I could use a bracer, at that," David said. "For medicinal purposes only, of course."

"Absolutely," Randy said, flashing a four hundred watt smile. "I don't think you've met my manager, Brian Benetto?"

The bodyguard-type shook hands perfunctorily. Up close, he was even bigger than David had first thought, square-jawed, with a faint blue beard shadow, and hard eyes. He looked like a movie mobster on steroids. "Nice to meet you, Doc. Look, Randy, you can't waste any more time here, you hafta talk to the promoters—"

"All I *have* to do, is breathe, Brian," Randy said, cutting him off. "Everything else is optional. And right now I want to talk to the doc, here."

"I'll put Bobby Boa in the van," Ilena said, stepping between them to cool things. "Why don't you come with me, Brian?"

"Good idea," Randy said, his smile fading. "Babysit her, Brian. No telling how many other loonies might be hanging around. Come on, Doc, let me get you that drink."

"What did you want to talk to me about?" David asked, following Castle into the pub.

"Ilena and I are in the middle of a tour," Castle said, taking a corner booth in the shadows. "And frankly the crowds could be better. We've always used snakes in our act and since this animal rights thing's heated up, we've been drawing a lot of media attention doing shows like today's."

"Not quite like today's, I hope," David said.

"Wrong, today's was damn near perfect," Randy said gleefully. "That wuss falling over his chair will play on stations that wouldn't give me the time of day otherwise. I'd risk a dozen parking lot scuffles for that kind of publicity. Thanks again for steppin' in. Maybe I can return the favor."

"How do you mean?" David asked.

"I've been thinking about maybe adding some game animals to our act, Doc. Z.Z. Topp toured with an honest-to-God buffalo a few years ago, and I figure a few big animals on stage might give our show some pizzazz, especially if I could get 'em to react to the music somehow. I figure on using a couple of deer, maybe even an elk. What do you think?"

"Frankly, I think it's a lousy idea," David said. "Deer and elk seldom adapt very well to captivity, to say nothing of traveling. They wouldn't be suitable at all."

"Why not?" Randy said, his charm fading like a mist in sunlight.

"They're ungulates," David said. "Their reflexes are geared to running at the first hint of danger or even anything out of the ordinary. If you put them in a situation where they're agitated but unable to run, like a traveling cage, they'll destroy themselves. They'll hyperventilate until they die of stress."

"Couldn't they be drugged to keep 'em calm?"

"There are drugs that'll sedate them for a short time; Xylazine, for instance. But even drugging them for a single move entails a serious risk. You couldn't do it for a whole tour."

"So we have to replace a few of 'em. If you came along to keep 'em zonked to the gills they'd last awhile, right? I'd be willing to pay you a pretty good salary."

"A good salary for what?" Brian Benetto asked, taking the seat next to David as Ilena Castle slid into the booth beside her husband.

"The doc's gonna look after the zoo I'm planning to add to the road show," Randy said.

"A zoo? And a zookeeper?" Brian Benetto said. "Randy, are you nuts? We haven't been able to book half the dates we need to break even as it is. We can't afford to hire anybody else."

"The point's academic anyway," David said, rising. "The animals you mentioned wouldn't survive a tour, Mr. Castle. They might not survive the first move. I wouldn't take the job myself and I doubt that any other reputable vet would either."

"Get real, Doc," Randy sneered, all pretense of civility gone now. "How much money can you be makin' in a rinky-dink town like this?"

"Enough that I can tell you to stuff your offer where the sun don't shine, jack," David said evenly. "It's a bad idea. Forget it. And Mrs. Castle, you'd better be careful about overfeeding your snake. He looked sluggish and his eyes were a little dull."

"I prefer him sluggish when I'm carrying him under my coat," she said, unoffended.

"Carrying him there isn't a good idea anyway," David said. "Snakes are carnivores, not fashion accessories. I'll skip the drink, Mr. Castle. See you around."

David spotted a client on the far side of the pub, wandered over to say hello and stayed to chat a few minutes. On his way out, he glanced at the corner booth. Randy was gone, but Ilena and Benetto were still there, sitting closely together, talking. Judging from their interlocked knees, it wasn't a business conference. More like love or a facsimile, David guessed. Life in the fast lane. Ilena glanced up and met his eyes. She smiled, and pointedly caressed Brian's cheek. David waved goodbye.

✳ ✳ ✳

"I can't believe you turned down the offer," Yvonne said, over a very late supper. David had been out until ten o'clock helping a mother Chow with a difficult delivery. They were alone now, in their kitchen, just shy of midnight, lights low, Nat King Cole murmuring on the radio.

"Why? Would you want me to go?"

"Of course not, but sometimes I think you feel restless working in Algoma. Didn't it sound exciting?"

"Alligator wrestling sounds exciting. That doesn't mean I'd like to try it. Besides, from what the manager said, it sounded like a low budget adventure anyway."

"Ilena Castle looks . . . very attractive on television."

"Benetto certainly seemed to think so."

"And you didn't?" she said carefully. Yvonne was barefoot, wearing a shapeless bathrobe and her glasses, her hair a tousled shambles. She looked utterly adorable but David knew better than to say so. Women seldom feel beautiful unless their hair is perfect and their clothes are impeccable. It's a miracle the race has survived.

"Ilena Castle is a very handsome package," David admitted. "But that's also the way she struck me. Like a commodity. A new car or a refrigerator, and about as sexy as a fiberglass mannequin. Besides, the lady wears snakeskin accessories with the snakes still aboard. I prefer my reptiles in terrariums, thank you. Or better yet, on video. And I prefer my ladies winningly rumpled. The way you look now."

"I'm rumpled, all right, which reminds me, I have a bath waiting. Turn off the lights when you're finished. We'll pick up in the morning."

"I'm finished now," he said. "But since I doubt that you'd care to bed down with someone who's spent the last four hours groveling in a kennel coaxing Chow pups into the world, I'll flip you for the bath. Unless, of course, you'd care to share."

She eyed him, her expression neutral. "I don't have a coin," she said.

"Neither have I."

"You didn't even look."

"I'm positive I don't have one. You don't think I'd lie about a thing like that, do you?"

"I would certainly hope so," she said.

So they shared the bath, and made love, long and languorous. And fell asleep in each other's arms.

But sometime before dawn he jerked awake, shaken and sweating. He'd been dreaming about the death of his father, ten years before. And he lay there in the dark, with his love at his side. Feeling haunted and alone. And a little afraid.

Even the light of morning couldn't dispel the dream. Its shadowed images lingered like a mist. And on the way to his office, he listened to the news. And learned that Randy Castle's home had been riddled by gunfire in the night. Randy had been wounded. His manager, Brian Benetto, had been killed.

✲ ✲ ✲

"It wasn't much of a fight, Stan," David said. "I tackled Feicke before he even landed a punch, and then Randy Castle and his manager . . . what was his name?"

"Benetto. The late Brian Benetto," Sheriff Stan Wolinski said. The two of them were alone in David's surgery. Wolinski was a cement block of a man, squarely built, with attitudes to match. His uniform and brush cut were similar shades of gray.

"Right." David nodded. "Benetto. Anyway, the three of us just held Feicke until the security guard came. It wasn't exactly World War Three."

"And Benetto didn't rough Feicke up, particularly, or have words with him?"

"No. I doubt Feicke even knew who he was. Benetto wasn't on the panel. I wasn't introduced to him until after the scuffle. Why?"

"Because Benetto's the man who got killed," Wolinski said simply. "Feicke says he was trying for Castle and Benetto must have caught one by accident. I have no reason to doubt that; I'm just gathering facts. Maybe you shouldn't have tackled him. If the poor bastard had landed one solid punch, his honor or whatever might've been satisfied and he wouldn't have shot up Castle's house like some gang-banger. And he wouldn't be in my slammer looking at murder one."

"There's no doubt Feicke did it?"

"He's admitted it. Hell, he seems proud of it. Turned himself in first thing this morning and his only regret was that he'd only wounded Castle."

"Well, if you're looking for more nails to drive in his coffin, I can't help you," David said. "After the scuffle he was almost in tears. The studio rent-a-cop ran him off with no trouble. He didn't make any threats . . . Wait a minute. If he's turned himself in, what are you doing here? What's the problem?"

"A small one," Wolinski admitted. "He's confessed all right, I'm just not sure I believe him."

"Why not?"

"For openers, he's doesn't seem like the type. He's a nice kid, well educated. Still, the ugliest killing I ever saw was a sixty-year old grandma who took a neighbor apart with a golf club."

"Okay, maybe he's not the type. What else?"

"The gun. Or rather, the lack of one. It was an automatic rifle, .223, with full metal jacket ammunition, probably military surplus. Feicke's a little vague about the kind of gun it was. In fact, he doesn't seem to know much about guns, period."

"You don't need a college degree to pull a trigger."

"True, but he not only can't tell me what gun he used, he doesn't know where it is. He says he ditched it in the river but he's not sure where. If you're going to confess, why bother to ditch the gun? Why not just turn it in?"

"If he's shooting up people's homes, maybe he's a couple of bricks shy of a load."

"Did he seem crazy to you?"

"I'm a veterinarian, not a shrink."

"You're qualified to spot mad dogs, right? Did Feicke strike you that way?"

"If Jerry Feicke was one my patients, he'd be a rabbit," David conceded. "No, I didn't think he was crazy. He's definitely a zealot about animal rights, though. If he'd shot Castle to prevent him from harming an animal, I might buy that."

"Well? Was Randy Castle harming any animals?"

"Oddly enough, he was considering it. He had a cockamamie idea about working game animals into his act. Deer, or maybe an elk. He asked if I'd be interested in touring with the show to handle the animals."

"So? Were you?"

"Hell, no," David said, exasperated. "It was a crazy idea. The animals wouldn't have survived a week and I told him so."

"Could Feicke have known about these plans?"

"I doubt it. I think it was something Randy came up with on the spur of the moment. His manager was as surprised to hear about it as I was. He thought it was a lousy idea, too, but for a different reason."

"What reason?"

"Money. He said something about the tour not having enough bookings to break even. Said they couldn't afford anyone else."

"It's a moot point now. Castle's canceled the tour. In fact, with the hole he's got in his arm, he may be through touring, period."

"How badly was he wounded?"

"It didn't look like much to me. A hole in the back of his right bicep. The doc in the emergency room told me Randy was lucky Feicke used jacketed ammo. It went through clean without expanding. They were willing to release him but Randy wanted to stay in the hospital until they can fly in a specialist to check for nerve damage. And speakin' of second opinions, I need one from you."

"On what?"

"A case like this, rock singer gettin' plugged by some guy he offends on a TV show, it's gonna draw serious media attention. My phone's already ringin' off the wall with questions from reporters."

"So? It's an open and shut case, isn't it?"

"It looks like it, sure."

"Then what's the problem?"

"It's two problems. And I want to be off the record here, okay? Doctor-patient relationship?"

"You hardly qualify as one of my patients."

"You know what I mean. The thing is, the emergency room doctor told me Castle was stoned when they brought him in last night. Cocaine, he thought."

"Gee, a rock singer using drugs? I'm shocked."

"Yeah, but Castle's no ordinary singer. He's got this squeaky clean outdoor image. I've never heard any local rumbles about him usin' dope, and I think my local sources are pretty good. But if he's into dope, I don't want to get blindsided. Was anything odd about his behavior yesterday? Like he was high?"

David considered the question. "No," he said slowly. "He seemed pumped, maybe a little edgy, nothing out of the ordinary."

"What do you mean, edgy?"

"He overreacted when I turned him down. Instantly nasty, when there was no reason for it. I got the impression he was feeling some pressure."

"What kind of pressure?"

"Maybe a tour that wasn't going very well. But maybe more than that. Ordinarily I wouldn't say anything about this, but since we're talking about a killing . . ."

"And I'm your patient, sort of. What is it?"

"As I was leaving the pub, I noticed Ilena Castle and Benetto sitting alone. They looked awfully cozy. Maybe it was nothing, but . . ."

"But if you really thought so, you wouldn't have mentioned it, would you?"

"No, I guess not. It definitely looked like something was going on between them. But it couldn't have anything to do with what happened, right?"

"I don't see how."

"You said there were two things bothering you. Okay, Castle was stoned when they brought him in. What's the other?"

"I don't know if you'll understand this," Wolinski said, shaking his head. "You're not a hunter. I don't hunt much anymore myself. But this is huntin' country and I grew up here and took a lot of game when I was a kid. The thing is, sometimes you're making a perfect stalk on an animal; you're downwind, haven't made a sound or showed yourself. And yet suddenly that whitetail or elk or whatever, will look up, right at you. Somehow it knows exactly where you are. It's like a voice on the wind whispered to it. Look out, pal. Something nasty's headed your way."

"What are you saying? That Castle should have sensed trouble coming because he's a hunter?"

"Maybe he did, I don't know. Maybe that's why he lived and his manager didn't. But I'm not talking about him, I'm talking about me. I'm the one who's hearing a voice on the wind. It's telling me there's something wrong about this."

"Like what?"

"I don't know," Stan said, shrugging his massive shoulders. "It's just a feeling. A bad one. That this could blow up in my face if I'm not careful."

"If you're hearing voices, maybe you really do need a doctor."

"If I do, it won't be a vet. Thanks for your time, Doc."

* * *

The day returned to normal. Almost. David saw the usual run of patients, canine, feline, one goat with mastitis and a lop-eared rabbit who'd been savaged by a feral cat. Two hours and forty stitches later, the rabbit was in one piece, though minus the tip of an ear.

Saving a patient usually gave David a lift, but the dark mood from the talk with Stan and the dream of his father persisted. It was probably the power of suggestion, but David could almost feel a shadow hovering near him, just out of view. Terrific. He'd be hearing Stan's voices on the wind next.

Just before closing, Bettina, his veterinary assistant, stuck her head in the surgery door. "I've got a lady out here who says she needs to see you, a.s.a.p. Says it's an emergency, but doesn't have an animal with her. Ilena Castle? Do you know her?"

"We've met. Are you sure she doesn't have an animal? She's been known to carry a snake under her fur coat."

"Trust me, this lady isn't hiding a thing under her clothes, including underwear," Bettina said dryly. "Shall I send her in?"

"I'll see her in my office," David said. "All we have left are a couple of vaccinations, right? Why don't you handle them and then take off. I'll close up."

Bettina arched an eyebrow, then closed the surgery door without saying a word. Which was a considerable commentary in itself.

David went into his small office, and a moment later there was a rap on the door and Ilena Castle stepped in.

Bettina was right. Ilena wasn't concealing anything. Her ecru t-shirt fit like a snake's skin and her faded jeans seemed too tight to walk in. But she managed. Quite well, in fact.

"I'm afraid I've barged in under false pretenses," she said. "I don't have a sick animal, I'm the one with the emergency."

"No problem, I thought it might be personal. Sit down, you must've had a tough day."

"It's been grim," she admitted. She eased down into the battered chair beside his desk, glancing warily around as though she might take flight at any moment. "I just finished talking to Brian's parents about what happened. They were . . . Well, you can imagine."

"Actually, I'm not sure I can. What did happen, exactly? The news reports have been pretty vague."

"That crazy bastard from the TV panel shot up our home, that's what happened. He killed Brian and wounded Randy, all over that stupid prank with a snake! He must be insane."

"He may have some problems, all right," David said. "But haven't we all?"

"I certainly have my share," she said, meeting his eyes and taking a deep breath. "That's why I'm here."

"How can I help?"

"Have you, ah, talked to Randy since . . . all this happened?"

"No. Why?"

"Because you saw me with Brian yesterday, and I suppose it might have looked . . . Anyway, please don't say anything to Randy about it."

"I never intended to."

"I'm sure you didn't, I'd just feel better if I had your word."

"Of course," David said. "I doubt that I'll see your husband again in any case. We didn't exactly part friends."

"He may want to talk to you, though," she said, rising. "About the tour, I mean."

"I thought it was canceled."

"It was. But all the publicity's brought us a ton of offers. It looks like we'll be going on, only bigger and better. If you change your mind about taking the job I'll . . . see that you get your price. Anything at all."

"I won't change my mind," David said.

"Too bad," she said. "It might have been fun. Thanks for seeing me, Doc. It's been interesting." She swept out of the office like a model on a runway. A very worried model.

"Yeah," David said to the empty room. "It certainly has."

* * *

He closed the clinic, then took five minutes to pop the soft top off his Jeep and stow it in the back seat. He took the slow lane home, putzing along with the semis at fifty-five. It was a perfect autumn afternoon, warm, but with a crisp snap in the air that hinted at the chill of the coming night. The hills north and west of Algoma were showing the first dabs of color from the brush of the Master Painter, splashes of oaken gold, maple reds and oranges against the loden-green background of the tall pines.

He loved the northern Michigan countryside this time of year, reveled in the colors and scents. But it held no peace for him now. There was something tugging at a corner of his consciousness, like a mosquito droning in the dark. One you know will find you eventually . . .

And he realized it was the dream. Of his father, in those last months. Dying in the veteran's hospital in Grand Rapids. Dying by inches. The ulcers on his legs turned septic, then gangrenous. And so they'd amputated. His left ankle first. Then his knee. Then his right ankle. Sweet Jesus. And the worst of it was that he'd scarcely known it. Alzheimer's Disease had stolen most of his memory and much of his consciousness before his diabetes entered its final, lethal stage.

David and his dad had never been close, and even the stench of death in that sterile, anonymous room hadn't changed things between them. When his father was lucid, their conversations were generic; the politics of forty years ago. Or business. Or baseball. Man talk. Subjects of general interest discussed dispassionately, with no emotional involvement. And in this fashion, they both managed to avoid comment on the obvious. That the surgeons were cutting his father's legs away, and would continue to do so until . . .

God, the horror of it. He hadn't thought about it in years. Had deliberately repressed it.

And yet here it was, back again, in a dream. As though it had happened only yesterday. And the odd thing was, he had a definite sense that the dream was no coincidence. That somehow, something had called the memory of his father back. But why? What triggered it? He wasn't feeling lonely or maudlin. Nor was it the season for remembrance. His father had died in the spring. April. The twenty-first.

What was the old saying? Dream of the dead, hear from the living? Well, he'd certainly been hearing from the living. And the day wasn't over.

When he pulled into the driveway of the country home he shared with Yvonne, a gleaming red Jaguar was parked beside his wife's Range Rover. It looked like a car a rock star might drive. It wasn't.

Helena Massey was sitting at the kitchen table with Yvonne, sharing coffee and small talk. They were both wearing scuff clothes, jeans and blouses and boots. And both managed to exude elegance anyway. A valuable talent. One David admired greatly without having a clue as to how women manage it.

"Hi," he said. "Am I interrupting anything?"

"Actually Helena came by to see you," Yvonne said, giving him a peck on the cheek. "I have to see to my horse. You're sure you won't join us for dinner, Helena?"

"No, I really can't, but thank you. It was wonderful to see you again."

"You, too," Yvonne said. She winked at David as she ducked discreetly out the kitchen door.

"I'm sorry to bother you at home," Helena said, "I, ah, wanted to talk to you privately."

"No problem," David said. "What's up?"

"It's about what happened at the studio yesterday. Have you been interviewed about it yet?"

"Sheriff Wolinski talked to me this morning."

"I meant by the press. Have any reporters talked to you?"

"No, why should they?"

"I don't think you understand what's happened here, David," she said earnestly. "This will be the first major trial focused on the struggle for animal rights. No one's taken us seriously up to now, but Jerry's trial will change that. With Randy Castle involved, the trial will draw national attention. We'll be able to present the issues every single day to the world. Jerry will be the kind of symbol that James Brady was for the anti-gun movement."

"Brady? You mean the guy who was wounded with President Reagan?"

"And who went on to testify before Congress and helped get meaningful gun control legislation passed."

"Right, but James Brady was the victim, not the shooter, Helena. I doubt people will see Jerry in the same light."

"Once the American people are made aware of our viewpoint, they'll feel the same revulsion for the slaughter of animals that we do," she said doggedly. "And after the trial, Jerry will . . . Well, what really matters is that the issues will be forcefully presented."

"You may be right, Helena. I've never been much on politics. But I can't change the statement I already gave Stan Wolinski, if that's what you want."

"I wouldn't dream of asking you to, David. Tell me, do you think I'm crazy because I believe in animal rights?"

"Of course not. I don't agree with you totally, but I'm not unsympathetic to your viewpoint."

"And Jerry? Didn't he seem rational to you? Right up until those bastards shoved that damned snake in his face?"

"I suppose so. He seemed a lot less rational in the parking lot afterward, though."

"But his behavior was certainly understandable, wasn't it? After all, he'd been provoked."

"I'm no expert on rationality, Helena. What is it you want from me?"

"Only the truth. That the trouble in the parking lot was caused, at least in part, by Castle's provocation of Jerry earlier. You can say that honestly, can't you?"

"But the parking lot scuffle is hardly the issue now."

"All I'm asking is that you don't give the press the impression that Jerry is some wild-eyed maniac. We want the media to give our cause a fair shake."

"I see," David said. "All right, I won't tell reporters that Feicke's a lunatic, if that's what you're asking. I'm not qualified to comment one way or the other anyway."

"Good," she said, rising to leave. "I knew we could count on your honesty, if not your wholehearted support, David. Perhaps that will come later. I've got to get back to the jail now. There's an evening visiting hour at seven. Tell Yvonne goodbye for me."

She swept out, obviously cheered by the conversation. Leaving David shaking his head. He took two fluted wineglasses down from the cupboard, carefully filled them both with a light chardonnay, drained one at a gulp and refilled it.

"Has Helena driven you to drink?" Yvonne said, coming into the kitchen. "She's been known to have that effect on people."

"How do you mean?"

"She's always been a great one for causes," Yvonne said, taking a glass from him. "Her heart's in the right place, but all that earnestness can be a bit wearing sometimes."

"She's got me more confused than worn," he said. "Believing in a cause is one thing. Sacrificing people for it is another."

"Who's being sacrificed?"

"Her pal Feicke. I'm no legal expert, but he's confessed to shooting up Castle's home and killing his manager, right? So it seems to me his only hope is to plead insanity or something like it. And yet Helena wants me to tell people what a rational guy he is just to be sure their cause gets a fair hearing. She sees him as a martyr, for God's sake."

"Oh, I think she sees him as considerably more than that," Yvonne said. "They're lovers, you know."

"Lovers? You're kidding. She must be, what, fifteen years older than he is?"

"If their genders were reversed, you wouldn't think anything of it, and in a way, it makes perfect sense. They're both so passionate about animals, why shouldn't they feel some animal passion for each other?"

"But if she loves him, then what she just said makes even less sense."

"Maybe they think his conviction is a foregone conclusion and they're trying to salvage what they can."

"She seemed awfully cheerful for someone whose lover will be spending his happily ever afters in prison," David said doubtfully. "Besides, she said something . . ."

"What?"

"She was talking about James Brady, comparing Feicke to him. Saying he could be as effective for animal rights as Brady was for gun control. But Brady addressed Congress and spoke around the country. Does she think the Senate's gonna hold hearings on visiting days?"

"I don't know," Yvonne said. "I know Helena well enough not to underestimate her, though. She may be overzealous for her cause of the moment, but she's no fool."

"Right," he said, frowning, "she's not. So what's wrong with this picture? Her lover's in jail. Any publicity they get for their cause will be negated by his conviction, yet she's happy as the proverbial clam. It doesn't make sense. Unless . . ."

"What is it?"

"Unless she knows he won't be convicted."

"But he's confessed."

"So he has, but right now his confession's the only evidence against him. And Stan Wolinski has doubts about it. Feicke doesn't know anything about guns and he didn't produce the gun he said he used when he turned himself in. Okay, let's suppose he didn't ditch it? Suppose he never had it at all? Because he didn't do the shooting."

"But if he didn't, why would he confess?"

"Well, he's a bone deep fanatic about his cause. Suppose his confession's some kind of a . . . ploy? Let's say Feicke and Helena are together last night, maybe with a few friends from the animal rights movement. And they hear on the radio that somebody used Randy Castle's home for target practice. They've been looking for a forum to publicize their cause, and this is it. Feicke confesses to the shooting, the trial draws national publicity for weeks, maybe months, and at the end, they announce that his confession was a hoax and can prove it."

"But wouldn't Feicke be in trouble?"

"He might be charged with obstructing justice or something, sure. Maybe all of them would be. They'd be fined, maybe do a few nights in jail. But trust me, Feicke and Helena are serious enough about animal rights to serve some time for it."

"I don't know," Yvonne said doubtfully. "It seems hard to believe they'd go to such . . . extremes."

"Extreme's the operative word when it comes to animal rights. Both sides see it as life and death struggle, for the animals or their own lifestyle. It's almost as volatile as the abortion issue and people are killing each other over that one."

"Still, all this is speculation. We have no proof."

"Maybe not, but if Feicke didn't pop Castle and his manager, then whoever did it is still on the loose and the police aren't looking for him because they think they've got their man. I'd better call Stan Wolinski about this, even if I'm wrong."

"Fair enough, you call Stan, and I'll grill a couple of chicken breasts for dinner. A quiet evening at home tonight? No pups to deliver?"

"I'll do my best," he said, checking the directory for the number of the sheriff's department.

Ten minutes later he wandered into the kitchen, somberly sipping the last of his wine.

"What's wrong?"

"Wolinski says the idea of Feicke faking his confession isn't off the map. The preliminary ballistics report on the shooting came back and it's possible two weapons were involved. The slug that killed Benetto may be slightly different from the ones recovered from the house. They're the same caliber and they're deformed from the impact, so they can't be sure."

"What's Stan going to do?"

"All he can do is continue to question Feicke and try to break down his story."

"You know, there may be another explanation for this. Suppose Feicke's taking the fall for someone else?"

"Like who?"

"Helena. She feels as strongly as Feicke does, and as I recall, she and her first husband were both expert shots. Competitive skeet shooting, not hunting. She didn't get active in the animal rights movement until after he died."

"Do you think she's capable of a thing like that?"

"I think a strong, intelligent woman is capable of anything she sets her mind to," Yvonne said wryly. "Even killing, to protect herself, or someone she loved."

"She was pretty upset when she stormed out of the studio yesterday. On the other hand, there are two sides to this thing and we've only been considering one of them. Hunters are as adamant as the rights activists. And they're the ones who own guns."

"But Castle couldn't have shot himself."

"No, not in the left bicep with a rifle. It would be physically impossible. Still, all things considered, he's ahead of the game. His rival's dead, his wife is intimidated, his tour's back on track and he'll get national media attention for months."

"I'd hardly call getting shot a lucky break."

"Maybe luck had nothing to do with it. Not if he had a guardian angel."

"I don't understand."

"I'm not sure I understand it myself. The thing is, Stan told me he had a bad feeling about this, like a voice on the wind, warning him something was wrong. And I've been having the same feeling myself, only it's been . . . personal. I even dreamed about it last night."

"About what?"

"About my father's death. It's been on my mind all day."

"Your father? But . . . do you think it was some kind of a warning?"

"From beyond the grave, you mean? No, it wasn't like that. And anyway, my father and I didn't communicate that well when he was living, I can't imagine that he'd be a voice on the wind all these years later. No, it was more like a . . . reminder. To help me remember something important. It may be nothing, but I'd like to follow it through. I have to talk to someone. Save my supper, I won't be long."

"Where are you going?"

He hesitated in the doorway. "To visit an old friend," he said. "I hope."

✳ ✳ ✳

The Jaeger place was a Centennial Farm, so designated by the state with a handsome bronze plaque mounted on a post in the front yard. A hundred years of being worked by the same family. Actually it was closer to a hundred and forty years, but it wouldn't matter much longer. Hutch Jaeger's only son died in Vietnam. There would be no Jaegers after him on this land.

It wasn't really a farm anymore, in any case. It had been eleven hundred acres once, but Hutch had ceded a thousand acres to the state in his late wife's name for a preserve for deer and elk and a small herd of American bison.

Only the house and outbuildings remained on the last hundred acres now. The house was a mammoth old three-story Victorian pile, painted a cheery Christmas red with white trim to match its barns and silos. A shaded front porch stretched the full width of the building, complete with swings, café tables and chairs that overlooked the sprawling grounds. If you wanted to miniaturize a farm for children to play with, this would be the one.

David had been here many times to tend sick animals. Hutch still kept a small herd of dairy cattle. They were long since past their productive years but he maintained them anyway, like friends who'd retired. He'd also converted one of his barns to a kennel for greyhounds, after reading about how the animals were mistreated or killed when their racing days were over. His farm was a halfway house for them now, a place where they could run free and frolic and enjoy a puppyhood they'd never known.

A half dozen of the lean, lanky dogs surrounded David's Jeep as he pulled into the yard, yapping a greeting that brought Hutch to the front door.

"David? What's up? Has one of those damned hounds been playing with my cellular phone again?"

"Strictly a social call, Hutch. Have you got a few minutes?"

"Sure, let's sit on the porch here. House is a mess anyway. Join me in a beer?"

"I'd like one, thanks." David eased down at one of the café tables. Hutch disappeared into the house for a moment, then came back with two beers. He tossed one to David, but didn't join him at the table. He rested a haunch on the porch railing instead, a few yards away. He looked drained, and he was wearing a canvas trench coat, though the evening wasn't at all chilly yet.

"So," he said, looking out over the yard, "what brings you all the way out here?"

"Just wanted to talk. The panel yesterday turned out to be a lot more exciting than I expected."

"That's a fact," Hutch acknowledged, sipping his beer. "That Feicke has to be totally out of his tree."

"And Castle's not?"

"There's a difference," Hutch said evenly. "Castle's on my side."

"Or you thought he was."

"Randy may not be an ideal NRA poster boy, but I think his interest in the hunting life's genuine. And he definitely knows how to attract media attention to the sport."

"And to himself as well," David noted.

"Well, who do reporters want to talk to? A rock singer or an old fuddy-duddy like me?"

"That depends the kind of story they want. What do you suppose Feicke wants?"

"Publicity," Hutch said bitterly. "That's what they all want nowadays. Go on TV and say your mama slept with your brother, or you shoot a rock star. And reporters shove a microphone in your face and ask you how it felt. Everybody yells at everybody else, and in the noise the things that matter are drowned out . . ." Hutch's voice faded, and his gaze seemed to lose focus, in the terribly familiar way it had done on the show the day before . . .

The same way David's father had faded in and out in the last days of his life. And there it was.

David rose casually, and moved to the railing near Hutch.

"Hunting was our way of life for a hundred thousand years and more," Hutch continued softly, almost to himself. "Helena and her friends think the world's a giant zoo and we're the keepers. Well, maybe they're right. But there are a million deer in this state. Ban hunting for a year and there'll be two million. A year after that their numbers will double again and we'll have to slaughter them like vermin or they'll devour their habitat and destroy themselves and every creature they share it with. You know it's true."

"I know," David acknowledged. "But I also know you've kept your dairy cattle long past their useful years and you've gone to a lot of expense and trouble to bring these greyhounds up from Florida to make a home for them. Where's the logic in that?"

"I didn't say it was simple," Hutch said dryly, gathering himself. "If savin' a few dogs makes me a hypocrite, I can live with it. There's room for both sides in this, if we can just find some kind of balance. But that isn't how it's been goin' the last few years. The anti-hunting mob's growing and the press is on their side because it's an easy story; hunters are neanderthals and every deer is Bambi."

"And Randy Castle said he could change the balance? By volunteering to be a martyr for the cause? Is that what happened?"

Hutch eyed him a moment, then nodded slowly. "Randy came to me with the idea after Feicke jumped him in the parking lot. He said he was willing to take a flesh wound for the cause if I could deliver one safely. Everybody'd assume Feicke or one of his loonie friends did it and maybe we could sway public opinion our way for a change."

"It was a crazy idea."

"No," Hutch said levelly, "it was a very brave idea, I thought. And it would have worked. Only . . . it went wrong. He was supposed to be alone. I would never have fired into the house if I'd known anyone else was there."

"I don't think it was a mistake, Hutch," David said carefully. "I think it worked exactly the way Randy meant it to."

Hutch turned slowly to face him, as if he'd just remembered David was there at all. "What does that mean?"

"That Benetto's death wasn't an accident. A minute ago you said that Randy's plan was a brave thing to do. Maybe it wasn't so brave. For one thing, he was stoned when he arrived at the emergency room. I doubt he even felt the wound. But even if he did, it was probably worth it. His musical career was on the skids, his concert tour was losing money and his wife was having an affair with his business manager. And then bang! You solved all of his problems with a few shots. He's a media hero, his tour's red hot again, his rival's dead and his wife is so terrified she wouldn't dream of leaving him."

"You're wrong. Except for the shot that grazed Randy's arm, I fired at random. There's no way he could have arranged for Benetto to get hit."

"You're underestimating him. Did he know what kind of weapon you were going to use?"

"We discussed it, sure. We needed one that'd be accurate and seem lethal without doing too much damage. The .223 fit the bill. The military full-metal jacket ammo would make it look like the shots came from an assault weapon, but the main point was that they wouldn't expand so his wound would be as clean as possible."

"So the ammunition was his choice?"

"That's right. I didn't have any jacketed ammo so Randy gave me a box."

"But not a full box?"

"There may have been a couple of rounds missing . . . My God."

"Right. He killed Benetto himself, using ammo from the same box you fired at the house. A perfect match. A perfect crime. You've got to tell Stan Wolinski what happened, Hutch."

Hutch fell silent, mulling it over. "No," he said at last. "I don't think I can do that."

"Hutch, you have to. If you don't, Castle's going to get away with murder."

"He might anyway. That crazy Feicke's already confessed to it, and even if I come forward now, I won't make much of a witness.

You remember when I had that . . . lapse, yesterday in the TV studio? It wasn't the first. I have them fairly often now, and they're getting worse. It's Alzheimer's, David."

"I know," David said, nodding. "I sensed something was wrong yesterday. I even dreamt about it last night. My father had Alzheimer's, too."

"Then you understand my situation. I can't go in with you to answer a lot of questions. I'll just get confused and make a muck of it. Hell, I was probably having a lapse when I let Castle talk me into this in the first place. So I'll give you the gun I used, David. You give it to the sheriff. The bullets fired from it and the one that killed Benetto will be different. But I'm not going in with you. If Stan wants to talk to me, I'll be here."

David hesitated.

"I give you my word."

"All right, Hutch." David nodded. "Your word's always been good enough for me."

* * *

Dusk was settling over the hills as David drove slowly down the farm lane out to the highway, lost in thought. It was going to be a mess, any way you looked at it. Feicke and Castle and the law tearing at each other with Hutch caught in the middle. They'd rip into the old man like—David hit the brakes on instinct, startled by a sound. A faint, too familiar, pop.

He sat there, engine idling, hoping he'd hear the sound again, hoping it was a backfire, a blowout. Anything. Hoping he was wrong.

But he wasn't. An eerie wailing gradually arose, from the dogs kenneled near the house at first, then spreading to the others, each of them lifting their voices in a timeless lament.

They were greyhounds, not hunting dogs. They had no way of knowing what that muffled shot meant. And yet they did know, all of them. As though a voice on the wind had whispered it to them. And so they howled, howled as though it was the end of the world. Howled, as though they'd lost their best friend.

Perhaps they had.

* * *

"I should never have left him alone," David said. "I should have known."

"That diploma back at your office says you're a veterinarian, Doc," Stan Wolinski said. "It doesn't say anything about bein' a mind reader." They were in Stan's prowl car, following the ambulance slowly back to Algoma. There was no hurry.

"No, it was in his voice, his whole attitude," David said. "If you'd talked to him, you would have guessed."

"All I know about suicides is that if they're really determined, and Hutch was, then there's not much anybody can do about it. Except make themselves crazy broodin' about how they might've done this or that differently. The bottom line is, you couldn't have prevented it. And you damn sure can't change it now."

David eyed him a moment.

"No. I guess not."

"What matters now is, that it counts for something. Hutch left a letter explaining what happened, how Castle came to him with the idea of making himself into a martyr, and how they worked it. At the end, what Hutch feared most was that by the time Castle came to trial, his condition would have deteriorated so much that he'd embarrass himself. And let Castle get away with murder because of it."

"It still won't be easy to convict him, will it? I mean, he's still the guy with the hole in his arm and Feicke's confessed to the shooting."

"When Feicke hears what's happened, I doubt he'll stick to his story for long. And if Castle's wife was as frightened as you said, maybe I can talk her around once he's in jail. A big part of it will depend on you, though."

"On me? Why?"

"You're the last person Hutch talked to," Stan said carefully. "You're the only one who can testify that he was calm, and rational. And how sorry he was about what he and Castle tried to do. Will you have any problem with that?"

"No," David said. "That's how it was."

"Good," Stan said grimly. "In that case, we'll be able to put Mr. Castle where he belongs for a long while."

"This is personal with you, isn't it?"

"Damn straight it is. Hutch Jaeger was a friend of mine. The way I see it, Castle's as responsible for his death as if he'd shot him himself. I want him to pay for it. One way or another."

Neither of them spoke for awhile, riding in silence, each adrift in his own thoughts.

"Somethin' I wanted to ask you about," Stan said at last. "Somethin' in your line, for a change."

"What is it?"

"That sound those hounds were makin' when the medics carried Hutch's body out? I've heard dogs howl before, plenty of times. But I've never heard anything quite like that. Is there a special name for it?"

"Animal rites," David said.

"Animal ri . . . ? You're putting me on, right? Is that really what it's called?"

"No," David said. "But it should be."

Puppyland

The bitch had golden eyes, liquid and deep. Her coat was sleek, a lustrous liver color with white ticking on her shoulders and rump. She was a four-year old German Shorthaired Pointer, weight, about seventy-five pounds. She looked exhausted. She was lying on her side on a red velvet pillow in an elaborate wicker dog basket. Her name was engraved on an ornate brass plate on the front. Hilda Von Holzweg. Five squirming furballs were suckling at her swollen breasts.

A sixth wasn't squirming anymore. She'd pushed it to the edge of the basket away from the others. David picked up the dead pup. It was already cooling. Hilda raised her head a moment and glowered at him, but didn't growl. Probably didn't have the energy.

"How long was she in labor?" David asked.

"I'm not sure," Ted Crane said. "She had them in the night. I checked her at eleven just before I went to bed. Then this morning, about seven, there they were."

"And this pup was alive then?" David said, turning the small body over, examining it for injuries or obvious flaws.

"I believe so. I can't say I honestly took special notice of it, I mean, they all look pretty much alike, except for the solid white one. Is it an albino?" Crane was a bit of an albino himself, a handsome one, tall and fair, with sandy hair and nearly invisible eyebrows. He was dressed for the office in a mocha brown three piece power suit. His Sulka tie probably cost more than the loden-green corduroy sportcoat David was wearing.

"I doubt he's a true albino," David said. "His nose is dark. Can't be certain until its eyes are open, though. Solid-white Shorthair pups are quite valuable, I understand. Did the dead pup try to suckle at all?"

"I think so. I didn't really pay any special attention to it until I noticed it was just stumbling around, kind of wheezing. And then it died. The other one was wheezing too, but it was all right afterward."

"The other one?"

"Another pup was behaving oddly. My wife has it in her room, feeding it with a bottle."

"And it's taking the bottle?" David frowned.

"Seems to be. But only when she holds it. It stops trying when she puts it down."

"I see. Is she cradling it? Like a baby, I mean?" David demonstrated what he meant by cradling the dead pup in the crook of his arm, with its head upright.

"Something like that," Ted acknowledged, wincing at the casual way David handled the tiny corpse. "But she can't hold it for long. She's . . . quite ill herself. Look, I can't hang around here all day, I have to get back to the office. I have a luncheon meeting at one."

"I'll just be a few more minutes," David said, examining the dead pup's face more carefully. There were bubbles of dried milk in its nostrils. He tried to force its mouth open with a fingertip but it was locked shut. Rigor mortis had already set in. "I don't think this is anything serious, Mr. Crane. The mother and rest of the pups look healthy as horses. I'd guess this fella's problem was a birth defect rather than an illness. I'd better examine the other sickly pup, though, if you don't mind."

"My wife's room is at the head of the stairs," Crane said impatiently. "I really have to go. Will you, ah, take care of the dead one?"

"You mean dispose of it?" David said.

"I'd appreciate it," Crane said. "I don't like having to mess with . . . dead things."

"I thought you worked at the hospital," David said.

"I'm Director of Public Relations," Crane said, trying not to sound smug, and failing. "I deal with fund raising, not patients. Frankly, I try to have as little to do with corpses as possible."

"I'll see to this one," David said. "Do you have a plastic bag?"

"In the kitchen. Thanks for coming by, Dr. Westbrook. I really have to go." Ted Crane hurried off. Grateful for an excuse to be away from the messy business of life and death, David thought.

David left Hilda and her pups in their basket and wandered into the living room. The Crane home was a mansion, really, filled with antiques. The Persian rugs were rich, but showed signs of wear. The

Tudor furniture covered in white damask, and an honest to God *Gone With the Wind* staircase swept up to the floors above. The stairway had been modified with metal tracks to accommodate a wheelchair lift. David followed the lift rails up to the second floor. The first door was ajar and he rapped lightly.

"Mrs. Crane?" No answer.

"Hello?" He peered cautiously around the door. A woman was propped up in bed, surrounded by pillows, cradling a puppy in her arms. "Hi," David said, "I'm Dr. Westbrook, the veterinarian. Your husband said you were having a spot of trouble with some of the pups. May I come in?"

She nodded, closing her eyes a moment. Her hair was auburn and very fine, like a wispy halo of fire. She was wearing a jade-green embroidered silk bed jacket. It matched her eyes, which were a deep, deep emerald. And very sunken. She was probably in her mid-thirties, but illness was aging her. There was a rack of medical equipment beside her bed, a humidifier, a heart monitor, and a respirator the size of a small microwave. A length of flexible tubing connected the respirator to a breathing mask on the pillow beside her.

"I'm sorry," she whispered, "I have some difficulty talking. How's Hilda?"

"She's fine," David said. "So are her pups. How's this little guy doing?"

"Not well. He'll only eat if I hold him."

"May I?" David took the pup from her arms. He stepped over to the window for better light, then worked his finger into the hinge of the pup's jaw, pried it open and peered in. Damn. There was a narrow schism in the roof of its mouth. Double damn.

"What is it?"

David hesitated.

"Just say it, Doctor. I'm used to hearing bad news."

"He has a birth defect, Mrs. Crane, a cleft palate. I expect the one that died had the same problem. I'm sorry."

"Call me Inga, please. How bad is it?"

"It's usually fatal, I'm afraid. They can't suck very well, you see, so they either starve, or milk gets into their airways. The pup downstairs probably suffocated."

"But this one seems to be feeding all right."

"That's because you were holding him upright. He doesn't have to suckle. The milk's trickling down the back of his throat."

"Well, what's wrong with that?"

"Nothing, for now. But he won't be able to eat solid food that way, or even drink water normally. He could choke, or get fluid into his lungs and die of pneumonia."

"Isn't there anything you can do?"

"Well, on an adult dog, I could repair the palate by inserting a plate, perhaps, but the procedure's not practical on a pup. It would simply outgrow it and the surgery would be both risky and expensive in any case."

"But it would be possible? On an adult dog?"

"Mrs. Crane, Inga, forgive me for being blunt, but pups with this problem rarely reach adulthood."

"Really? Take a look at all the machinery beside my bed, Doctor. Do you know what it's for?"

David glanced at the rack of equipment on the left side of the bed against the wall. "A heart monitor," he said. "And . . . some kind of a respirator?"

"That's right. I have ALS, Lou Gehrig's disease. I had an auto accident nearly three years ago, shattered my right shoulder and hip. And while I was in the hospital, in traction, they diagnosed the ALS. They gave me eighteen months to live, or less. That was three years ago. I need a wheelchair to get around now, and the respirator breathes for me much of the time, but I'm still here. Maybe that's why life seems very precious to me these days. If I care for this pup properly, will he have a chance to live?"

"That depends. He won't be a pup for long, you know. He'll only drink milk for a few weeks, then he'll need solid food and it'll have to bypass his mouth. Are you up to feeding him through a tube? Several times a day?"

"If that's what it takes to save his life, then I'll either do it myself, or see that it's done. I'm not alone here; my mother can help, and my niece. And you? Are you willing to help?"

"I don't know," David said. "What you're suggesting would be difficult for anyone, let alone someone in your condition. No offense, ma'am, but you seem to have troubles enough of your own."

"Trust me, a few puppy-sized troubles will make a pleasant

change from the rest," she said, smiling. It was a wan, but fine, smile.

"Then I guess we'll all have to do the best that we can," David said, handing her the pup.

"Good," Inga Crane said. She cradled the pup to her breast. "Can you sit a minute? I don't have much company. You're the newcomer Yvonne LeClair married, aren't you?"

"Not such a newcomer," David said, easing into the chair beside her bed. "I've been practicing in Algoma about four years."

"In northern Michigan, unless you're born here you're a flat-lander forever. Ted, my husband, moved here . . . My God. Is it five years now? It seems like so much longer. We hadn't been married long when . . . this happened." She indicated her wasted form with a wave of her free hand. "He tries, but he's such an active man, he has a little trouble dealing with illness, I think."

"On the other hand, you seem to be handling it well enough," David said.

"But I have no choice, have I," she countered. "Oh! Is something wrong? The puppy's twitching."

David peered at it intently, then relaxed. "No, nothing to worry about," he said. "He's just dreaming, that's all."

"Dreaming? What about?"

"What do you mean?"

"Well, he was just born last night. He hasn't been any place or done anything yet. His eyes aren't even open," Inga said. "So what can he possibly be dreaming about?"

"I don't know. I guess I never thought of it that way."

"Maybe he's dreaming about Puppyland," she said.

"About what?"

"Puppyland. My family has always had dogs, so my mother never told us the stork story. She said that baby dogs came from Puppy-land, kind of a hound heaven, where they can run and play all day. When I was a girl, this house was my Puppyland. My grandparents built it and I grew up here. Ted thinks we should sell it now. I know it's expensive to maintain, but I doubt my mother'd be happy any-where else and I love it too. God, I used to run like a deer in the hills out back when I was a kid. I still dream about it sometimes. I'm running, flat out with the wind in my face and I can breathe easily again. I almost hate to wake up. I hope this little guy won't be too dis-appointed when his eyes open and he finds out he's not in Puppyland anymore. He's stuck in our world now." She smothered a cough with her hand. She was clearly tiring.

"At least he'll have a friend," David said, rising to leave. "What are you going to call him?"

"I don't think I'll name him yet," she said, thoughtfully tracing his silken ears with her fingertip. "It will be harder to lose him if he has a name. I'll wait a few weeks. See how he does. Thanks for coming by, Dr. Westbrook."

"Call me David," he said. "Would you mind if I stopped by now and again? No charge."

"I'd like that," she said. "Maybe you can help me choose a name. If he . . . needs one."

"He's going to need one, " David said.

✶ ✶ ✶

She named the pup Hector, after the old phrase "since Hector was a pup." Neither of them could remember who the original Hector the pup was, but it didn't matter. Inga's Hector soon developed a quirky personality of his own. Despite his defect, he cheerfully adapted to his circumstances, learning to feed and drink in Inga's arms, first liquids, then solid food through a tube. Over the next several months, as spring warmed into summer, David stopped by once or twice each week to check on the pup and to chat with Inga Crane. The visits often stretched into an hour or more, talking about dogs, or mutual friends, or just life in general. David rarely saw Ted on these visits, but he did meet Inga's mother, Clare, a charming, drifty old soul who seemed to wander through the house like a ghost. She'd obviously been a beauty once, but her mind was as cloudy now as Inga's was clear.

Most of the scutwork and heavy lifting involved in caring for an invalid fell to Inga's niece, Cindy, a stolid, pudgy girl, of twenty or so. She wore her dun colored hair in an MTV-style shambles and her ears were pierced with three studs each. She never complained, but David sensed that she resented his visits a little, so he generally took her arrival as his signal to leave.

The truth was, his visits had become more personal than professional anyway. Hector was healthy and growing like the national debt and David really couldn't afford the time away from his practice, but there are some things you have to do for yourself. For your soul.

In any case, he knew that the visits wouldn't continue for long. He was a vet, not an M.D., but it was clear that even as Hector was flourishing under Inga's devoted care, Inga herself was wasting away, as though the fire of her spirit was consuming her shrunken body. It should have been depressing, but he found her struggle an inspiration instead. He'd read Dylan Thomas in college, but he'd never truly understood the line "rage, rage, against the dying of the light," until he met Inga. Her thirst to savor every last drop of her life, however bitter, personified the indomitability of the human spirit more than anyone he'd ever known. And in the end, she did not "go gently into that good night . . ." Not gently at all.

✳ ✳ ✳

The phone dragged David up from the depths of a dark dream. He glanced at the nightstand as he fumbled for the receiver. Four-thirty. What the hell?

"Hello."

"Dr. Westbrook? This is Sheriff Wolinski. I'm sorry to bother you this time of the morning, Doc, but I've got a special problem. Are you awake?"

"I am now. What is it, Stan?"

"I'm at the Crane place on Stillmeadow Road. Do you know it?"

Damn. "Yes, I know it," David said. "Is it Inga?"

"Yeah, she's gone all right. Thing is, it looks like her dog may have killed her."

"What?"

"Look, Doc, I can show you a helluva lot faster than I can explain it over the phone. Can you get out here, please? Now?"

"Right," David said, fully awake now. "I'm on my way."

✳ ✳ ✳

The emergency flashers of the Algoma County Sheriff's patrol car and the EMT van were already being washed out by the first light of dawn when David pulled into the red brick drive of the Crane estate. Sheriff Stan Wolinski was waiting for him on the porch, pacing impatiently. Stan's concrete-block build and gray uniform were both in perfect order and his eyes were clear. A grayish stubble of beard was his only concession to the early hour. David wondered if he ever actually slept, or just caught catnaps at his desk at the county jail.

"Morning, Doc," Stan said, leading the way into the house toward the winding staircase. "Sorry to drag you out like this but I've got a bit of a situation here."

"What's happened?"

"Mrs. Crane's mother called 911 about three a.m., said her daughter'd passed away, then started mumbling. When the EMT techs got here they found the mother sitting by the bed. The dog was on the bed, guarding the body. The old lady seemed to be pretty much in a fog."

"She's on quite a bit of medication," David said.

"Anyway, Mrs. Crane was dead, probably had been for an hour or so. The bedclothing was disarranged a little, as though she'd thrashed around some at the end. And as the technician was checking over the body, he noticed the respirator was unplugged."

"The respirator?"

"Right. Apparently she could only breathe without it for short periods. I guess she was in pretty bad shape. Thing is, the machine's quite close to the wall, and there's other equipment near it. The mother said she hadn't touched it and the tech thought it was unlikely it could have been unplugged by accident. It looked odd to him, so he called me."

"And you called me? What the hell for?"

"I'm coming to that. By the time I got here, the husband had showed up—"

"What do you mean, showed up?"

"Came upstairs. He said he was asleep but the EMT guys had been there half an hour at that point, and hadn't been particularly quiet."

"Maybe Crane's a heavy sleeper."

"Maybe. He said he'd had a few scotches before he turned in and I believe him. He smelled like a brewery. On the other hand, he was wearing street clothes. I ask you, if you had a sick wife and heard noises in the night, would you bother to get dressed? Anyway, when the tech tells Crane the respirator was unplugged, he goes ballistic. He says the dog must have pulled it out, that he'd been prowling around back there before. And there are some marks on the plug that coulda been made by a dog. So I called you."

"To look at a plug?"

"Dave, what I got here is a dead woman who probably would have passed away naturally in a month or two anyway. Maybe a few things don't quite add up about it, but that's not unusual. Death is a messy business sometimes. I've got no real reason to doubt the husband's story, I just want to be sure. If the marks on the plug look like toothmarks to you, we can all go home."

"What the hell is he doing here?" Ted Crane bellowed. He was blocking the head of the stairway in his stocking feet. His shirt tail was half out of his dark, dress slacks. His was weaving and his face was flushed. "This is his fault!"

"Mr. Crane—" Stan began.

"He knew that damned dog had a birth defect! If he'd done the right thing and put it down before my wife got so attached to it—"

Crane lunged at David, swinging wildly at his head. Stan grabbed his arm but the force of Crane's rush carried all three men down in a heap, struggling dangerously at the top of the stairs.

"Damn it, Crane, get hold of yourself!" Stan roared, twisting Ted's arm behind his back and hauling him to his feet.

"Let go of me, you bastard! This is my house!"

"This is a crime scene until I say otherwise!" Stan said, forcing Crane against the wall. "Now you settle down or I'll cuff you and lock you in the back of my patrol car. Are you all right, Doc?"

"I'll live," David said, getting to his feet, more shaken than he cared to admit. He touched his cheek with his fingertips. They came away bloody. Terrific.

"You've got a nick on your cheek."

"It's nothing," David said. "Crane's cufflink grazed me, that's all. Mr. Crane, I'm terribly sorry about your wife, and I know this must be an awful time for you. So why don't you let me take care of my business and I'll get out of here."

"You'd better take that dog with you," Crane snarled over his shoulder. "You get it out of here or I'll kill it! I swear I will!"

Stan marched Crane over to a chair and parked him in it, none too gently. David left them in the hall and stepped into Inga's room. A burly uniformed medical tech was standing just inside the door, his arms folded. Inga's mother was sitting beside the bed in her robe and slippers. One of her hands was beneath the sheet that covered Inga's body and David guessed she was still holding her daughter's hand.

He touched the elderly woman's shoulder. She glanced up at him without a hint of recognition, then looked away.

David eased cautiously around the bed, knelt beside the respirator and picked up the plug. Toothmarks. He'd seen them a thousand times on everything from fine furniture to briar pipes. Puppies test their strength against the world by grabbing and tugging on things. Or they just chew things up for the sheer joyful hell of it. There were several other cords plugged into the multiple socket, for the other medical equipment and her bedside lamp. They'd been chewed as well. He examined the respirator plug closely to be sure, but there was little doubt. Damn it. Sometimes it seems like the Almighty has an almighty warped sense of humor . . .

He rose slowly, dusting off his hands.

"What do you think?" the medic asked. The tech was a heavyset man with a beer-barrel build and a dark stubble of beard. He looked tired, probably nearing the end of his shift.

"I'd say her husband is right. There are toothmarks on that plug," David said, gazing down at the shrouded body. "How did she . . . die?"

"Heart failure, I think, triggered by anoxia. Actually, in her condition that mask was barely adequate to keep her going anyway. Her doctor wanted to hospitalize her weeks ago to have a ventilator tube inserted. She refused."

"Can't say I blame her for that," David said. "It can be a pretty uncomfortable situation."

"True blue," the medic agreed, "and it's not like it would have cured her. It only would have prolonged her dyin' a bit. Maybe it's best this way. If she woke up at all, she was probably too groggy to realize what had happened."

"I hope so," David said. "She was quite a lady."

"Well?" Stan Wolinski said from the doorway.

"They . . . certainly look like toothmarks to me," David said. "Proper depth, proper spacing. Maybe a lab could tell you more."

"Do you think a lab's necessary?"

"No," David said. "They're toothmarks all right."

"Anything wrong, Doc? You look a little bummed."

"Just upset," David said. "The lady was a friend of mine."

"In that case, considering Crane just decked you, I'll assume your opinion's as close to objective as I'm likely to get. Thanks for coming down."

"I'll send you a bill," David said. "Where's Hector?"

Hec—oh, the dog, you mean?"

"We shut it up in the next bedroom," the medical tech volunteered. "He wouldn't let us near her."

"You gonna take him with you, Doc?" Stan asked.

"I think I'd better, under the circumstances, don't you?" David said. "There's been enough trouble here for one night."

He collected Hector from the adjoining bedroom. Ted Crane was still in the hallway chair where Stan had left him, sitting with his head in his hands. He didn't look up as David passed.

David put Hector in the back of his Jeep. He clipped a lead to the pup's collar, but it wasn't really necessary. Hector made no move to escape. He seemed dazed and disoriented, barely aware of his surroundings. And David knew exactly he felt.

✳ ✳ ✳

During the course of the day, David tried to feed Hector several times. He'd seen Inga do it, cradling the pup lovingly in her arms, slipping the feeding tube into the corner of his mouth to bypass the schism in his palate. Hector had seemed to enjoy every moment of it. Why not? It was the only way he'd ever been fed by the only mother he'd ever known. When David tried it, though, the pup snapped out of his apathy long enough to snarl at him and spit the tube out. An hour later David's second attempt failed as well. He decided to have his assistant, Bettina, try the next one. Perhaps a woman's touch . . .

"Doctor?" Bettina stuck her head around his office doorjamb. "There's a Cindy Meyers to see you. She says it's urgent."

"Meyers? Oh, that would be Inga Crane's niece. I'd better see her now, if no one's bleeding to death on the waiting room floor."

"Nope, everything out front's routine. I'll send her back."

David met Cindy at the door. She was wearing a Def Leppard sweatshirt and jeans. Her eyes were red, but she seemed more nervous than sad. She scanned the office warily, as if she was scheduled for some uncomfortable procedure.

"I'm very sorry about your aunt," David said, taking her hand and leading her to the chair beside his desk. "If there's anything I can do . . ."

"Actually, maybe there is," Cindy said, glancing uneasily around the office. "I need to talk to you privately. Would you mind closing the door?"

David hesitated, then complied. "What is it?" he asked.

"Ted called me around ten this morning," she said. "I was visiting a girlfriend over at Central Michigan. He . . . he sounded pretty loaded, you know, drunk?"

"I suppose that's understandable, wouldn't you say?"

"I guess it is," she said, taking a deep breath. "Anyway, I drove straight back, but the more I thought about it, the more I thought I'd better talk to you before I went home."

"I don't understand."

"The thing is, Ted said that Hector killed Aunt Inga. That he'd been chewing on the respirator plug and pulled it out somehow. He said the sheriff even called you out to look at it."

"That's right. There were toothmarks on the plug—"

"How many marks were there?" Cindy interrupted. "I mean, was it all chewed up? Or were there just a few?"

"Well, I didn't actually count the marks but the cord wasn't badly chewed. They were definitely toothmarks, though."

"I know they were," she said. "I've seen them."

"What do you mean you've seen them?"

"Hector's been chewing up things for the past few weeks," Cindy said carefully, her voice tautly controlled. "Slippers, shoes, table legs, anything he can reach, really. And Inga caught him chewing on the cord a couple of days ago. She had me paddle his bottom good."

"He's just a pup," David said. "Sometimes one lesson isn't enough."

"You don't understand. Inga and Ted had a big fight about it. He wanted her to get rid of the dog, said if it happened again, he'd get rid of it whether she agreed or not. So she was real careful to watch Hector when he was with her, and she's been shutting him out of her room at night."

"What are you saying?" David asked.

"I'm not saying anything," Cindy said. "I'm just trying to . . . understand how Inga died. Ted said it must have happened during the night, right?"

"I believe the EMT people got there about three-thirty," David said.

"And Inga seldom went to sleep before midnight," Cindy said. "So, let's say Clare forgot and left the door open or something and Hector got in. The first thing he would have done was jump on her bed to say hello. He always did."

David started to speak but she waved him off.

"I know," she said. "He's only a pup. So maybe he didn't say hello. Maybe he went straight to that cord and chewed on it until he pulled it out. But he couldn't have done that without drooling on it, could he?"

"No," David said, "I suppose not."

"So? Was the plug damp?"

"No," David said slowly, remembering. "It was dry. A little dusty, in fact. I . . . brushed my hands off after I handled it." Neither of them spoke for a moment, each of them considering what the other had said.

"You don't think the pup unplugged that cord, do you?" David asked at last.

"I don't know what to think," Cindy said. "You've got to understand, I'm in kind of a shaky situation here. Inga took me in when my parents died, but everything will belong to Ted now and he can put me out in a heartbeat if he wants to. I wouldn't mind so much for myself, but who'll take care of Clare? She can't fend for herself and she loves that house. So I don't want to make waves, but I think I'd better take a look at that cord. After all the fuss about it earlier, I'm pretty sure I'll be able to tell if Hector chewed on it again. The thing is, I think I should have a witness, but if I ask the sheriff to go with me and nothing's wrong, Ted might . . . Look, these past weeks you've been the closest friend Inga had. Would you come with me? Please."

"I—of course," David said abruptly. "Let's go."

∗ ∗ ∗

Cindy entered the house without knocking. "With any luck we'll be in and outa here before anybody knows it," she said quietly. "I'm probably just making a fuss over nothing anyway."

David followed her quietly up the main staircase. He felt a bit like a burglar, but he hoped to avoid trouble with Ted Crane if possible. Clare was still in Inga's room, sitting beside the empty bed where David last saw her, hours before. She might have been there the whole time, except that she'd exchanged her bathrobe for a prim gray housedress and sensible shoes.

"Hello Dr. Westbrook," she said vaguely. "Inga's not here now."

"It's all right, Gran," Cindy said, swallowing. "Everything will be all right. We'll just be a moment." She moved around the bed, knelt beside the respirator and examined the plug. Her mouth narrowed to a thin line. She rose slowly.

"I can't be absolutely positive, of course," she said grimly, "but I'd swear the plug doesn't look any different than it did before. Gran, when you . . . found Inga last night, was Hector in the room with her?"

"Hector?" the old woman echoed.

"Just tell us what happened," Cindy said impatiently. "One step at a time. You came into the room, right?"

"Yes, something woke me . . . The phone? Or the doorbell? I can't remember. I thought at first it was morning. The pills I take . . . usually I sleep very soundly. But when I woke up I had a bad feeling about Inga. And so I went to her room. But . . . she wasn't there anymore. She was gone." Clare looked away.

"The room," Cindy prompted. "Tell us about the room."

"It was . . . a little messy," Hilda said. "And you know how fussy Inga was about things being neat. So I straightened up a bit. I didn't want . . . strangers to see it like that."

"And Hector?" Cindy asked. "Was he in the room?"

"Hector? No," Clare said. "He was on his blanket in the hall. He came in with me and jumped on the bed but . . . he didn't get all excited the way he usually does. He just . . . licked at Inga's face a little, and then he curled up at the foot of her bed. He didn't move after that until the . . . ambulance men came. He got excited then, tried to keep them away from her, so they put him in the next room."

"So he was out in the hall until you let him in," Cindy said. Her eyes met David's for a moment.

"Yes." Clare nodded. "Hector was outside."

Cindy took a deep breath. "You said you straightened up the room? Why, Gran? Was it messed up?"

"The . . . bedclothes were disarranged," Clare said vaguely. "As though . . . she must have had trouble at . . . the last."

"And is that all you did? Fix the bedclothes?"

"No, I . . . her book was on the bed," Clare said. "It was open and I knew she wouldn't want people to read it, so I put it away."

"Her book?" David echoed.

"Her diary," Cindy said, moving to the bookcase and picking out a slim volume.

"You shouldn't touch that," Clare said. "Inga will be angry. . ." Her voice trailed off as she realized what she'd said.

Cindy leafed through the diary, then froze. She passed the book to David. The paragraph at the top of the page was dated and neatly written in a careful hand. But below it, was a wobbly scrawl that covered half the page. *Ted unplu* . . . The line sagged away at the end. Unfinished.

There was a rustle from the hallway, and suddenly Ted Crane was standing unsteadily in the doorway, his face flushed, his hair disheveled. "What's going on here?" he mumbled blearily. "What are the hell are you doing here, Westbrook?"

David carefully closed the journal. "What I'm doing, Mr. Crane," he said, picking up the bedside phone, "is calling the police."

✳ ✳ ✳

Crane made it easy. When Stan Wolinski tried to question him about the diary Ted was so outraged he took a swing at the sheriff. A big mistake. Stan took him into custody for attempted assault and hauled him off in the back of his patrol car.

David left Cindy and her grandmother on the porch, arm in arm. The elderly woman didn't seem to comprehend what had happened, and David recalled Cindy's earlier question, "who'll take care of Clare?" Perhaps the answer was beside her now. He hoped so.

David hadn't liked Ted Crane all that much initially and his recent behavior hadn't helped matters. Still, the thought that Ted might have killed Inga or contributed to her death was hard to stomach. People killed each other in Detroit or New York or L.A., not in Algoma. Folks moved to the north country to live happily ever after. Maybe that had been Ted's problem. Knowing that he and Inga would never have a happily ever after. David didn't know what to do about Hector. The pup was still rejecting the feeding tube. If he didn't start eating in the next few days, force feeding him while he was sedated would be the only option left. It was a tough choice. Hector wouldn't be mature enough for a surgical repair of his palate for another twelve to fourteen months, minimum. David doubted the pup could survive more than a few weeks of force feeding, to say nothing of a year. Besides, he'd seen this behavioral syndrome before.

Dogs that are strongly attached to their masters or their mates will sometimes mourn their deaths so keenly that they lose their own will to live. They don't whine or howl or carry on, they simply sink into a numbed apathy and refuse to eat. Exactly as Hector was doing.

David was in a black mood for the rest of the afternoon, curt with his clients and Bettina. His temperament didn't improve when his last client at the end of the day turned out to be Stan Wolinski.

"Doc," the sheriff said, following David back to his office, "I think I need another favor, or rather, Ted Crane does."

"I don't owe Crane any favors," David said grimly, waving Stan toward the chair beside his desk. "I don't owe you any either, for that matter. What's happened?"

"Well, for openers, I've caught Mr. Crane in a half-dozen lies," Stan said. "At first he said he was home, asleep, but when I showed him Inga's diary he changed his story. Swore he was with a lady friend whom he preferred not to name. I told him chivalry was a helluva nice idea but it wouldn't do him much good in the state pen. Them hardcase cons ain't big on mother may I, you know? At which point he caved in and named . . . a prominent local lady. Who happens to be more'n slightly married to a prominent local gentleman."

"Who?" David asked, his curiosity piqued.

"I'm coming to that," Stan said. "I called the lady in question. She told me she barely knew Crane, couldn't even remember his first name."

"So what's your problem? It sounds open and shut to me."

"That's the problem," Stan said. "It is open and shut. Now maybe Ted Crane's not one of my favorite human beings at the moment, but he's an educated man. He's not stupid. So why would he give me an alibi that was so easy to disprove? For that matter, why would he bother to murder his wife? She was dying anyway. All he had to do was wait, and probably not for very long, either."

"Maybe he got tired of waiting."

"Maybe so. But that still leaves me with his alibi. He claims he can prove he and the lady were more than acquaintances. He says he gave her a puppy as a gift. Says it was a pure white one, worth a lot of money. Do you know anything about it?"

"There was a pure white pup in the litter," David acknowledged. "And he's right about it being worth a lot of money. White German Shorthairs are rare. I'd guess it would be worth at least a thousand dollars, probably more."

"So if the lady in question actually has this dog, then she and Crane are probably better friends than she wants to admit."

"I suppose they could be," David said. "Where are you going with this?"

"It's not where I'm going, Doc, it's where you're going. Would you recognize this dog if you saw it?"

"A white shorthair? Probably. But so could you. Why not just go check?"

"Because I've already asked the lady and she said she doesn't know Crane. So if I show up on her doorstep asking to inventory her dogs, she may just infer that I doubt her word."

"So? Since when did you get sensitive about offending a suspect?"

"But the lady isn't a suspect, she's only a witness. And she also happens to be Senator Holcomb's wife."

"Diane Holcomb?" David whistled. "She's Crane's alibi?"

"So he claims. And since I have to run for election in this county, the Senator and his wife aren't people I'd care to tick off unless it's absolutely necessary."

"So you want me to tick them off instead?"

"I'm hoping to avoid offending anyone, period. The Holcombs have a kennel attached to their guest house. If you drive past you can probably spot the dog from the road. If it's there, then I'll make an official call on Mrs. Holcomb."

"And if it's not?"

"If you don't see it, then it comes down to her word against Crane's and he's already lied to me. The funny part is, you're the reason I tend to believe him. That nick on your face you got in the scuffle this morning? He grazed you with his cufflink. Most guys don't wear cufflinks except on special occasions."

"Like a hot date with someone else's wife, for instance?" David said, touching the cut gingerly with his fingertips. "All right, I'll take a drive past the Holcombs' kennel, but that's all I'm doing. Don't expect me to stick my neck out for Ted Crane."

"All I'm asking for is a look, okay?"

"Right," David said grimly. "A look."

✳ ✳ ✳

Easier said than done. The Holcombs lived in a rambling brown brick ranch house that sprawled along a ridge west of Algoma. There was a four car garage behind it with guest or servants' quarters above and a kennel attached to its rear wall. The impeccably landscaped grounds were enclosed by a decorative split-rail fence. It was an expensive home, but most of the homes nearby were equally posh, built on ten acre lots with three-car garages standard and rolling lawns large enough for polo. Which meant it wasn't a neighborhood where a strange car could linger for any length of time without being noticed.

Fortunately, the next home was a Windsor manor set well back from the road. Its long driveway ran parallel to the rear of the Holcombs' guest house, which gave it a clear view of the kennels.

David swung the Jeep into the driveway, slowing as he approached the kennels. Beagles. The first three runs held pairs of Beagles. The dogs raised their heads to watch him pass, but otherwise ignored him. The last two kennels were a problem. They were larger than the Beagles' pens, but one stood open and empty. No way to be sure what lived there, except that it was probably larger than a Beagle. The last pen held a white dog. It was the right size to be Crane's pup, but it was sleeping in the afternoon sun with its back to him and David couldn't be sure one way or the other.

He stopped the Jeep abruptly and climbed out. He vaulted the low fence and trotted to the kennels. The Beagles came to life, raising the alarm, yawping and yapping as he approached.

The white pup in the last kennel stirred and rose to check him out, but it didn't deign to join in the clamor. Barking was for Beagles, and this pup was no hound. He was a German Shorthaired Pointer, a solid-white male. And he was almost certainly Hector's one time litter mate. David knelt for a closer look, to be absolutely sure. The pup approached him curiously and sniffed his hand.

"What are you doing here?"

A woman had appeared at the corner of the building. She was strikingly attractive, with fine, aquiline features and honey-blonde hair tied back in a lustrous ponytail. Her eyes were hidden behind dark glasses. She was dressed for country life, riding breeches, boots and a flannel shirt, but there was nothing working class about her. She oozed the confidence that comes with old money and social position. Or perhaps her confidence came from the fiery-eyed Doberman that was straining at the short leash she held in her gloved hand. The dog wasn't growling or even baring its fangs, but its gaze was locked on David's throat. All business. Probably a trained attack dog.

David rose slowly. "I guess I could say I was just passing, Mrs. Holcomb, but I'm not much at fibbing, even in a good cause. My name is Dr. David Westbrook. I'm a veterinarian. Sheriff Wolinski asked me to stop by in order to verify some information, an alibi actually."

"This has to do with that . . . Crane person, doesn't it? I've already told the Sheriff that I scarcely know him. My husband and I may have met him at some function, we're quite active socially—"

"Mrs. Holcomb, you don't have to convince me of anything," David interrupted. "I'm not a policeman. On the other hand, this is a very unusual pup you have here. Pedigreed and AKC registered, I imagine."

"What business is that of yours?"

"None at all, ma'am. But if you wouldn't mind an observation by your friendly neighborhood veterinarian, this dog will be awfully easy to trace which means you're likely going to be involved in a murder investigation whether you like it or not. Ted Crane named you as his alibi. He also said he gave you this dog and here it is. Rather an expensive gift from a man you scarcely know, wouldn't you say?"

She started to reply, then bit it off.

"Ma'am, if you really want to get clear of this thing, the smart thing to do is to just tell Stan Wolinski the truth. He may seem like a rube to you but you can trust his discretion. He doesn't want to cause any . . . problems for you, and he certainly doesn't want trouble with your husband. That's why he asked me to stop by instead of coming himself."

"And what's your part in this?" she asked coldly.

"I don't have one. I'm only here because I can identify the dog."

"But I'm supposed to rely on your discretion too?"

"I can only give you my word for that, but I live in Algoma now, and practice here. I'm not looking to make enemies either."

"No," she said, releasing a long, ragged breath, "I suppose not. All right then, Ted was here last night. My husband is in Lansing for the week. He spends much of his time there, and I . . . Anyway, Ted arrived about midnight, I believe, and left a few hours later. I'm not really sure of the time, we . . . were drinking quite heavily." She took a deep breath and squared her shoulders. Her eyes were coldly unreadable behind her smoked glasses. "That's really all I have to say on the matter," she said firmly. "I'd appreciate if you'd pass it along to Sheriff Wolinski for me. I'm leaving for Lansing within the hour to join my husband. We're dining with the governor tonight."

She tugged the Doberman's leash and turned away, but then hesitated. "Please tell Sheriff Wolinski that I am relying on his discretion. And yours. And by God, I'd better be able to. Do you understand?"

"Yes, ma'am," David said, eyeing the Doberman. "Definitely."

* * *

"I don't like it," Stan Wolinski said. "I should have questioned her myself." They were in Tubby's Restaurant in downtown Algoma, seated at Wolinski's favorite table. The room was paneled in knotty pine, the furniture was dark oak and the only decorations were trophy mounts of white-tailed bucks. The chandeliers were made of elk antlers. North country chic.

"You can still question her if you like," David said, sipping his coffee. "Lansing's only an hour and a half away. If you leave now you can probably roust her in the middle of the governor's after-dinner speech."

"Very funny."

"Sorry. The truth is, I'm a little disappointed too. I was hoping Crane was lying."

"Maybe Mrs. Holcomb's lying. Maybe she's covering for him."

"I doubt it," David said. "She didn't strike me as the sacrificial lamb type. I got the impression that she only bothered to tell me the truth because it was expedient. If it had been more convenient to let Ted hang, she would have."

"Poor Crane. He doesn't seem to have much luck in love, does he?"

"That depends on how you define luck," David said. "I'd say Inga Crane, as ill as she was, was ten times the woman Diane Holcomb is. And a lot better than Ted deserved."

"But as you say, Inga was in rough shape and that can be a terrible drag, emotionally and financially," Stan said. "Personally, I don't think Crane has the backbone to carry the weight. Alibi or not, I still like him for the killing. And he's the one Inga named."

"Yeah, so she did. I've been chewing about that all the way back to town. Why did she name him?"

"Maybe because he did it," Stan snorted. "Or at the very least, she thought he did."

"You mean she woke up in the night, suffocating, realized her respirator was shut down, and just assumed Ted unplugged it? I doubt that. She couldn't function without the machine for long and she couldn't get out of bed without help. So with her dying breath she managed to scrawl his name? Very dramatic."

"Sometimes death is dramatic."

"But she didn't want to die. At least, not yet. So why did she bother to scrawl his name? Why didn't she just pick up the phone and dial 911? Her bedside phone worked, I used it to call you today."

Stan stared at him a moment. "Are you sure about that?"

"Absolutely."

"Then maybe whoever unplugged the machine did the same to the phone, or at least moved it."

"Or perhaps Inga simply never woke up. The machine stopped breathing and a few moments later, so did she. But either way, she couldn't have written the note blaming Ted."

"Why not?"

"Because her mother said the book was open on the bed. She put it away to protect Inga's privacy. If Ted killed her, he must have either unplugged the phone or moved it out of her reach and then replaced it afterward. But if he did that, he would have seen the diary."

"But the only other person in the house was Inga's mother. Surely you don't think she could have done this thing?"

"If she had, she'd hardly have put the diary away, would she? No, I think the person that killed Inga knew Ted would be visiting his ladylove and knew Clare would be too zonked on medication to hear the machine's alarm or any sounds Inga might make. Inga once told me that Ted was worried about how much her care was costing, that he wanted her to sell the house. With Ted out of the picture and the old lady clearly incompetent, I wonder who will inherit the estate?"

"You mean the niece? But she was out of town, staying with a girlfriend."

"Was she? Did you actually check her story out, Stan?"

"No, I didn't," the sheriff said slowly. "I had no reason to. Until now."

✳ ✳ ✳

David was in his kitchen making a cup of midnight cocoa when he heard the crunch of tires the driveway. He poured a second cup as Stan Wolinski eased quietly in the back door.

"Thanks, Doc," Stan said, gratefully accepting the steaming cup. "Thought you might be waiting up for news. I've arrested Cindy Meyers. She claims it was a mercy killing. Says poor Inga was suffering and she only wanted to put an end to it."

"Maybe that's how it was," David said, waving Stan to a seat at the kitchen table.

"She'll have a tough time making that fly," Stan said. "She arranged an alibi for herself and forged that death note to frame her uncle. I doubt a judge will buy the idea that she did Inga in out of the goodness of her heart. The friend Cindy claimed she stayed with in Alma folded like an accordion when she learned it was a murder case. She admitted Cindy'd told her she was seeing someone secretly and borrowed her car to drive back here."

"A secret lover? Maybe she got that idea from Ted."

"Possibly, although she's certainly sly enough to have thought of it on her own. She stuck to her story about being out of town until I hit her with the phone record."

"Phone record?"

"Sure. The thing is, Cindy knew about Ted's little midnight visits and she wanted to be sure the EMT guys would find Inga's respirator unplugged and Ted gone. So I figured she must have made a call to wake Clare on the way back to her friend's place. I checked the records, and there was call from a gas station pay phone just outside of Algoma to the Crane home. Cindy even used her credit card."

"Not very clever of her."

"She didn't have any change," Stan said wryly. "And she didn't want to ask the attendant for any. She was afraid he might remember her. And now I've got a question for you, Doc. Something's been bothering me all day. You don't have to answer if you don't want to."

"Maybe I won't," David said. "What is it?"

"This morning at the Crane place when I asked you about the toothmarks on that plug? I got the feeling you had some doubts."

"No, they were toothmarks all right."

"I'm not saying you lied about anything, only that you might have had some doubts."

"It did seem awfully. . . convenient," David conceded. "There were several cords back there and Hector'd chewed on all of them. It seemed odd that the only one he unplugged was the one that really mattered."

"But you didn't say anything."

"No. It was early in the morning and I hadn't had time to think. It occurred to me that Crane might have pulled the plug, but if so, I wasn't sure I should point the finger at him."

"Why not?"

"Because Inga was my friend and she was in a lot of pain," David said evenly. "It cost her every time she drew a breath. To be honest, I'd thought about pulling that plug myself more than once."

"I see. But later, when Cindy asked for your help in implicating Ted, you went along."

"I'd thought things through by then," David said with a shrug. "And I realized that if Inga wanted to end things, she could have done so anytime just by leaving her mask off. But she didn't. I think she intended to live long enough to see Hector healthy and strong and able to stand on his own. Maybe it was a foolish idea, but no one had the right to take it from her, not her friends, nor her family. Only Inga."

"That's straight enough," Stan said, rising. "But next time, if you have any doubts, you tell me about 'em, okay?"

"I hope to God there won't be a next time," David said. "At least not like this one."

"It came down pretty hard, I'll admit," Stan said, pausing in the doorway. "But at least one good thing came out of it. Your friend was in a lot of pain, and now it's over."

David nodded without answering. But he knew it wasn't true. It wasn't over. Not yet.

* * *

Four days after Inga's funeral, Hector died. At the end, David eased his passing with an injection. The pup wouldn't accept food from anyone but Inga and he was wasting away. David decided against trying to anesthetize Hector in order to force feed him. It would only have prolonged the inevitable, and he couldn't find it in his heart to compel Hector to abide in this world when he so clearly wanted to be gone.

Later that afternoon, David placed the pup's small body in the Crawford furnace behind his office and cremated it. His ashes barely filled an envelope. Dusk was falling and a hint of rain was in the air as David drove his Jeep through the gates of Holy Cross Cemetery. He parked near the entrance, then followed the tiled walkway to Inga's grave. Her resting place seemed more final somehow than it had the day of her funeral. The flowers were gone now and fresh strips of green sod had been neatly laid down over the mound of raw earth.

He knelt in the grass beside her grave for a moment. He didn't pray. He'd never been a religious man and it would have seemed hypocritical. After a few moments, he glanced around to be sure he wasn't being observed. No one was near. The cemetery stretched away to the foothills beyond. The only other mourner in view was an elderly woman in a dark raincoat and she was far off and lost in her own thoughts.

David carefully raised the corner of a sod strip and slid the small envelope of ashes into the soil beneath, then gently patted the grass back into place. He wasn't sure if what he was doing made any sense, even to himself. But he hoped that it might mean something to Inga.

He lingered awhile as the shadows lengthened, waiting in silence for . . . something. Anything, really. A sign, perhaps. Some indication that he'd done the right thing. But nothing happened, nothing changed. He'd thought that burying Hector's ashes here might give him a sense of closure. It didn't. It felt like an empty, futile gesture. Maybe the cynics are right. Maybe the grave is truly the end of things after all.

Eventually he tired of waiting, and rose on stiffened knees. But he hesitated. Something in the distance caught his eye. A movement. Probably just the wind in the trees. The Algoma hills rolled away into the dusky distance like shadowy waves, bathed in the blaze of the lowering sun. And in the dying light, the hills seemed to glow from within, as though they were being magically transmuted into gold, like the hills of Oz or . . .

Puppyland. That's what Inga'd said those hills meant to her when she was a child. And perhaps that was why he felt no sense of her presence at the grave. She wasn't here anymore. If she was anywhere, she would be there, in those shining hills, running free. Breathing free. But not alone. Hector had been so eager to follow her, surely he must be with her now. Perhaps he'd gone to show her the way back to the place he'd come from. Puppyland. Where the air is sweet, and the hills are so lush and lovely that puppies are born dreaming of them.

The Beaches of Paraguay

It was one of those perfect evenings, the kind you never forget. Pete Boothe and I were sitting on the back deck of my wife's home, watching the sun melt into the Algoma hills, shadows lengthening, the sky darkening to gold, then copper, and then a deeper purple. We'd had a few beers, but nothing heavy, not like our college days at Michigan State when we could drink horse dribble till dawn and still cope with classes. Sort of.

We were older now by a decade and more, but holding up fairly well, I thought. Pete was still lanky, with the same rumpled puppy looks that used to melt coed hearts. I'm shorter, more intense, and a lot less lovable.

"I'm thinking of quitting the business," Pete said. "Of getting out."

"Why? I thought you liked your work."

"I used to. You know me, David. I've always been a . . . cautious guy. Being a legal investigator is the perfect job for me. Running background checks, interviewing witnesses. A little excitement, but not too much. I like rubbing elbows with dangerous people without being in danger myself. But lately I feel like I'm losing my edge."

"How do you mean?" I asked.

"I can't seem to concentrate the way I should. I'm like a guy who works on skyscrapers or TV towers who starts to wonder what it would really be like to fly."

"You want to clarify that a little?"

"Okay, a couple of weeks ago we needed a deposition from a crack dealer named Gumpy. He'd been gunned down in a drive-by a few weeks earlier, took six rounds in various parts of his body. When I tracked him down, he was holed up on the third floor of a crack house from hell, homeboys with AK-47s and Uzis in every doorway. I must have been braced ten times on my way upstairs, frisked, my briefcase rifled, the whole drill."

"Some career you picked," I said.

"At least it's never dull. Anyway, when I finally meet Gumpy, he's laid up in a hospital bed. The kind that changes positions electrically? He's got a home-care nurse, and a motorized wheelchair, all installed in this crack house. The place had enough medical gear in it to qualify for Blue Cross."

"Why didn't he just stay in a real hospital?"

"Maybe he was afraid the guys who popped him would be back. Or maybe having a deputy standing guard outside his room cramped his drug deals. In any case, he's in bed, bandaged up like the mummy's curse. So I ask him the questions I need and get the hell out. So far, so good. Except halfway down the stairs, I changed my mind and went back up there."

"What for?"

"I honestly don't know. A whim. That's what's scary about it. Anyway, I just said, man, look at yourself. You've got more holes in you than a cheese grater, you're jammed up in this rattrap with guards at every door. You seem like a bright guy and you must have a few bucks in the bank to afford a setup like this. Maybe you should consider another line of work."

"What did he say?"

"He just looked me over and said, 'you're the one in the wrong job, whiteboy.' And on my way out, it occurred to me that we were both right."

Something in his tone troubled me and I glanced at him. The dusk was deepening the lines in his face. He was my best friend. And I wondered how well I really knew him anymore. College was a long time ago. "Okay," I said. "Maybe your crack-dealer career counselor had a point. So why not change careers? You're only thirty something, you've still got the dregs of your youthful looks and you're rich. What's the problem?"

"Rich?" he echoed.

"Well, you had a trust fund in college, right? What happened to that?"

"Nothing," he said curtly. "Money doesn't go as far as it used to. You, on the other hand, seem to be doing fine. I envy you, David. You've got a neat wife, a lovely home."

"Marrying Yvonne was the luckiest thing I ever did," I said simply. "But what about Jolene? You two have been together quite a while now, right?"

"Nearly four years. Good years." His mouth narrowed to a thin line. "But Jo and I are coming to the end of things. Marriage isn't in the cards for us."

"I thought you were serious about her."

"Serious is a good word," he said dryly. "Things have definitely gotten serious with us. Let it go, David, okay? So, how do you like working up here in the boondocks?"

"Being a small town vet's no way to get rich."

"You never cared about money anyway," Pete snorted.

"Sure I did. Once. Remember my career as a gambler?"

"Gambler?" Yvonne said, tousling my hair as she joined us on the deck. "I thought I knew most of your vices."

"Gambling wasn't a vice with David," Pete said. "It was a death wish. There were some jocks with room temperature IQs in our dorm who used to play high stakes poker. David figured since he was brighter than they were, he could clean up."

"Only they knew I didn't have any money," I put in. "They wouldn't let me into the game unless Pete would play too."

"I told him he was crazy," Pete said. "He threatened me with physical violence. Greed does terrible things to a man."

"What happened?" Yvonne asked.

"David was winning big, only he was so busy concentrating on the cards he didn't notice the thugs we were playing with were getting seriously surly. A couple of them were muttering about card sharps and getting ready to tear us limb from limb. I tried to break up the game, but they said nobody quits until everybody's broke."

"So Pete claims he's too drunk to play anymore," I continued. "He pushes his stack of chips over to me, hands me his cards, and goes staggering out. The bastard left me to die."

"One of us had to be alive to call 911," Pete countered. "I thought the worst they'd do was break your arms and legs."

"And?" Yvonne asked eagerly. "Did they?"

"Not quite," Pete said. "Your lovin' husband not only got out alive, he kept every cent we'd won."

"But how?"

"I bluffed," I said simply. "My so-called friend here left me no choice. The jocks were still laughing over how drunk Pete was, so I said I was in no better shape, and offered to bet everything I'd won against everything they had left. One of 'em called me a cheat and grabbed my cards. And I had nothing. Pete's hand was a busted flush, I only had a pair of treys. I figured they'd take the bet, clean me out and let me live. As it was, since they caught me bluffing, I obviously hadn't been cheating. So they let me walk."

"How much did you make that night?" Pete asked.

"Two hundred and fifty-three dollars. A small fortune in those days."

"It's not chump change now," Pete said. "And you're right, leaving you to die or get maimed was a lousy thing to do. Send me a bill for what your life is worth and I'll stick a check in the mail. Anything up to ten bucks."

But I never got the check. Instead, four months later, I got a phone call at my office.

"Dr. Westbrook? Dr. David Westbrook?"

"Speaking. How can I help you?"

"My name's Favio Andretti. I was Peter Boothe's partner."

"Was?" I said. "Isn't Pete working with you anymore?"

There was a long pause. I could hear static on the line, and suddenly I felt a terrible sensation of vertigo.

"I, ah, I take it you haven't been informed," Andretti said carefully. "I'm sorry, but Peter's dead, Dr. Westbrook. He was killed a few nights ago."

I didn't say anything. Couldn't.

"Dr. Westbrook?"

"I'm here," I said numbly, pulling myself together. "What happened?"

"A mugging went wrong, apparently," Andretti said. "He was found in an alley off the Cass Corridor in Detroit. He'd been shot. Police think it may have been gang related."

"I see," I said, though I didn't. What I really saw was Pete sitting on my deck in the fading light, talking about life, and laughing. "My God. I can't believe . . . I mean, he was just here a few months ago. God. When's the, um, the funeral?"

"Day after tomorrow."

"I'll be there," I said. "Thanks for . . . wait a minute. If you didn't call to tell me what happened, was there something else?"

"As a matter of fact there is. Pete's will names you as the executor of his estate."

"The what?"

"His executor. You'll have to inventory his property and—never mind. Just come on out to the office after the funeral, and I'll run you through the drill."

"But you're a lawyer, aren't you? Why me?"

"You knew Pete. His brother's an attorney, his partner's an attorney, so naturally he'd name a veterinarian as his executor."

"Right," I said. "I guess that does make sense. Knowing Pete." I hung up. I can't remember if I said goodbye.

* * *

The funeral was in Highland Park, a section of the Detroit metropolitan area that's almost entirely black now. I skipped the ceremony at the funeral home. I didn't want to see Pete in a silk lined box with canned organ music in the air. I didn't want to be here at all, really. Especially not alone. But Yvonne is in the fourth month of her pregnancy, and her doctor recommended against the trip.

I hate funerals, hate the terrible communion of grief and . . . loss. I considered skipping it, but Yvonne pointed out that funerals aren't for the dead, they're for the ones who have to go on. And so I stood on a knoll on a chilly November afternoon with a cluster of strangers and watched the plain pine box that held my best friend disappear into a hole in the ground.

I couldn't make it compute. The whole scene seemed as surreal as a doper's dream. For one thing, the coffin was really crude, rough planks pegged together like a prop from a Clint Eastwood western. Orthodox Jews are sometimes buried in plain pine boxes but the Boothes were WASPs. And Pete was probably the only WASP ever buried in this cemetery. The Boothes weren't big rich, but they had money. A grandfather had founded a pharmaceutical company back at the turn of the century and they'd been financially set ever since. I was sure there must be a Boothe family plot somewhere, but Pete had arranged to be buried beside Jolene Greene's family. Okay, he was in love with Jolene, even if they weren't married, and wanted to spend eternity near her. Only he'd have to wait. Jolene wasn't present.

Of the seventy so people at the graveside, I only recognized a handful, mostly guys I'd been in school with. I couldn't remember many names. We exchanged nods or shook hands. We didn't talk much. We were too damned young for this. And always would be.

Pete's family was there, of course. What there was of it. His brother Arnold looked heavier than I remembered, forty pounds at least. His suit was probably hand-tailored but he was already bulging its buttons. Arnold never approved of me. I was just Pete's wastrel roommate. Still, he greeted me civilly and invited me to the family home after the services, which surprised me.

I hadn't seen Pete's mom in ten years. She'd always been a striking woman, tall, ash-blonde, aristocratic. She'd aged thirty years in the past decade. Her hair was dull gray and her once flawless skin was as roughened and red as though she'd been lashed to a mast in a hurricane and scoured raw by the wind. As always, Pete's younger brother, Donnie, was at her shoulder. Donnie alone seemed unchanged, his vacant eyes and massive frame unmarked by the years. The aging process seemed to be ignoring him the way most people ignored him. He had to be twenty-seven or eight, I suppose, but his bland, puddin' face didn't look a day over eighteen. Mentally, he'll always be eight or nine.

The person I wanted to see most, Pete's sister Amanda, I only glimpsed. She was there when I arrived, on the far side of the crowd, but when I looked again, she was gone. Which was pretty much the story of our relationship.

After the ceremony, I followed Arnold Boothe's Mercedes to the family home in Grosse Pointe, a three-story brick Victorian box on a huge lot with a long, curving drive that leads around back to a four-car garage with servant's quarters above it. The house is a few blocks from Lake St. Clair, which probably makes it middle class in this neighborhood. Still, the grounds and garden out back were beautifully maintained. Like the house, they reflected a lot of tender care, and radiated an aura of warmth and gentility and safety. Home sweet home. I'd come home for weekends with Pete a number of times during our college years. It was the poshest place I'd ever seen, at the time. His family was always civil enough, though I sensed an undercurrent of disapproval. I was a mongrel kid without kin or connections, studying to be a vet so that I could take care of other people's pets. I didn't exactly fit into their social set. And after I flipped over Amanda and made a sophomoric attempt to woo her, it was clear I'd transgressed a social line. I never felt welcome again.

Nor did I feel particularly welcome now. The long drive was lined with cars and a wake of sorts was obviously in progress, but when I entered, Arnold met me at the door, and hustled me off to the den, away from the others. A leper at the feast.

"David," he nodded, shaking my hand. "How have you been?"

"Fine," I said, glancing around. It was a comfortable room, floor to ceiling bookshelves, leather chairs, a fire glowing in the grate. "I'm sorry about Peter—"

"Yes, we all are," he said, cutting me off. "Would you like a drink? Scotch, wasn't it?" I nodded and he filled two tumblers to the brim with Aberlour single malt. He handed me one and slugged down a third of his own with a single gulp. "God, I needed that. What a mess. Typical of Peter."

"How do you mean?"

"To leave things in a shambles. The funeral. Being buried in a colored cemetery, with the services in a colored funeral home. And dragging you all the way down here, of course."

"I was glad to come."

"Well, for the services, yes," Arnold said, sipping his drink, wincing at the bite of it. "But there's no need for you to stay on. I understand you live up north now."

"In Algoma." I nodded. "I have a practice there."

"Which I'm sure you're eager to return to. Bloody inconvenient affairs, funerals. As for Peter's estate, such as it is, I can at least take that burden off your hands. I've taken the liberty of having the papers drawn up. You can take them with you and look them over or we can just have them witnessed now."

"What papers?"

"Transferring the executorship to me. The probate court will have to approve it, but that's only a formality."

"That won't be necessary," I said, warming myself at the fire. "I don't mind handling it, and since it was Pete's wish . . . "

"He may have wished it back in college," Arnold said, "but be practical. You no longer live in the area, David. But it's not just a matter of convenience, it's business. I'm an attorney with an established reputation in this town. How will it look if my clients learn that my own brother left his affairs in the hands of a stranger? If the money's a problem, just say so. I'm a reasonable man. Let's work something out."

"What money?"

"The executor's fee, of course. You're entitled to five percent of Peter's estate, plus expenses. I'm afraid it won't amount to much. I took the liberty of running a check on Peter's finances. It didn't take long. He was totally irresponsible when it came to handling money. Absent his stock, which is in trust, I doubt his net worth is more than ten or twelve thousand, which would make your fee less than a thousand. Suppose I up that a bit, let's say . . . an even five thousand?"

"That's very generous," I said, "but it's not necessary. I don't want the money and if Pete's estate is small it shouldn't take long to clear up. I'll take care of it."

Arnold eyed me over his drink. "All right," he said mildly. "Make me an offer. How much do you want?"

"I don't want anything. Look, you're an attorney, you probably see cases like this every day. It's just another job to you. But your brother was my friend, and he asked me to do this last thing for him. And so I'm going to."

"Very noble," Arnold sneered.

"Not at all," I said tiredly. "Excuse me, I'd better offer my condolences to your mom and hit the road."

"Wait a minute, we're not through talking yet," Arnold said, grabbing my arm. Our eyes met and held a moment, then he looked away. And let go of my arm. "Look, it's a bad day and we're both upset," he muttered. "Let's not be hasty. Stay and talk. Let's work something out. Besides, you haven't finished your drink."

I glanced down at the cut glass tumbler and the liquid smoke it held. "I've think I've had enough," I said, placing the glass on the mantel, untasted. "I'm sorry about Peter, Arnie. As for the rest of it, I'll be in touch."

I left him in the den, refilling his glass. The crowd in the living room fell silent when I walked in. They were apparently old family friends, with the accent on old. I didn't know a soul. I offered Peter's mother my sympathy. She accepted graciously, though I doubt she remembered who I was.

Donnie, on the other hand, surprised us both by remembering me. Not my name, of course, he doesn't remember anyone's name, but he remembered that I once gave him a ride on my motorcycle. The memory seemed to brighten his day a little. And mine. He was the only one who noticed when I said my goodbyes and made my escape.

Favio Andretti's office was on Beaubien, a few blocks down from Detroit Police headquarters. It was a third floor walk-up, two rooms and a couple of desks. Andretti was on the phone when I walked in. He waved me to a chair. He was a stumpy man, short, squat, and powerful, with square features and thinning black hair. His tie was askew and his tweed sportcoat was draped carelessly over the vinyl sofa against the wall.

He rose and offered his hand. "How are you, Doc? I'm Favio. Pete mentioned you often over the years, mostly about how much trouble you two used to get into. A helluva thing to finally meet like this. You want a drink or something?"

"No, thanks. I've had my limit, actually."

"I skipped the funeral," Andretti said. "I hate the damned things. Besides, they're for the family. Pete and I worked together for almost eight years. I've been to the family digs a few times, but I never really felt comfortable there. I'm second generation Sicilian, not exactly their kind of people."

"You were Pete's kind, though," I said. "He valued your friendship."

"Yeah, well, he must have," Andretti said, swallowing and misting up. "He sure as hell didn't hang around here for the big bucks. Oh, we made a living. We mostly do legwork for outstate law firms, affidavits, depositions, the kind of scutwork they don't want to pay fulltime staffers to do. I handle the legal paperwork; Pete did most of the interviews. He was good at it too, had a way with people. They'd tell him the damnedest things." He shook his head, smiling at the memory.

"Is that how he got killed?" I asked carefully. "The work?"

Andretti eyed me quizzically a moment, reading me. "Not exactly," he said at last. "He was on a job but apparently he was just in the wrong place at the wrong time. He finished an interview in a flophouse off the Cass Corridor and got taken off walking back to his car."

"Do the police have anyone in custody?"

"Not yet, but I know the detective who's handling it, a guy named Garcia. He's a good man. He told me he's got a couple guys he likes for it. Nearly half the homicides in this town go unsolved, but I don't think this one will."

"Well, that's something anyway."

"But not much," Andretti said. "Tell me, Doc, when you and Pete talked last, did he seem depressed?"

"He was . . . a little more thoughtful than usual. Why?"

"I don't know, I'm just trying to make sense of what happened. Pete and I were friends. Maybe I feel guilty for not pressing him harder."

"About what?"

"That's just it, I don't know. He got a bad case of the blues last summer, not himself at all. When I asked him about it he blew me off, said it was nothing. But I knew better. So I looked into it. For his own good, you understand."

"What do you mean, looked into it?"

"I asked an investigator I know check him out."

"And? Did he find anything?"

"Pete was having woman trouble, but not the usual kind. His ladyfriend, Jolene? She had a drug habit. Nothing heavy, mostly tranquilizers. She's a singer and part time model. Tranqs are like popcorn with that crowd. Problem was, she apparently got pregnant while she was using, miscarried, and nearly died herself."

"My God," I said softly. "I never knew."

"Neither did I," Andretti said. "Pete never said word one to me about it. When I found out, I figured I'd back off, cut him some slack and let him work his way through it. But he didn't. At least not right away."

"How do you mean?"

"He got pretty flaky. Started keeping odd hours on the job. A week after Jolene got out of the hospital, Pete took off alone for a week to South America. Needed to get away, he said. Well, maybe he did. After he came back he seemed even more down than before. Until he drove up to see you."

"He never mentioned a word about South America to me."

"He wasn't saying much about much at that point. Seeing you seemed to settle him down, though. He got back to business and moved back with Jolene. The only odd thing was that he had me draw up a new will for him, and made you his executor."

"You mean this will is new? I assumed it was something left over from college."

"Nope, brand new about ninety days ago. So. You were his friend, what do you think? Did I miss something?"

"I don't know," I said. "Pete was an easy man to like, not so easy to know. Maybe none of us are, really."

"Sad, but true blue," Andretti said, shaking his head grimly. "Anyway, here's the will." He fished a manila envelope out of his desk and slid it over to me. "It's properly drawn, signed and witnessed, in case Pete's brother gives you any guff about it. Not that he should. Pete leaves almost everything to dear Arnold."

"Everything?" I said, opening the folder and scanning it. "I never thought they got along very well."

"They didn't," Andretti said. "In fact, they had a major blowout a few months ago about the family stock portfolio. Pete wanted to sell his shares and Arnold was dead set against it. Well, he doesn't have to worry about that anymore. The will divides Pete's shares between Arnold and his mom, about three hundred grand worth. The rest of his estate goes to Jolene, but it doesn't amount to much. Their car and checking and savings accounts were held jointly. He'd blown some money recently, the trip to South America and some other cash withdrawals. There's about seven grand left, all told."

"No insurance?"

"Not that I'm aware of," Andretti said, "and I witnessed most of his legal transactions. Jolene may know more about that, though. There was a keycard for a National Bank of Detroit safety deposit box in his effects. The stock certificates are probably there. Is there any reason you can't be bonded?"

"Bonded?"

"Michigan law requires that executors be insured for roughly the amount of the estate. Ever been convicted of a felony or a misdemeanor involving embezzlement?"

"Nope."

"Good. Sign this form at the bottom, I'll notarize it, then take it over to the county courthouse to have it recorded. Do you have a place to stay? I've got a spare room."

"Thanks, but I'm already registered at the Holiday Inn downtown and I know my way around from there."

"Suit yourself," he said. "If I can help in any way at all, give me a call, okay?" He rose and offered his hand. "I'm sorry we didn't meet years ago, Doc. Good luck."

"Thanks," I said. "For everything."

✳ ✳ ✳

I took the paperwork to the county courthouse. A bored clerk scanned it, then swore me in, and I officially became Peter Boothe's executor.

I suppose the proper order of business should have been to meet with Jolene next, but I wasn't quite up to it yet. I decided to check the safety deposit box instead.

I went to the National Bank of Detroit branch listed on the card, showed another clerk the executorship paperwork, signed my life away and then used Pete's card to retrieve his deposit box. A clerk ushered me into a small, well lighted cubicle that contained only a table and four wooden chairs. I placed the box on the table and opened it.

I don't know what I was expecting, family jewelry, or maybe mementos, a christening spoon or a pocket watch. The box held nothing but a stack of personal papers. I began sorting it out.

A frayed manila envelope held a packet of family pictures from his childhood. Pete and Arnie in Little League uniforms, Amanda on a swing looking utterly angelic and heartbreakingly young. There was a shot of his mother and father arm-in-arm in the living room of their Grosse Pointe home. I studied the photo curiously. Pete's father had died of a coronary before I met Pete and I couldn't recall seeing a photo of him before. He'd been a handsome man. I could see his resemblance to Pete, less so to Arnold. It was a pretty shot, sunlight glowing in the background, framing an attractive couple. Happier times.

I put it back in the envelope with the others, started to set it aside, then hesitated. It was just a packet of family photos. So what was it doing in a safety deposit box? Well, boxes are for valuables, and I suppose the photos were something Pete valued; therefore, here they were. I'd long since given up any hopes of being able to follow Peter Boothe's mental processes. "Pete logic" simply didn't compute for me.

The next folder actually was valuable. It contained five one-thousand-share certificates of Quatermain Pharmaceuticals stock, plus a prospectus and a corporate financial statement. I'm not knowledgeable about the stock market, nor was Pete. The stocks were part of his father's estate and came to Pete as a lifetime trust. The holdings were worth about sixty bucks a share, three hundred grand total, and generated an income of roughly twenty grand a year. Pete had always worked, even in college, but the extra twenty thou made him big rich to me. Well, now it would be divided between Arnold and his mother. But not Amanda? Why not? Had they had a falling out? Or was it just more "Pete logic"?

There was a school folder with "HOW I SPENT MY SUMMER VACATION" printed in block letters on the cover. I flipped it open but it was only photographs, beaches, street scenes. I set it aside.

Next was a nicely engraved folio with Detroit Metropolitan Life on the cover. I opened it, began to scan it, then slowed down and read it more carefully. It was a term life insurance policy, complete with copies of the application and the physical exam Pete had taken to get it. The beneficiaries were Amanda Boothe and Jolene Greene, equally. And the value of the policy seemed to be two and a half million dollars.

I flipped back to the application. Pete had bought the policy in August, roughly four months before. A thousand down, five hundred and twenty one bucks a month for five years. He'd passed the physical with no problems. It looked like the policy was valid, a done deal.

I leaned back in the chair, trying to make sense of what I was seeing. And for just a moment I was sitting on my own back deck in the afternoon sun, and Pete turned to me and said, "I think I'm losing my edge."

I felt absolutely chilled, as though I'd been drenched with a barrel of ice water. Had he known? Had he tried to tell me? Had he been asking me for help? Did I miss that somehow? And let my best friend down? Let him die?

Sweet Jesus. I massaged my eyes with my fingertips, trying to recall more of our conversation that day. All I could come up with were bits and snippets. A typical talk with Pete, topics changing like light dancing on a pool of quicksilver. Serious talk, about things that mattered, life and love and work, but nothing heavy, nothing ominous. Or at least, not that I remembered.

But Yvonne had been there. It was the first time she and Pete had met and it was important to me that my wife and my friend like each other. Had I been subconsciously managing the conversation to avoid touchy subjects? All I could remember clearly was Pete's attitude. There had been an air of . . . melancholy to it. He'd always been mercurial, it was part of his charm, but I couldn't recall seeing him in that particular mood. We'd talked a lot about old times that day and he seemed to remember them fondly. I recalled them as a struggle to survive, to get through my classes, get by the exams, get my degree, and get the hell out. At the time, that's how Pete saw it, too. Something must have changed to make them look better to him. To give them a gloss of nostalgia. Something must have gone seriously wrong in his life, and I'd been too full of myself and my own problems even to notice.

Suddenly the figures on the insurance policy blurred, and my eyes were stinging. And for the first time since I'd heard the news, I sat in that tiny, anonymous room, and wept for my friend. And for myself. Because my world would be a darker place without him.

A clerk stuck his head in the door. "Is . . . everything all right, sir?"

"Fine," I said, pulling myself together. "Could I have a paper bag, please? I'll be taking this stuff with me."

"A bag, sir?" he said, arching an eyebrow. "As you wish."

✳ ✳ ✳

I drove directly to the Holiday Inn downtown and checked in, then placed a call to the insurance company and verified that the policies were valid. The agent seemed genuinely distressed about Pete's death, though the prospect of a two-and-a-half-million-dollar payout may have darkened his mood a bit.

I quickly sorted the policies and the stock certificates into a separate envelope and deposited them in the safe in the hall closet. Then I stripped and stepped into the shower. I stood in the spray for a very long time, trying to wash away aches and tear tracks. It didn't work. I was toweling dry when the phone rang.

"Yes?"

"Dr. Westbrook? My name's Garcia. I'm with the Detroit Metro homicide squad. Favio Andretti said you were staying here. Can I come up and talk a minute?"

"I'm not dressed," I said. "Why don't we meet in the coffee shop in the lobby. Ten minutes?"

"Fine. See you there."

"How will I know you?"

"Don't worry, Doc. I'll know you."

＊ ＊ ＊

The coffee shop was sparsely occupied in the middle of the afternoon. As I entered, a tall, strikingly handsome Latino rose gracefully and waved me over to his booth. His suit looked like an Armani, a perfect fit. On a cop's salary. Ah, Motown.

"Dr. Westbrook, I'm Sergeant Garcia."

He showed me his identification. "Sorry to bother you; I know my timing's lousy."

"No problem," I said, sliding in across from him. "How can I help?"

"I just have a few routine questions. For openers, do you know of anyone who had reason to kill Peter Boothe?"

"No one," I said positively. "He wasn't a man who made enemies."

"I understand you're handling his estate. Is there anything I should know about?"

"I don't think so," I said. "The bulk of it, his stockholdings go to his mother and brother, and a life insurance policy will be divided between his sister Amanda and his lady, Jolene Greene."

"How big a policy?" Garcia asked.

I hesitated. "Two and half million," I said.

Garcia smiled, ruefully, and shook his head. "It's almost like a lotto jackpot, isn't it? What a sorry way to hit it."

"The insurance company didn't seem to think it was out of line."

"It probably isn't," Garcia said with a shrug. "Funny that neither Miss Greene nor Miss Boothe mentioned it, though."

"Maybe they don't know," I said. "Andretti didn't know about it."

"Odd. According to Favio, they were pretty open with each other."

"Let me ask you one, Garcia. Why are you here? I thought this was a street crime."

"We're quite certain it is," Garcia conceded. "In fact, I expect to make a bust by the end of the week. On the other hand, I'm nosy by nature and it never hurts to ask."

He rose, glancing at his watch. "Thanks for seeing me. Sorry to hassle you and run, but I have another appointment."

"Will you let me know if anything develops?"

"If you like," he nodded. "Tell me, do you remember a TV show when we were kids called *The Millionaire?* About a guy who gave away a million bucks every week?"

"I think I saw it once. Why do you ask?"

"Because I think you're about to act it out in real life," he said wryly. "Too bad it couldn't be under nicer circumstances. Take care, Dr. Westbrook. Motown's no town to let your guard down."

"So I gather," I said.

✳ ✳ ✳

Pete's home address was a duplex townhouse in Westland, sandy brick, separate balconies, covered parking. Nice, but not spectacular. I rang the buzzer, waited, then tried again. I was about to give up when the door opened. Jolene Greene and I stared at each other for what seemed like a very long time. We'd never met. I'd only seen her in Pete's pictures of her. They didn't do her justice. Barefoot, wearing a lime green blouse half tucked into a matching skirt, she was tall and willowy as an eland, with high cheekbones, a golden café-au-lait complexion and dark, hawk's eyes. A bust of Nefertiti come to life. She looked like she hadn't slept in a week and yet somehow it didn't diminish her appeal one whit.

"Do I know you?" she asked at last.

"I'm David Westbrook, Pete's old roommate from college? Can we talk for a minute?"

"Don't feel like talking," she said, turning away. She didn't close the door so I followed her through the living room to the kitchen. Her purse was on the table, with some of its contents spilled beside it. There was an open bottle of Southern Comfort and a single glass. A few yellow pills were scattered loose on the table. She scooped them into a neat pile beside her glass and sat down.

I eyed the pills and the liquor a minute, then took a seat across from her. "Those won't help."

"Sure they will. It'll just take 'em a little longer than usual. You want a drink, help yourself. You want to preach a sermon, Reverend, take your act on the road."

"No sermons," I said, glancing around. The kitchen was bright and airy, the table and cabinets were golden oak, the real thing, handcrafted. It must have been a happy room. Once. "Look, I know this is a bad time—"

"Damned straight it's a bad time," she said, cutting me off. "And you don't want a drink and I don't want to talk. So say your say and say goodbye, okay?"

"All right." I shrugged. "Pete made me the executor of his estate. The apartment, the car, and the bank accounts are yours now, free and clear. Are there any other effects of his I should see? Papers, insurance policies, anything like that?"

She eyed me a moment, then shook her head, carefully, as though it was loosely attached. "Not here," she said. "Not anymore. He kept things in a shoebox in the bedroom closet. Took it with him when he moved out. I haven't seen it since."

"He moved out?"

"I kicked him out. Right after I got out of the hospital. I blamed him for what happened. I lost my baby. And the rest of me. I had a hysterectomy. Did he tell you that?"

I shook my head.

"It wasn't so bad," she said grimly. "I'm tougher than I look. And it must've eased Mama Boothe some. She didn't have to worry about any little beige Boothe babies shockin' the relatives at family reunions."

"I doubt she felt like that," I said.

"Then you don't know her very well, do you? Anyway, Pete moved back home to mama. It was probably best. We weren't much good for each other at the time. He took the box with him when he left. I don't recall seeing it after he moved back. He said something about a safety deposit box once. Maybe that's where it is."

"Do you remember what was in it?"

"Papers," she sighed. "Some stocks, old pictures, stuff like that."

She picked up one of the yellow pills, examined it a moment like a grape at a supermarket, then popped it in her mouth and washed it down with a sip of Comfort.

"What are those?" I asked, gesturing at the handful of pills beside her purse.

"You don't know? I thought you were a doctor."

"I'm a vet. An animal doctor."

"They're quarries," she said. "Quaranes. Mellow yellows. Try one. They're harmless. No side effects. Unless you happen to be pregnant. Then there are a few side effects. Internal bleeding, fetal anoxia. In the end they had to abort my daughter and gut me like a trout. But on the upside, I don't have to worry about that particular side effect. Not anymore."

"I'm sorry," I said. "I truly am."

She stared at me a moment, then slowly shook her head. "No. I'm the one who's sorry. None of this is your fault, and I know Pete cared about you. He talked about you a lot, especially lately. Like he was trying to remember happier times, you know? So what do you want from me, Doc? How can I help you?"

"I should be asking you that," I said.

"I don't need help. I'm fine."

"You don't look fine to me."

"I'm not a horse and you're not my doctor. Was there anything else?"

"Just one thing," I said. "Pete was acting . . . well, he wasn't himself the last time I saw him. I'd like to know why. Andretti said he went to South America, but Pete never mentioned it. What was that about?"

"I honestly don't know. He went there after I kicked him out. He said it was a vacation, but I don't see how it could've been. He was only gone a week, hit about five countries and it's not exactly Disney World down there, you know? But Pete said it was great. Even talked about moving there. Living was cheap, we could toast on the beaches and run in the surf. Even the drugs were cheap. Good stuff, too. Brand names. Like the junk that killed our daughter. It was the ugliest thing he ever said to me. He never mentioned it again. Just as well."

"Still," I said, "I can see how he might have blamed you a little for what happened. You were popping yellows then, right? And you still are."

"Blamed me?" she said, surprised. "For these?" She picked up a fistful of pills. "You must be a horse doctor. You really don't know what they are, do you?"

"Quaranes?" I said. "They're tranquilizers, right?"

"Right. But do you know who makes them? Quatermain Pharmaceuticals, a big German drug company. But they didn't develop them. They bought the manufacturing rights twenty years ago from a small American company. Boothe Pharmaceuticals, Pete's family firm. It's almost poetic, isn't it?"

Her eyes were brimming, but there was so much rage in her gaze that I couldn't face her. I looked away. "My God," someone said. Me, I guess

"So you see, Pete didn't blame me for losing our baby," she said after a while. "Or at least, he didn't blame me alone. Considering what happened, if he was acting a little crazy the past few months, maybe he was entitled to."

"Yeah," I said, "I guess he was." I rose slowly, feeling a hundred years older than when I'd arrived. "Look, I know it doesn't mean much, but I can't tell you how sorry I am about everything. If I can help . . . "

"All you can do for me is leave me be. It's easier to handle alone. And I'd better get used to it. You know where the door is."

I nodded. I reached out to touch her shoulder, but she turned away. I was halfway to the front door before I remembered. "Jolene," I said, retracing my steps, "there was an insurance policy in Pete's safety deposit box. Did he tell you about it?"

She shook her head numbly.

"It's quite substantial, and you and Amanda are the beneficiaries. Your share will be a million and a quarter. It'll take ten days or so to process the paperwork. They'll contact you." She didn't react. Her dark eyes were molten but her face as wooden as a tribal mask. I could read nothing in it.

I let myself out and stood on the stoop a minute to catch my breath and gather my thoughts. *The Millionaire.* Right. No wonder the show was canceled. As I started down the steps, I heard an odd sound. It sounded like a dog yowling somewhere in the building. But

I'm a vet. I've heard a lot of howls. This was a wail of pure animal anguish, but it wasn't a dog at all.

✳ ✳ ✳

Amanda Boothe had an apartment in the older section of Eastpointe, née East Detroit. The house was a huge old saltbox, circa World War I, subdivided into flats. I rang the doorbell marked Boothe/Pearson, and someone buzzed me in. Amanda was waiting on the landing at the head of the stairs, looking as blonde and slender and angelic as I remembered. She was a few years older perhaps, but wore it well. I was so busy basking in her welcoming smile that I was halfway up the stairs before I realized she was holding herself upright with a pair of Loftstrand crutches, aluminum canes with wrist braces.

The surprise must have registered on my face. She grinned wryly and shook her head. "I knew it," she said. "I knew exactly how you'd react. That's why I made Pete promise he wouldn't tell you."

"But . . . what happened?" I asked, taking her shoulders and giving her a peck on the cheek.

"A fall," she said, leading me into her apartment. "I was waterskiing in Florida a few years ago, and got tangled with a submerged stump. Actually, I'm doing pretty well now. I can walk with a little help from my friends here, though it's still easier to get around in my chair." She lowered herself into a black canvas wheelchair with a frame of anodized aluminum.

"How about you? Pete told me you finally got married."

I nodded, trying not to stare at her legs and the wheelchair. I forced myself to glance around the room instead. The living room was sunny and bright, with bone berber carpeting, creamy walls, freshly painted, and Queen Anne furniture, delicate as china, all arcs and curves.

"And?" Amanda prodded. "Are you happy? What's she like?"

"She's terrific. Her name was Yvonne LeClair and she's your diametric opposite, dark and, um, not slender. And conning her into marrying me was the luckiest thing I've ever done."

"Second luckiest," she said, shaking her head. "My turning you down was first. We're an unlucky clan, David. Look at us. Arnold's stuffy as a Victorian closet; mom will be saddled with Donnie until she dies and then it'll be my turn. Pete was our best hope, our last candle in the wind. Out. Just like that." She snapped her fingers with finality.

"Actually, I've been getting the impression that he'd been having some pretty serious problems, too."

"You mean Jolene losing their baby? Yeah, that was rough. Pete even moved home for a while after that. But it didn't work out."

"Why not?"

"I don't know. He was pretty unsettled at the time. He took off for South America for a week and afterwards he and mom had a major blowout."

"What about?"

"Neither one would say but it must have been pretty grim. It even got physical. Donnie went after Pete with a shovel and banged him up. He didn't mean it, of course; he was crying two seconds later begging Pete to forgive him. Donnie's always been protective of my mom, but I never dreamed he'd try to hurt Pete."

"He must have been pretty upset."

"Seems like he gets upset a lot more easily lately. Maybe he's getting to be too much for mom to handle. She's a great lady, my mom. She's been a saint with Donnie. But she's got flaws, too. She never liked Jolene, probably because she's black, and she still thinks this wheelchair is a phase I'm going through, like hula hoops or Beatlemania. That I could get out of it if I wanted to badly enough."

"Maybe you will. They're doing great things nowadays."

"I'll survive even if they don't. When they told me I'd never tango again, I went into a tunnel so black I thought I'd never crawl out. But I did. And I managed to whack together a new life for myself out of the pieces of the old one. I survived. And I'm not going back into that tunnel again. Not even for Pete. Does that seem cold to you?"

"No. Just honest, and you always were. Pete would have wanted you to keep pushing."

"I'm not so sure. The last six months, it was like I hardly knew him anymore. He'd come over here half loaded and say he needed to talk. But he wouldn't talk. He'd just stare off into space, a thousand miles away. When I asked him he'd say he was dreaming about South America, especially Paraguay. What a great place it was, great beaches, cheap living. He said I ought to see it sometime, that I'd love it there."

"Maybe you can, if you like. Pete left you some money from an insurance policy. It'll take a week or so to process—"

"Insurance?" she said, cutting me off. "What kind of insurance?"

"Life insurance," I said. "A two-and-a-half-million-dollar policy, divided equally between you and Jolene."

She looked away for a moment, and when she turned back her face had gone gray. "When did he get the policy?"

"About four months ago. Why?"

"That would have been about the time he and Jolene were having all the problems," she said grimly. "What about Pete's stock?"

"He divided it equally between Arnold and your mother."

"Arnie? But why? Pete and Arnie never got along and after Pete's blowup with mom they were barely speaking. Why would he leave his stock to them?"

"I don't know," I said. "His will doesn't explain anything; it just expresses his wishes."

"But it doesn't make sense. Look, Pete never bothered with insurance. We didn't need it. You see, none of us can sell our Quatermain stock. The shares are locked up in a lifetime trust, non-transferable. It was an arrangement my dad made when he sold the company to the Germans. He wanted to guarantee us an income without taking any chance that we'd blow it. So Pete and I made a deal. Whichever one went first would leave our stock to the other, and we'd look out for each other's loved ones. We figured it was all the insurance we'd need. Why would he break his promise to me?"

"I don't know, Amanda. After what he'd been through this past year, I'm amazed he was rational at all. Maybe he was more aware of how fragile life is because of what happened to Jolene, so he arranged things so you'd be okay if anything happened."

"What are you saying? That he was suddenly psychic? That he sensed something was coming?"

"I don't know what to think. He visited me a month after all this happened and we had some pretty heavy conversations, but he didn't mention any of this, not the insurance or the lost baby or even South America. Maybe he'd been down that tunnel you mentioned and was working through it."

"No," she said quietly, "I don't think so. This is all too strange. I think he went into that tunnel and never came out. And now he never will."

We stared at each other in silence. A cellular phone gurgled softly in a pocket of Amanda's chair. She lifted it to her ear. "Yes?" She listened a moment, then nodded. "I see. That's good news, Sergeant. Thanks for letting me know." She rang off and replaced the phone. "That was Garcia," she said numbly. "He's arrested the guys who killed Pete. Three teeny bop gang bangers from the Corridor. A random street crime. I think I'd like to be alone now, David. It was good to see you." She turned and wheeled herself into another room. And out of my life. Somehow I knew I wouldn't see her again. Maybe Pete wasn't the only one who was psychic.

＊ ＊ ＊

I went back to the Holiday Inn but the thought of spending the night there was too damned grim. I decided to pack, grab a quick bite, and then head home. I'd done as much as I could and I wanted to be away from Pete's city and its pain. I wanted my own bed. I wanted to hold Yvonne, and tell her everything was okay. And even if she knew I was lying, she'd let it pass. Sometimes lies become true that way.

I packed my bags, then trotted downstairs to the hotel restaurant, found an empty table in the corner and ordered a BLT and coffee, and a double coffee to go. A moment later, Sergeant Garcia walked in, scanned the room, and made his way to my table.

"Doc, glad I caught you. I checked at the desk and they said you might be here. Can I join you for a minute?"

"Please, sit down. Can I buy you dinner? I think you've earned it."

"No, thank you, I'm on my way home. And I'm not sure I earned very much. The schmucks tried to peddle Pete's credit cards. Master criminals they ain't."

"Then you're sure you have the right people?"

"Positive. They had his wallet, his watch, and one punk's already cut a deal to roll on his buddies. They did it all right. Why do you ask?"

"I don't know. I've been hearing some odd things today about Pete."

"Like what?" Garcia was eyeing me curiously.

"Only that he's been going through a rough patch. It doesn't matter now."

"No," Garcia agreed. "I guess not. But there are a couple of points about this case that bother me, too. Maybe you can help me out. The family's already circled the wagons, you know? All I get from them is St. Peter Boothe."

"He really was a terrific guy." I said.

"I'm not saying he wasn't. And I'm sure as hell not looking to help the punks who took him off. I just want a few answers, for my own peace of mind, okay? Just between us?"

"Ask away," I said.

"You were his friend, right? Knew him pretty well?"

"We were friends. I'm not sure how well I knew him."

"Do you know if he was into street drugs at all? Like crack? Or cocaine maybe?"

"Not a chance," I said.

"What about his ladyfriend, Jolene. Rumor has it she's a pill popper. Would he try to score for her?"

"Again, no chance. They'd already had a major blowup about drugs. There's no way he'd help her get them. Why?"

Garcia sighed. "I'm just trying to make sense of the setup. Boothe was down on the Corridor to talk to a witness, a guy named Washington. Wash lives in a flophouse on Montcalm. There were plenty of empty parking spots out front; it's not like the area gets much traffic, you know? But Boothe didn't park in front. He parked three blocks over, on Ligett. That's a rough area at night and Pete must've known that. So why make the walk? Unless maybe he was trolling for drugs, looking to score?"

"No way. None at all."

"Okay, maybe not. Do you know if he was ill? Epileptic, anything like that?"

"He couldn't have been," I said. "He passed an insurance physical a few months ago. Why? What are you getting at?"

"I don't know; that's what bugs me. Boothe's autopsy bloodwork didn't turn up a damned thing, no drugs, no booze, nothing. But the three punks that killed him said he was stoned to the bone. That's why they decided to take him. He was staggering, so drunk he could hardly walk."

I didn't say anything for a moment. It was as though time had ground to a halt. "This . . . Washington?" I said at last. "The guy Pete interviewed? What did he say?"

"That Boothe was fine when he left. Sober as a judge. Any ideas, Doc?"

"No," I said. "Sorry."

Something in my tone must have given me away. He glanced up at me, reading me openly. He knew I was lying. He listened to lies for a living. But apparently he decided not to call me on it. He rose, curtly wished me luck, and stalked out. My dinner arrived a moment later. I left it on the table.

I walked slowly up to my room in a mood as dark as Amanda's tunnel. My memory kept flickering back to that poker night in college, when Pete pulled his drunk act, staggered out and left me behind. To play out his hand. And my imagination countered with a second image, of Pete staggering along the Cass Corridor late at night. Setting himself up? But why?

I picked up my suitcase, flopped it on the bed and opened it. I found the accordion folder that held the contents of Pete's safety deposit box, emptied it onto the dresser and switched on the overhead light.

I set aside the envelope of family pictures, the stock certificates, and the insurance policies. The answer wouldn't be there.

The folder with "HOW I SPENT MY SUMMER VACATION" printed in block letters on the cover was next. I flipped it open and glanced through it. Ordinary vacation photographs, beaches, street scenes.

The beach shots looked typically touristy, sunbathers and swimmers. The street scenes, though, were nondescript. Traffic, pedestrians. But they all had street signs in the shot, in Spanish. Each shot was identified by country with a scrawled abbreviation below it. I checked the dates on the edges of the photos. They corresponded to Pete's August vacation.

So what was the folder doing in the safety deposit box? I finished flipping through the pages, and found something I'd missed earlier. His canceled plane ticket. Some vacation. He'd spent one day each in Panama, Ecuador, Peru, Bolivia, Paraguay, and finished in Argentina. Wrong, not one day each. He spent two days in Paraguay. Whoopee.

What on earth had he been doing down there? After the death of his child, he must have been at one of the lowest points in his life. Maybe running away made a kind of sense. But to do a lightning tour of second-rate South American beaches?

No, not beaches. He's said something to Jolene about . . . Paraguay. About what a great place it was. Great beaches. And good dope. Something about that had bothered me when she said it, but I'd let it pass. Beaches. There were beaches in Ecuador and Peru and Argentina. But none in Paraguay. The country's landlocked, right?

Sarcasm? And the crack about good dope? The real thing. The junk that had killed their daughter. The cruelest thing he'd ever said to me, Jolene said. The real thing? Quaranes?

I opened the packet that held the Quatermain Pharmaceutical stocks, and found the prospectus. I flipped through it to the section on foreign sales, and there it was. Pete's itinerary. Quatermain had sales operations in each of the countries he'd visited. So? Quatermain was a German conglomerate; they had branches all over the world, including most of the countries of South America. At a glance, it looked like they did a fair amount of business there; the sales figures accounted for half of the corporation's gross, with each of the countries contributing its fair share—including Paraguay.

I rechecked the street scenes in the photos. Each shot had focused on a street sign, but in the background, each had a Quatermain Corporación building. All looked substantial but one. The shot of the street in Nueve Bavaria, Paraguay, was a row of ramshackle storefronts. Quatermain headquarters was the size of a mom and pop bodega. A mail drop, nothing more. I double-checked the prospectus. The street address was correct; it was the only Quatermain address in Paraguay. And according to the prospectus, corporate sales for Paraguay were roughly equal to those from Argentina.

I was a little rusty on my geography, so I made a quick call to the information desk of the Detroit Public Library. Argentina is roughly eight times larger than Paraguay, in size and population.

Pete logic and Pete humor. There are no beaches in Paraguay. And there was no Quatermain Pharmaceuticals operation there either. At least no legitimate one. The corporation was dumping drugs in Paraguay, but they weren't being used there. A lot of the stuff was being shipped north. All the way to Detroit.

And Pete had walked off and left me to play his cards for him again. Maybe because in college, I'd been lucky, and I'd won. But I couldn't see any way of winning this game. No way at all.

* * *

It was nearly nine when I arrived at the Boothe home in Grosse Pointe. The house was brightly lit and the long driveway was still lined with cars. It was raining, so I kept my Jeep to a crawl and double-parked near the front door. I blocked some people in, but I wasn't concerned about it. I didn't expect to stay long.

Arnold answered the bell. He was in a vest and shirtsleeves with his tie loosened. In fact, he seemed pretty loose generally. I guessed the tumbler of scotch in his hand wasn't his second. Or even his fourth.

"Sorry to bother you again," I said. "I'd like to talk to you, and to your mother. Privately. It's about Pete's estate."

He glowered blearily a moment, then shrugged. "Come in." He showed me into the den again, then left to fetch his mother. I stood at the french doors, staring out into the dark. The drizzle was increasing. The end of a perfect day. A few minutes later Arnold returned with Mrs. Boothe and Donnie in tow. Mrs. Boothe looked tired, but there was a grim set to her mouth. Perhaps she'd been expecting me. She took a chair by the fire with Donnie at her shoulder just behind her chair. Arnold walked unsteadily to the bar to freshen his drink.

"I'll have to ask you to be brief, Dr. Westbrook," Mrs. Boothe said. "We have guests. This isn't the proper time for . . . business."

"It's the only time I have," I said. "I'm leaving tonight, and I have a big problem. Pete left me with a decision to make, one he couldn't make himself. You see, he's willed his shares of the Quatermain stock to the two of you, equally. But he also left enough clues behind to point me to an ugly truth. One that affects you both."

"What truth?" Mrs. Boothe asked.

"That the Quatermain Corporation is dumping massive quantities of drugs, mostly Quaranes, in South American markets. Those drugs are being funneled back into this country. They're as easy to get as popcorn."

142 / *All Creatures Dark and Dangerous*

"And no more dangerous," Arnold protested. "I've used them myself. By prescription, of course."

"But most of them are being sold illegally. And when a pregnant woman takes them, as Jolene Greene did, the results can be disastrous, both to the fetus and to the mother."

"You can hardly hold a corporation or its shareholders culpable for the actions of a few drug addicts," Mrs. Boothe said coolly.

"I didn't come here to debate morality with you, Mrs. Boothe. I just wanted to tell you something, and ask you something. For openers, I don't believe Pete's death was a random crime. I think he meant it to happen. Not suicide, exactly, more like Russian roulette. He put himself in harm's way by arranging his schedule to be in rough parts of town at night, and then he invited an attack by pretending to be a drunk."

"That's nonsense," Arnold said. "Pete was immature, but he wasn't crazy."

"No, but he was in a terrible jam," I said. "The death of his daughter set him off on a search for answers, but when he found them, he realized he couldn't blow the whistle on Quatermain without bankrupting his entire family. So he found a way to resolve it. He bought a small fortune in life insurance for Amanda and Jolene. It wouldn't pay off for suicide of course, so he found a way around that too."

"I don't believe you," Mrs. Boothe said coldly. "Peter would never have done such a thing. He hadn't the . . ."

"Courage?" I said. "Maybe not. The Pete I grew up with wasn't particularly brave. But that was a long time ago. Perhaps the death of his daughter and the . . . maiming of his lover changed that. But it wouldn't explain the way he rearranged his will. So I have to ask you something. After Pete's 'vacation' in South America, did he tell you about Quatermain and the drugs? And ask you what he should do?"

Neither of them answered me for a moment. They glanced at each other instead. And that glance was all the answer I needed.

"Thank you for your time," I said, turning to leave.

"Wait a minute," Arnold snapped. "Where are you going? What are you going to do?"

"I don't know," I said honestly. "Play out the hand, I guess."

"You mean make these ridiculous charges public? And reduce our family to poverty?" Mrs. Boothe said. "Surely Peter wouldn't have wanted that."

"No, he didn't," I said. "But it's not his problem now. He left it to me. I'll have to work it out on my own. And frankly, it doesn't pose the same dilemma for me that it did for him. Goodbye, Mrs. Boothe, and again, my condolences."

"Wait, please," Arnold pleaded, but I closed the door behind me, cutting him off. I could hear them arguing fiercely as I made my way out. I paused on the porch. The rain was a torrential downpour now. I turned up my collar and ran to my Jeep.

I motored slowly down the drive, squinting into the streaming darkness. I was halfway to the street when I glimpsed a figure off to my left, running through the rain. It was Donnie. His black suit was drenched and his hair was plastered against his skull. And he was carrying a shovel.

He was trying to cut me off at the gate. It was a suicidal move. Even if he made it he'd have to step aside to avoid being run down. Unless I got there first. If I could beat him to the gate I could get out on the street and be gone before anyone got hurt.

I matted the gas pedal and the Jeep surged forward, charging toward the gate like a crazed buffalo. But he was faster than I thought. He made it to the gate first and wheeled to face me, blocking my path. And by the manic look in his eyes in the headlight glare I could see he wasn't going to move. His mother had told him to stop me, and he meant to do it. Or die trying.

I was too close and the driveway was too slick. If I swerved to avoid him now I'd ram the concrete gateposts that flanked him. I had to hit him. No choice. I had to. I even tried to, I think. But I didn't.

At the last second I cramped the wheel hard right, sending the Jeep into a full-blown skid. It bucked, started to flip and then slammed broadside into the gatepost, driver's side first.

The world exploded into a welter of shattered glass and torn metal, and then winked out as my head banged off the doorsill.

Something was in my face, smothering me. I tried to brush it off and it gave way. The airbag. The airbag had gone off.

I was dazed, my nose was bleeding, maybe broken. And then Donnie was beside me, raising his shovel to finish me off. And I was too groggy to move. Trapped in my seat by the airbag and my safety belt, I couldn't even avoid the blow. I closed my eyes . . .

And there was light. A glare on my closed eyelids. And I could hear sirens. And road noise. I opened my eyes. Donnie was gone. A woman was kneeling beside me, wiping blood from my face. She was wearing some kind of a blue uniform. Her face was squarish and her blonde hair was cut very short. I blinked, trying to take in my surroundings. Ambulance. I was in an ambulance.

"Where's Donnie?" I asked.

"Who's Donnie? You were alone in the car." She stared into my eyes, checking my pupils for dilation.

"Donnie was . . . outside. With a shovel."

"You mean the mentally handicapped guy? He's okay. You're lucky he was there. He pried your door open with his shovel. He said you gave him a ride on your motorcycle once."

"Once," I agreed. "Long time ago."

"You'd better save your strength. You've got a nasty gash on your forehead, maybe a concussion. You rest now, we'll be at the hospital in a few minutes."

"Right," I said, sagging back against the pillow. The glare from the overhead light was irritating so I closed my eyes again. And after a while the thrum of the engine became the thunder of waves. And I could feel the sunlight on my face. And I saw Pete off in the distance, loping through the foamy breakers, leaving me behind.

I tried to call his name, but I had no voice. And so I put my head down and ran after him, pounding desperately through the surf, chasing my best friend down the golden, glistening beaches of Paraguay.

Cedar Savage

Curt eased his battered pickup truck off on the shoulder of the road, checking both ways as he did so.

"All clear," he said quietly. "There's a car parked back there a ways, though."

"It was here earlier," Jack Lamotte said. "It ain't about nothin', probably broke down. You get the dogs out, gimme their leads, then get the truck out of here. There's a turnoff about a quarter mile ahead. Turn down Grissom Road, pull into the trees out of sight then hotfoot it back here. When I seen the bear, he was movin' through that copse o' cedars over there. I got a piece of fur he lost on some bob wire when he raided Colfax's sheep pen. I'll set the dogs on his scent and head 'em in before anybody spots us. Think you can catch us up in the dark?"

"No problem," Curt said. "Uncle Jack? Be sure to keep a tight hold of Brummie. When he gets excited—"

"Boy, I was runnin' bear dogs before you was a shine in your mama's eye," Jack snapped. "I may be short a pin or two but I ain't ripe for no rockin' chair yet. You just try to catch us up before your hounds tree that rogue or I'll feed your share of the bounty money to your dogs."

"Don't worry, I'll catch up," Curt said, piling out of the truck. He quickly released the gates of the kennels built onto the pickup bed, solid, well-insulated doghouses that kept the hounds comfortable even on long trips in winter weather.

The two Walker hounds leapt out of their cages to the ground, eighty pounds of lean musculature and floppy ears, tails up, eyes alight, wired up and ready for the hunt. Trooper immediately sat at Curt's feet like the soldier he was named for but Brummie danced around with excitement before he let Curt snap on his lead.

Curt handed the leashes to Jack. The older man showed the hounds the bit of black bear fur, then led them across the drainage ditch into the trees. Curt watched them go, shaking his head.

Jack was dressed for the woods in an old green army jacket, corduroys and logger's boots. He moved surefootedly for a man minus an arm, an eye, and most of one leg, but Curt thought his limp seemed more pronounced than usual. Probably needed to get his prosthesis refitted again. Problem was, Jack hated VA hospitals. Claimed to be afraid they'd whack off his other arm and give it to some wet-eared second louie.

Jack glared back over his shoulder, spotted Curt watching him and angrily waved him off. Right. Time to go.

Curt scrambled back into his pickup truck, gunned it along the shoulder of the road to the turnoff and concealed it well back in the trees. It was the spring of the year and nothing in northern Michigan was in season, so any DNR officer who spotted a truck with dog crates aboard would immediately get suspicious.

Keeping to the shadows at the edge of the woods, Curt trotted back toward the cedars where Jack had disappeared. His boots sank into the moist leaf mould of the swamp as he ran. The spongy soil made the footing tricky, but it also made tracking Jack and the two bear hounds a snap.

Curt overtook his uncle about seventy yards into the trees. Jack Lamotte was keeping pace with the dogs, but he'd been paying a steep price. His face was ashen, slicked with sweat. When Curt took the leads from him he didn't protest.

"They're actin' birdy," Jack panted. "Bear can't be more'n a hundred yards ahead or so."

"Damn, we're still awfully close to the road if the bastard decides to tree around here," Curt said.

"Gunshots in the swamp roll like thunder," Jack said. "Nobody can tell where they came from. We'll be all right. You just think on your half of the bounty money, plus if his hide's half decent it'll fetch another three hundred, maybe more."

Brummie suddenly lunged at the end of his leash as though he'd been hit with a cattle prod. "Yawp! Yawp!"

"Turn 'em loose!" Jack hissed. "Mr. bear's gotta be right ahead of us in them trees."

"I can't see nothin'," Curt said, unleashing the hounds. And then it was too late for talk. He sprinted after his dogs, leaving Jack to follow along as best he could.

Curt switched on his flashlight, hoping they were far enough from the road so it wouldn't be seen. The penalties for poaching were severe, but crashing into a five-hundred pound rogue black bear in the dark could cost a man a helluva lot more than money.

He could hear the dogs singing now, yelping excitedly ahead. Their tones told Curt they had their prey in sight. No sounds of combat yet. Maybe the bear had treed.

He glimpsed a flash of Brummie's rump forty yards ahead or so but as he picked up his pace to overtake the dogs, their barking suddenly trailed off. What the hell? The hounds had to be on top of the damned bear, but they weren't growling or snapping. And he still couldn't hear any sounds from the bear.

A giant pine tree loomed out of the mist. Surrounded by a circle of smaller cedars, the clearing was defensible turf, a perfect spot for a bear to turn at bay. He could either climb the huge pine or make his stand with the tree at his back and fight the dogs one on one as they came at him. And if he was as big as Jack thought, he could kill both dogs faster than a bat could blink.

With his throat on fire and his heart hammering a drumbeat of fear and excitement, Curt burst through the outer ring of cedars into the pine clearing. The dogs were leaping and snapping at the air and each other, crazed with excitement, primed for combat. But there was no bear for them to fight.

In the shadowed clearing, it took Curt a moment to realize what the dogs were jumping at. A body. A man was hanging from a short piece of rope tied to a lower bough of the giant pine, twisting slowly in the dusk.

For a moment Curt thought the swaying man might still be alive but one glimpse of his purpled, distorted features blew that idea. The corpse was only moving because the dogs were nipping at its pantlegs.

"Holy Mary, Mother of God," Curt breathed. "What the hell is this?"

* * *

The dog standing on the examination table seemed to be in good physical shape. An eighty-pound, flop-eared Walker hound, four years old with his reproductive system still intact.

Frowning, Dr. David Westbrook gently ran his hands over the hound's flanks, checking for tumors or hidden abrasions. Zip. Zero.

Nada. The hound's coat had a glossy sheen, no fleas, no scars, and his tail was wagging slowly, which, in a bear dog, is an encouraging sign. Bred for ferocity and scenting ability, bear dogs could be a handful sometimes. But all in all, this hound looked like a healthy, happy camper.

His owner was another matter. Curt Lamotte was as jumpy as a field mouse in a frying pan. His dark eyes kept darting around the veterinarian's office as though he was scouting out escape routes.

Curt was at least twenty, but he seemed younger. Maybe it was his sparse beard. Like a lot of Algoma natives, Curt was of French and Ojibwa stock, dark hair and eyes, aquiline features, and scarcely enough stubble to warrant a shave every third day.

"Your dog looks healthy as a horse, Curt," David said, mussing the hound's ears. "If more of my clients cared for their animals the way you do, I'd be out of business. So why are you wasting my time?"

"What do you mean?" Curt asked, swallowing.

"You're too good a hand with hounds, Curt. You don't need a vet to tell you Brummie here's in the pink. So what's on your mind?"

"I just . . . needed to talk to you alone is all, Doc."

"I'll be breaking for lunch soon. I can meet you over at Tubby's if you like."

"No, I can't risk bein' seen. Look, you're pretty good friends with the sheriff, right? I mean, I see you guys havin' breakfast together most mornings at the café."

"Stan and I share a table now and again," David admitted. "Calling us friends is a bit of a stretch. What about the sheriff?"

"I need you to talk to him for me."

"About what? Look, Curt, I don't want to be rude, but I've got other patients waiting—"

"It's about a body," Curt blurted out. "We—ah—me and Brummie come on a body last night. In the swamp along Cullen Creek."

"A . . . human body, you mean?"

"Yeah." Curt nodded, swallowing. "Hangin' from a big white pine with a bunch of cedars around it."

"I see," David said, though he really didn't. "Do you—ah—do you know who it was?"

"I knew him, yeah. He's a shirttail relation of mine, second or third cousin. One of the Cadarette brothers. Norman. He's a couple years younger than me. It was hard to be sure at first. His face . . ." Curt swallowed hard. "His face was so swole up I couldn't hardly recognize him."

"But you're sure—yeah, of course you're sure he was dead," David said, answering his own question. "Look, I don't understand, Curt. Why are you telling me about this?"

"Because I can't go to the law, Doc. We was poachin' in there, huntin' outa season. I can't afford no fines and anyway the DNR will seize my dogs. I raised them dogs up from pups. I don't wanna lose 'em."

"So you want me to tell Stan about this? How the hell am I supposed to explain it?"

"I don't know. Tell him somebody called you, kinda anonymous like. I'd call him myself but I seen on TV where cops can tell who you are from your voice or somethin'. Please, Doc, you gotta help me out." Curt's voice was quavering, close to breaking. "Remember, you owe me one."

"Yeah, I guess I do at that," David conceded. A few years earlier, David had skidded his Jeep off an icy back road into a deep ditch. If Curt hadn't spotted the overturned vehicle and stopped to haul him out, he might have drowned or frozen.

"Okay, okay," David said. "I'll talk to Stan for you and I'll do my level best to keep you out of it. Fair enough?"

"More'n fair, Doc," Curt said, nodding gratefully. "I know you'll do what you can. I appreciate it."

"You'd just better hope we don't both end up in jail. Now, tell me about this body."

"It's back in the swamp near the creek. We went in maybe fifty, sixty yards west of the water. Norm's car was parked by the road there, but I didn't think nothin' of it, figured he was outa gas or broke down or somethin'. I set Brummie and Trooper on a bear trail and I followed 'em in. They started yawpin' and I figured they mighta treed the bear, but they'd come on ol' Norm's body instead. It's not far off the road. There's a path fishermen use along the creek. If you follow it back about a hundred yards you can spot that big pine easy. You can't hardly miss it."

"Famous last words," David grumbled.

✳ ✳ ✳

"Damn!" David's foot sank into the peaty muck halfway up his ankle. Naturally, his Weejun loafer came off when he tried to pull his foot free and he wound up dancing a one-legged jig as he fumbled in the mud trying to rescue his shoe. The chill swamp water cut at his ankles like a dull hacksaw.

"Watch your step there, Doc," Stan Wolinski said, not bothering to conceal a grin. "It's a tad damp out here." The sheriff could afford to be smug. He was wearing a pair of rubber barn Wellingtons he'd hauled out of the patrol car's trunk as soon as he'd realized where they were going. Stan was a sawed-off fireplug of a man, square-shouldered and square-faced. His hair was going prematurely gray but he still saw the world in stark shades of black and white. A man without nuances. Only a slightly off-center sense of humor saved him from being a total stick.

"Wet feet are healthy," David grated. "Cold water stimulates the circulation. That should be the tree up ahead, the big white pine with the cedars around it."

"Should be?" Wolinski snorted. "Be a whole lot simpler if who-ever it was came along to show us himself. Especially if this turns out to be a wild goose chase."

David didn't bother to answer. He picked up his pace, pushing through the huddle of cedars surrounding the huge old pine.

It was definitely the right tree. The ring of cedars formed a sort of woodland amphitheater, ringing the thick-boled pine like acolytes around an ancient priest. The pine's gnarled limbs were raised to the heavens in supplication. And a body was hanging from one of its lower branches by a short length of clothesline.

Norm Cadarette? Maybe. The corpse's bulging features were too distorted for David to be sure. It could have been anyone. He was wearing a loden-green and black checkered overcoat and torn jeans, but half the population of Algoma wore similar clothing this time of year, men and women alike.

Stan whistled softly as he moved past. He circled the body slowly, looking it over carefully. Then he knelt, examining the ground near the corpse.

"Looks like he stepped up on this busted cedar stump, then kicked it away," Stan said grimly. "And now I'm gonna have to tell his folks what happened. God, sometimes I hate this job, you know that? I really hate it."

"Why would he . . . do a thing like this?"

"Who knows why young people do anything these days?" Stan snapped, rising. "Christ, when I got outa high school our big career options were gettin' shipped to Vietnam or runnin' to Canada. Kids today aren't facing anything nearly that bad. You'd think life would look pretty good to 'em. Instead, the suicide rate keeps goin' up. Damn it to hell."

Spotting the boy's wallet and shoes at the edge of the clearing, Stan trudged over to them, knelt, and riffled through the wallet. "Norman Cadarette," he said. "Twenty-three freakin' years old."

"Did you know him?"

"I know his whole damn' family. Cedar savages. Work in the woods, trap some, do a little hardscrabble farmin'. Good folks for the most part. Work hard, pay their bills on time. Might get a little hammered of a Saturday night and bust up a backwoods tavern or maybe poach a deer out of season for meat, but otherwise they're not much trouble."

"Why do the locals call them cedar savages?"

Stan glanced at him. "Can't say I ever gave it much thought. I suppose it's because they work at loggin' or peelin' cedar posts, they don't wear ties and their fingernails aren't always clean. I thought young Norman here might turn out a bit different though. He was real bright in school. Won a scholarship to attend Westover College. Chemistry, I think."

"What happened?"

"Flunked out. Couldn't make the adjustment to college life. Too many buildings, too many girls, not enough hills or piney woods around. So instead of graduating and going on to a good job, he ends up decorating a lonesome pine. Sweet Jesus."

David glanced around the clearing. The grass was trampled down pretty thoroughly, probably by Curt's dogs. The stump Norm had stood on had fallen on its side. It seemed like a sorry way to die. He wondered if Norm had accepted the death he'd sought, or if he'd fought the rope at the end, and tried to claw his way upward for one last gasp of air.

David stepped back for a breath of air himself. The boy's bowels had voided in his final moments and the stench was potent when the breeze caught it just right. There was another scent mixed in with it too, something vaguely familiar that gave David a momentary flashback to his own college days. His dorm room, late at night. The image flickered a moment, and then passed. No sense to it.

The boy apparently hadn't struggled much. His hands were reddened by lividity as his blood settled in his lower extremities, but they were otherwise unmarked. If he'd been doing manual labor in the woods, he'd been damned careful about it. His hands looked as soft as a girl's, except . . .

For his right wrist. There was a line around it. Curious, David moved around the body to check the other wrist. A similar mark. Not a scar, a narrow bruise line. He'd seen it often on animals that had been tied too tightly. A rope burn.

Uneasy now, he knelt by the cedar stump at the boy's feet. Several broken branch stubs were sticking out of the stump, smeared with dark loam where they'd punctured the ground when the stump had been kicked away. But there were too many marks. The ground around the stump was dotted with a half dozen of them at least.

"Stan? Check this out, will you?"

Frowning, the sheriff carefully replaced the boy's wallet where he'd found it and joined David beside the body. "Check what out?"

"Look at the ground. Those marks."

"Where the stump dug in, you mean?" Stan said, kneeling to examine the wounded earth more carefully. He traced the gouges in the soil with his blunt fingertips, then touched one of the broken branch spikes on the stump. And when he glanced up, his square face was transformed into his cop mask. Unreadable.

"What the hell is this?" he asked evenly.

"I'm not sure. It looks like that stump was kicked over a number of times. And his wrists have rope burns on them. Maybe he tied himself up to be sure he couldn't change his mind."

"And then he jumped off the stump a half dozen times?" Stan asked acidly. "And then untied his wrists and tossed the cord away while he was dancing on air? And where's that rope now? I don't see it, do you?"

David shook his head.

"I think it's time to tell me who told you about this body, Doc."

"Stan, he had nothing to do with this. I'm sure of that."

"That's not good enough, Doc, not anymore. I think we may be lookin' at a homicide here, so all bets are off. I want his name. You're a veterinarian so you can't be protecting any doctor-patient confidentiality. Unless somebody's cat told you Norm was out here."

"Stan, I gave him my word."

"Damn it, Doc——" Stan turned away, visibly controlling his anger. "All right," he said, facing David again. "You gave him your word, now I'll give you mine. I'll have to call a State Police evidence team out here. It'll take 'em an hour to get here from Lansing, maybe two or three hours more to go over the scene and remove the body. Let's say four hours tops. Then I'll be heading back to my office. And when I get there, I want to see you and your anonymous informant waiting for me."

"But——"

"No buts. Either bring him in or bring your toothbrush along, Doc. Because you'll be a guest of the county until you produce your Mr. X. Do we understand each other?"

David nodded.

"Good. I'll stay here to protect the site," Stan said, taking a cell phone from a clip on his belt. "So why don't you go round up your witness and try not to trample any evidence on your way back to your Jeep."

Leaving Stan in the clearing, David made his way out of the swamp. He didn't retrace his steps to the path along the creek they'd followed in, though. Instead, he scouted around until he picked up the paw prints of Curt's dogs.

He was no Daniel Boone, but it wasn't difficult to follow the dog tracks in the moist ground. The trail came out only twenty or thirty yards from the banks of Cullen Creek, not far from Norm's abandoned car.

He spent a few minutes casting about the area looking for more signs, but didn't find any. From the position of Norm's car, he'd taken the same route the dogs had to that clearing. Had he been alone? No way to be sure now. But one thing was obvious. There were too many tracks, dogs and humans alike. Cursing softly, David climbed into his Jeep, fired it up, and drove angrily back to Algoma. He pulled into the lot at Shaeffer's garage and stalked around back to the service area.

Curt Lamotte was dressed in brown canvas coveralls, leaning over the fender of a Ford Taurus. He glanced up at David's approach but his smile of greeting faded fast.

"We have to talk," David said, grasping Curt's bicep and leading him to a shadowed corner of the garage.

"What's wrong?" Curt asked. "Did you find him?"

"We found him easily enough, Curt, but things didn't happen exactly the way you told me, did they? For openers, you weren't on that hunt alone. There were other tracks mixed in with yours. And worse, your friend Norman may not have committed suicide at all."

"I don't understand. I—"

"And lastly," David said, cutting him off, "you weren't even straight with me about the dogs. Brummie couldn't have found that body."

"Sure he did, him and Trooper both. They led me right to it."

"Did they? Funny, I thought they were good bear dogs, the best in the county, some say."

"They are!"

"Then why did they lead you to the body, Curt? You said you were after a rogue bear, right? One that had been killing sheep? Well I checked around that clearing. I'm no woodsman but that ground's so soft a field mouse would leave tracks, to say nothing of a five hundred pound bear. There weren't any bear tracks near that clearing. So if the dogs had really been on a bear's spoor, they wouldn't have left it to go check out that body any more than they'd go running off after a rabbit or a squirrel. They're bear dogs. Scent hounds. Once they're on a trail, they stay on it. So if they led you to that body, then they must have been looking for it."

"I swear that's not how it was."

"No? Then maybe you'd better tell me how it was, Curt. If you were after a bear how did the dogs pick up its scent? Where were its tracks?"

"I—don't know. It was dark. I didn't actually see its spoor."

"But you knew it was there? Who said so? Who really set your dogs on the scent?"

Curt hesitated, then released a long, ragged breath. "My Uncle Jack," he said quietly. "He come to my place yesterday afternoon. Said ol' man Colfax, the one with the big dairy farm, had offered him bounty money to take a bear."

"Why?"

"Colfax told him he'd been losin' sheep to a rogue bear but the DNR wouldn't issue him a nuisance permit to kill it. So he offered Uncle Jack two hundred bucks to get rid of the bear on the sly, like. Jack's got no dogs, so he offered me half the money if I'd help him out."

"And your uncle put them on the scent? How, exactly?"

"He had a little chunk of fur. Said he got it off a bob-wire fence where one of the sheep was killed. He let the dogs sniff it and they went off like rockets into the swamp, noses to the ground. They knew what they were doin'."

"But you never actually saw the bear's trail?"

"No, it was dark and it was all I could do to keep up with them dogs. And they led me right to Norman."

"And were they excited?"

"How do you mean?"

"Were they birdy? Yawping and jumping around?"

"Sure they were. You know how they get when they've . . . found what they're after." His voice died away, as though the import of his words had just registered.

"And where was your Uncle Jack while all this was going on? Could he have led the dogs to the spot?"

"No, way. He was way back behind us. He's only got one arm and half a leg, got blown damn' near in half over in Vietnam. He gets around pretty good, but he's kinda slow, you know? Me and them dogs was probably at that clearin' a good five minutes before Jack caught up to us."

"I see," David said. "Then he must have known the body was there beforehand."

"He couldn't have," Curt said. "The dogs led me to it, Doc. You think he whispered in their ears, told 'em where it was hangin'? He showed 'em a chunk of bear fur and that was it. Look, I'll talk to the sheriff, I can see where I'll have to now, dogs or no dogs, but I need to keep my uncle clear of this, all right?"

"Why should you?" David said, exasperated. "He's the one who got you into this mess."

"Not on purpose, he didn't," Curt said stubbornly. "He wouldn't do me like that. But Uncle Jack ain't so good with people. Especially the law. He's had a lot of trouble in his life. I'll be damned if I'll set him up for any more."

"Curt, it's a murder investigation. You can't keep him out of it."

"But we didn't do nothin'! We were tryin' to take down a rogue bear the DNR should've handled and I reported the body the best way I could. Why should we take the heat for doin' right? It ain't fair!"

"Okay, okay, calm down. The thing is, you can't lie to Stan without buying yourself a world of trouble, Curt. You'd better get hold of your uncle, and damned fast."

"I can't. He's got no phone and I can't just take off work to go chasin' out to his place. I'm barely hangin' onto this job as it is."

"All right then, I'll talk to him," David snapped. "I'm the one in the jam, here. Where does he live?"

"He's got a cabin way and the hell'n'gone back of the Silver River swamp. You take the second dirt road past the bridge, follow it to the end. Nobody else lives out there."

"Will he be there now?"

"He's always there," Curt said glumly. "Livin' back in that swamp all busted up like he is, he ain't exactly no social butterfly, you know? And you be a little careful comin' up on him, okay? Like I said, he ain't so good with people."

"I'll keep it in mind," David said.

✳ ✳ ✳

David found the dirt road that Curt had described with no trouble, but getting down it was another matter. After the first mile the trail narrowed to a rutted track barely wide enough for a single vehicle. If he'd been driving anything but his Jeep, he would have quit cold. The trail couldn't have been more than a few miles long, but it still took nearly half an hour to crawl back to Jack Lamotte's place in low gear.

The tiny cabin blended so naturally into the forest it seemed to be a part of it, as though it had sprouted and grown like a morel at the edge of the clearing. Perhaps it had, in a way. The log-framed, slab-sided building had probably been built from the pines that had been cut to clear the site.

Stacks of cedar logs stood in neat cords near the house. Some were peeled, but most still wore their hides. A sawhorse and a two-handed drawknife stood near a stack of skinned posts. Peeling cedars is the north country equivalent of a cottage industry. Loggers cut the posts to size then drop them off for local folks to shave to make fence posts or lawn furniture, one pickup truckload at a time. For ten cents a log.

Shadowed by the towering pines around it, the cabin looked deserted, its front door ajar, no lights showing inside. David eased warily out of his Jeep, remembering Curt's warning about his uncle.

"Mr. Lamotte? Jack Lamotte?"

A bearded figure dressed in overalls and a blue-black plaid shirt appeared in the shadow of the doorway.

"Who are you and what do you want?"

"I'm Dr. Westbrook, the veterinarian from Algoma. We have to talk. Your nephew Curt told me how to find you."

"I don't need no vet. Why'd Curt send you out here?"

"He didn't, exactly. I came on my own to keep Curt from buying himself a truckload of trouble by lying to Sheriff Wolinski about that body the two of you found last night."

Lamotte didn't react for a moment, then shook his head warily. "I don't know what you're talking about."

"I think you do. Curt told me what happened, Jack. He had the idea I could tip off Sheriff Wolinski about it and keep the two of you clear of it. I tried. It didn't work out."

"No? Why not?"

"Because that kid you found out there didn't commit suicide. Wolinski's fairly sure he was murdered, so you can forget about blowing this off, Mr. Lamotte. Wolinski gave me a couple of hours to produce my anonymous tipper. So here I am."

"I didn't tip you off about anything."

"True. And I can tell you up front that your nephew's all set to take the fall for you. He'll tell Wolinski he was poaching and found the body by himself. If you let him do it."

"He's old enough to vote. If he wants to do something that stupid, why shouldn't I let him?"

"Because I guessed Curt wasn't alone and so will Wolinski. Curt could end up in jail trying to cover for you and the law will come for you anyway. Look, I'm no cop but I do know dogs, and those two hounds wouldn't have found that body on their own."

"Why not?"

"Because Curt said you let them sniff a piece of fur and they led him straight to the body. The only way that could have happened would be if the fur and the body had a strong scent in common. I'm guessing you dusted it with something first. Something like amphetamines, right?"

Lamotte eyed him a moment without speaking. The older man was hawk-faced with a coarse salt and pepper beard. One eye was covered with a grubby black patch, but the other had a raptor's glint, shrewdly intelligent. "Maybe you'd better come in," he said at last.

Lamotte stood aside as David entered, or rather, he hobbled aside. Jack Lamotte's right leg ended just above the knee. His pant leg was pinned up and he was using a cane to steady himself. His left arm was missing altogether, the sleeve pinned up against his shoulder.

And yet he seemed far from helpless. And there were stacks of peeled cedar posts in the yard. David wondered how the hell a man could manage that kind of work with one arm. It was difficult enough with two.

The cabin's interior was a surprise. It was a crude, two room affair with a rough pine floor, a dry sink and a handmade table by its only window. An ancient cast iron woodstove stood in one corner, and a small bedroom was partly concealed behind a trade blanket hanging over the door frame. A huge black bearskin decorated one wall, and yet the cabin looked more like a library than a backwoods hovel.

Handmade bookshelves rose floor to ceiling on three sides, filled with an eclectic mix of hardcovers and paperbacks. Shakespeare and Freud stood shoulder to shoulder with John O'Hara and John D. MacDonald, Alexander Pope and Marcus Aurelius, but the majority of the books were history titles, Civil War, World Wars One and Two. And Vietnam.

"You read a lot of history, do you?" David asked dryly.

"When you get chopped up in a meat grinder, you get curious about who turned it on," Lamotte said. "Besides, I got no electricity out here, no radio or TV. It passes the time."

David crossed to the cast iron woodstove, but despite the chill of the autumn afternoon, it was unlit. The room was as cold as

Lamotte's unblinking stare. He left the front door ajar, standing in its shadow.

"How did you know about the speed?" Lamotte asked.

"I tried amphetamines in college. I was working two jobs, studying when I could, but speed wasn't much help. It doesn't matter much if you're wide awake in class if you're too wired up to remember your name. I caught a whiff of dust on Norm's body, but it didn't register until later. He must have been a heavy user for the dogs to find him so quickly."

"He was," Lamotte said. "He should have kept it that way."

"I don't follow you. What happened to him?"

"Reality happened to him, Doc. Norm was in the crank business. He started making it to feed his own habit and save a few bucks, you know? He put together a little lab in a shed behind his folk's farm and started cookin' up speed. Crystal Methedrine, high grade stuff. He was always a bright kid. Too bright, as it turned out."

"How so?"

"He realized that it wouldn't be much tougher to make a hundred pounds of the stuff than to make a few ounces. The chemicals are expensive though, so he hooked up with a couple of dealers who offered to front him the money and take the meth off his hands when it was ready."

"And you were one of the investors?"

"Me? Hell no. I've got no money and I don't screw around with drugs anyway. Saw too many friends get messed up on dope in Vietnam. Got a little messed up there myself," he added, indicating his empty pant leg.

"If you weren't involved, how did you know Norm was cooking crank?"

"I didn't know at the time, or I would've tried to stop him. He's my oldest sister's boy but we were never close. When it comes to family, I'm kind of a black sheep, livin' out here the way I do. I hadn't seen Norm since he went off to college, then a few days ago, he showed up here and asked to use my place."

"Use it for what?"

"Neutral ground, to meet with the dopers he'd gotten involved with. He didn't want them coming around his folks' farm. My place is a little farther off the beaten track."

"I noticed. Who were the guys he was going to meet?"

"Norm just said they were a couple of studs he knew from college. He went to Westover a few semesters before he flunked out. He said they were a little . . . flaky. He was afraid they might try to cheat him."

"Apparently he was right."

"Maybe not," Lamotte said, looking away. "That's the hell of it. Maybe not."

"What do you mean?"

"I may have screwed him up," Jack said, swallowing hard. "Norm asked me for a simple favor, to use my place. I was afraid if this deal went through there'd be no goin' back for him, that he'd get mixed in deeper and end up in prison. I did some time myself, once, right after I got back from 'Nam. I had a hard-on for the world in those days. Some guy messed with me in a bar; I cut him up for his troubles, and wound up doin' five years in Jacktown. Prison's not somethin' I'd wish on anybody, especially a punk kid like Norm. So I talked him into lettin' me hide his stash, to make sure he wouldn't get ripped off. He could show 'em a sample and make sure they had his money. Then he could contact me at the local coffee shop, and we'd make the exchange someplace public. If they tried to muscle him it wouldn't work. He couldn't tell 'em anything since he wouldn't know where the stuff was himself, you follow?"

"Sounds logical as far as it goes."

"Norm thought so too. The problem was, he was worried about his thug buddies but he thought he could trust me. Which was exactly backwards. Because I'm the one who shafted him."

"How?"

"I dumped the crank," Jack said simply. "As soon as he gave it to me, I drove out onto the marsh flats near the mouth of Cullen Creek and emptied it down a sinkhole. I figured I'd crash their meeting, tell them the crank was gone for good and to clear out or I'd set the law on 'em. But I never got the chance. When I got to Norm's place they were already gone. I headed back to town lookin' for 'em and spotted Norm's car by the side of the road. I guessed they took him back in the swamp to do a little persuadin'. I yelled, but nobody answered, but I still wasn't too worried. Figured they might have roughed him up, maybe left him out there to sweat. I never thought they'd . . ." He took a deep breath, collecting his thoughts. "He told me they were guys he knew from college. They must be majorin' in homicide. Did you see what they did to him?"

David nodded.

"I was afraid Norm might be out there hurt or tied up. I can't get around in the swamp too good on this one leg; I needed help. So I fed Curt a line about needin' his dogs to track a rogue bear. I'd kept one of the empty crank bags to prove it was gone. I let the dogs sniff a piece of it and they followed it straight to Norm."

"Why didn't you go to Sheriff Wolinski then?"

"And tell him what? That my nephew got offed by a couple of college punks? I don't know their names or even what they look like. And I'm the crazy Vietnam vet with the prison record livin' back in the woods. A cedar savage. He'd bust me for Norm's death in a heartbeat. And he'd be right. It's my fault."

"No, it's not," David said quietly. "Maybe you could have handled it better, but you were trying to do the right thing by him. The question is, what are you going to do now? Wolinski expects me to show up with the guy who told me where to find Norm. Even if Curt dummies up, I won't let him take a fall for you. I'll have to tell Wolinski about you."

"Yeah, I expect you will."

"Then why not tell him yourself? He'll come for you anyway, Jack. It'd look better if you came in on your own. Stan Wolinski isn't always the easiest guy to get along with, but he's a fair man. He won't try to railroad you."

"You don't understand. I'm an ex-con and that puts me at the top of Wolinski's list whether he's honest or not. The last time I trusted my government it cost me an arm and a leg. I'm not interested in donatin' any more body parts. I got none to spare."

"Then what will you do?"

"I'll wait," he said quietly. "The way I figure it, those bastards strung Norm up, then kicked a log out from under him a half dozen times trying to make him tell them about the stash. He couldn't tell 'em that because he didn't know where it was. But I expect one of those times when he was dangling from that damned rope tryin' for one last breath, he told 'em about me. I sure as hell would have in his place. And since they're still lookin' to score a crank stash, I figure they'll be along to talk to me any time now. So if I were you, Doc, I'd move along. You'd best be gone when they come."

"You shouldn't be here either. Look, no offense, but Norm was a strapping young guy and look how he ended up."

"Grown or not, Norm was a kid," Lamotte said evenly. "I haven't been a kid since a little Vietnamese girl tossed a grenade into my hooch back in '71. Maybe I'm not what I was, but I can still handle myself. Don't worry about me."

"Have it your way then," David said. "What should I tell Wolinski? Are you going to give him any trouble when he comes for you?"

"I hope not," Lamotte said, smiling faintly for the first time. "I'm hopin' it'll be over by then, one way or the other. No hard feelin's either way, Doc. Thanks for tryin'."

"Yeah," David said. "Right. Good luck, Mr. Lamotte. I think you're going to need it." He trotted grimly out to his Jeep, fired it up, gunned it into a tight U-turn and headed back out on the narrow track. The shadows in the swamp had lengthened in the time he'd spent in the shack. It was barely midafternoon, but the forest's leafy canopy dimmed the daylight to a muted green.

David reached for the headlight switch, but hesitated. He could have sworn he saw a faint flash of . . .

Light. Headlights. Flickering through the trees around a bend of the trail ahead. Someone was coming. He jammed on the brakes, skidding the Jeep to a halt. Maybe it was Wolinski. Could Curt have sent him out here?

Perhaps. But did he want to bet his life on that possibility? Not a chance. With no place to turn around, his only options were to blunder ahead or back up.

No choice. He jammed the Jeep into reverse and gunned it back along the trail as fast as he dared. Trees he'd barely noticed a moment before suddenly seemed to loom over the trail like sentries, clawing at the Jeep with skeletal branches as he passed. He risked a hasty glimpse down the track. The headlights were still coming on, definitely closer now, and moving one hell of a lot faster than he could drive in reverse. Damn it!

The cab clanged like an empty oil drum as David sideswiped a poplar sapling. Fighting the wheel, he managed to keep the Jeep on the trail, but he slowed down a little. Had to. If he hit something hard enough to jam up now . . .

Suddenly the gloom lifted a bit as the Jeep rocketed out of the woods into the clearing. David hastily parked the Jeep beside Lamotte's battered pickup truck, then piled out and sprinted for the shack while the Jeep was still rocking.

"Company's coming," he said, brushing past Lamotte into the cabin's dim interior. "It could be Wolinski, or maybe even Curt, but I don't think we can count on that. What should we do?"

"Do?" Lamotte echoed.

"Your plan," David snapped. "You were waiting for them, right? What did you intend to do when they showed up?"

"I figured Norm told 'em about me bein' crippled up, so I figured to sucker 'em in close enough to get off a shot. Havin' your Jeep out there'll probably blow that idea."

"A shot with what?" David said, glancing around wildly.

"This." With a move almost too quick for the eye to follow, Jack reached behind his back and came out with a revolver, a small six-gun that looked like something a kid would play cowboys with.

"But that's only a .22. A popgun," David said in disbelief. "Don't you have a rifle or a shotgun?"

"I'm a little short-handed to operate long guns, Doc, in case you hadn't noticed. The .22 will do the job up close. You'd better make a run for it while you can. Just book back into the swamp. They're city boys, they probably won't be able to track you."

"I'm afraid it's a little late for that," David said grimly as a dark green Range Rover eased to a halt at the edge of the clearing. Two men climbed out. If they'd ever been college boys, it was a long time back. Both were heavily built, wearing gangbanger duds, hunter green Carhartt work clothes that had never seen an honest day's labor.

At that distance David couldn't make out faces. One of them was wearing a black baseball cap turned backward, the other one had a blue kerchief tied over his hair, pirate style. And both of them were packing military surplus assault rifles with folding metal stocks and curved banana clips.

"College kids?" David said quietly. "From where? Beirut?"

"You know, I'm beginnin' to think maybe Norm may not have been entirely straight with me about a few details," Lamotte said.

"You shouldn't have gotten mixed up in this, Doc."

"You're telling me," David said, ducking farther back into the shadows.

"Yo! Jack Lamotte! We got business with you. Come on out, old man!"

Both gunmen were white, but the accent was strictly inner-city Detroit.

"What do you want?" Lamotte called back.

"You got somethin' belongs to us, pops. You got five seconds to give it up or we're gonna blow that shack of yours down around your ears."

"You try that you'll never find your stuff. It's all here. Why don't you come take a look?" Jack said, stepping into the open doorway. "You got younger legs. Don't be afraid. I won't hurt you none."

The two gunmen exchanged a glance. "Whose Jeep is that?"

"Belongs to a friend. Stopped by to do a little huntin'. He's off in the woods somewhere."

"He'd better stay gone," the gunman with the bandanna grunted. "If he shows up, we got enough ammo to go around." He said something inaudible to his buddy, who took up a firing position behind the Range Rover, resting the barrel of his rifle on its hood to cover the cabin and the Jeep. "You stay put, old man," Bandanna called, moving warily forward, one measured step at a time. "And if I see anybody else, you're gone." He kept his weapon waist high, its muzzle trained on Lamotte's chest.

"What can we do?" David hissed.

"We've gotta get 'em both in here," Lamotte said quietly. "We've got no chance, otherwise."

"We've got no chance anyway," David shot back. "You make one false move and he'll cut you in half with that thing."

"Get in the bedroom," Lamotte said. "When you hear him yell, come runnin'. It's our only shot."

"That's crazy!" David whispered. "Just tell them the truth, that the stuff is gone!"

"Dammit, get out of sight," Lamotte said. "If he spots you now he'll kill us both."

David started to argue, but it was too late. Lamotte turned away, ignoring him, and the gunman was getting too close to risk another word. David carefully sidled behind the trade blanket that shielded the bedroom.

The room held a cot, a single clothes pole, and more bookshelves. There was nowhere to hide and nothing that even looked like a weapon. Sweet Jesus. Shrinking into the shadows beside the doorway, David peered out of the narrow space between the blanket and the door frame.

"All right, pops, I'm here," Bandanna said, halting in front of the door, looking cautiously about him. "You'd best give me what we come for or I might just blow off your other leg and whittle you down to the size of home plate."

Up close, he was clearly no college kid. Bandanna was thirty-ish, hatchet-faced with hard gray eyes and a thin scar that trickled down from the left corner of his mouth.

"That's not good enough," Jack countered. "Norm promised me a cut. Since I'm the one holdin' the crank, I figure half of his share would be about right."

"Is the stuff here?" the gunman asked suspiciously.

"It's inside, but you'll never get it if anything happens to me."

"Hey, I got no beef with you, Pop. You're safe as a jailhouse as long as you give us what we want. Half of Norm's share sounds fair to me. Show me the stuff."

"It's in here," Jack said, limping away from the door, using his cane.

Without warning, the gunman lunged through the doorway and flattened himself against the wall, covering the room with his weapon. He fired off a dozen rounds, slugs slamming into the walls, scattering books, smashing the few bits of furniture. The gunman licked his lips, his eyes flicking around the room like a bat in a bonfire. "You see what this thing can do, old man? I can turn this dump into kindling in a heartbeat and you along with it. Maybe I ought to chop you up a little just to show you we're serious."

"Hell, I know you're serious," Jack said quietly. "I found Norman last night after you got done with him. What are you so nervous about?" Jack flapped his empty sleeve. "Afraid I might strongarm you?"

"Yeah, I'm shakin' in my boots," Bandanna said. "You said the stuff's here? Where? I don't see it."

"It's in the stove there, along with some kindling. If the law shows, it goes up in smoke before they can cross the yard."

"So tell me, old man, what's supposed to keep me from poppin' you right now and just takin' it?"

"For openers, you don't know whether I'm tellin' you the truth," Jack said evenly. "Maybe the stuff's not in there. Or maybe not all of it is. Maybe I'm holding some of it back until I see my share of the money."

"Yeah? You know, the last guy that held out on me didn't last very long. Just long enough to tell me about you. Maybe we oughta hang you up to one of these rafters, see how long you last."

"Okay, okay, cool it," Jack said, gulping. "I'm not jerkin' you around. The stuff's there. All of it."

"It damn sure better be," Bandanna snapped. "Now get over against the wall and keep your hands—'scuse me, keep your *hand* where I can see it. And I'm tellin' you right now, if you're lyin' to me—"

"I'm not," Jack said, completely cowed now, almost cowering. "It's all there."

"We'll see about that," Bandanna said, kneeling by the stove. He shifted the gun to his left hand, keeping the muzzle aimed in Jack's direction. He pulled the heavy cast iron door completely open and groped inside. There was a muffled *snick* and Bandanna froze, his eyes widening. "My arm!" Bandanna roared.

Jack lunged before the gunman could react, slashing him across the wrist with his cane, knocking the assault rifle out of his grip. Bandanna tried to pull his hand out of the stove, but something was holding it from within.

Jack slammed the metal door closed on Bandanna's arm with his cane. "Doc," he said quietly, "you'd better get out here."

"Kenny!" Bandanna shouted. "Get in here! Waste 'em! Kill 'em all!"

David charged out of the bedroom, wild eyed. "Hold him down and keep him away from that gun," Jack said, hustling back to the front door. Bandanna was writhing on the floor with one arm inside the stove, clawing for the assault rifle with his free hand. David tackled him, jerking his arm away from the weapon. Bandanna slammed him across the face with his elbow, bloodying his mouth, thrusting him away.

"Jack!" David gasped, grappling desperately with Bandanna to keep him from reaching the gun. But Lamotte was ignoring the struggle on the floor. He'd limped to the corner of the room, crouching in shadows away from the front door. And suddenly the doorway darkened as the second gunman burst through it.

David only glimpsed his face a moment, flushed with rage, teeth bared in a feral snarl as he raised his rifle . . . when Jack Lamotte calmly shot him in the head with his .22.

The pop of the small pistol was scarcely louder than a champagne cork. Kenny stumbled, apparently more surprised than hurt. He started to turn towards Jack, then crumpled slowly, like an inflatable figure with a puncture wound. Once down, he didn't move again.

In the momentary stillness, Bandanna drove his fist into David's midsection, doubling him over. Gagging, David managed to topple onto the assault weapon, trapping it beneath him as Bandanna kicked at him, trying to knock him away from the gun.

"That's enough of that," Jack said quietly, limping over to cover the trapped thug, keeping well clear of his swinging boots.

"You're dead!" Bandanna raged, rolling over to face him. "Both of you! The cops can't hang anything on me for this, and even if they do, I'll get out. I'll tear you apart, or my people will!"

"Maybe they'll try," Jack said, nodding. "But you won't, mister. Not after the way you did Norm." He raised the revolver, centering the muzzle between Bandanna's eyes.

The thug froze. "You're bluffin', old cripple," he began—

But Lamotte wasn't. David was still doubled over gasping for breath when he heard the report of the pistol. Bandanna shuddered at the impact, then went completely still. David rolled clear of him and struggled to his knees.

He stared at Bandanna's lifeless form for a dazed moment, then turned on Lamotte. "You killed him," he said in disbelief. "Jesus, he was helpless and you just—"

"Didn't sound helpless to me," Lamotte said, slipping the revolver into his belt. "You think this was like a boxing match, Doc? Queensberry Rules? You knock a guy down, then let him back up? It ain't. He would've killed us both, and anybody else who had the bad luck to be in his way."

"He nearly did kill us," David said, pushing the assault rifle away. "Why couldn't he pull his hand out of the stove?"

"Wolf trap," Jack said. "I imagine it smarted some, but it was a helluva lot better deal than he gave Norm. Or you. Looks like he popped you a pretty good shot in the jaw. You okay?"

"I think so," David said, gingerly touching his bleeding mouth with his fingertips. "I feel like I've been sledgehammered."

Lamotte rummaged in the wooden cupboard beside the sink, came up with an unbroken pint of Jack Daniel's Black Label and handed it to David. "Take a taste. You look like you need it."

David took a short pull from the bottle, wincing against the bite of the whiskey. "Whoa," he said, blinking and shaking his head. "Maybe that wasn't such a good idea." He set the bottle on the counter, gasping as he did so. Keeping his breathing shallow, he gingerly traced his ribs with his fingertips. "I can't feel anything broken, but it's definitely contused."

"You sure?" Jack asked dryly. "I thought you were a veterinarian."

"I try to be, when I'm not too busy being a punching bag for psycho dope dealers."

"You're gonna have a fat lip, maybe, but we came out way ahead of the game, Doc. Coyotes like these run in packs. We were damned lucky there were only the two of them or we'd be dead now. Hell, we still could be."

"How do you mean?"

"The late Mr. Bandanna there was right about one thing, Doc. When his friends find out what happened here, they'll come for us. Or for me, anyway. With a little luck you can still get clear of this."

"I don't understand," David said.

"I'm offerin' you an out," Lamotte said. "No matter how you look at it, I'm through here. I'll have to run like a scalded dog."

"What are you talking about? Why should you run?"

"For openers, I've got two dead men here, both shot in the head at close range and one of 'em was unarmed. The law's liable to take a dim view of that. Might even call it murder."

"That's crazy. No jury would—"

"—would convict you, Doc, but me? I'm not so sure. I'm a cedar savage. I live out here on my own away from folks. Maybe they'd figure I was mixed up in this from the first. Maybe they'd put me away awhile just to be on the safe side. The bottom line is, I'm not willin' to lay my freedom on the line for other people to decide about. There's somethin' about havin' an empty sleeve and pant leg that don't inspire much trust in the system. I'd rather try my luck on the road north to Canada."

"But I'll back your story, you know that."

"Don't be stupid," Lamotte said, exasperated. "The only chance you have to get clear of this is to tell the law that you found things the way they are, that it was all over when you showed up. If you admit you were involved the rest of their gang will be after you like a pack of wolves and you're an easy man to find. It's better this way for both of us. Give me a two hour start, then tell the law whatever you have to."

"I don't know," David said. "It's all happening too fast."

"Look, Doc, if you feel like you're honor bound to tell the truth, go for it, but you've gotta give me a runnin' start. I don't want to tie you up but I will if I have to. Will you give me your word you won't set the law on me for a couple hours?"

"No," David said slowly. "I don't think I can do that."

Their eyes locked for what seemed like a very long time, and David was suddenly aware that Jack Lamotte still had the gun. And that he'd just killed two thugs without blinking an eye.

Lamotte looked away first, shaking his head slowly. "What the hell, I guess I'll just have to take the chance you've got better sense than you've shown so far. We'll leave things like they are, but you'd better think on what I said. It's a bad road out to the highway from here. I'd take it slow if I were you."

"I'll keep that in mind."

"Thanks for tryin' to help us out," Lamotte said, using his cane to walk stiffly to the door. "Tell Curt I'm sorry I got him into this mess. I never meant for it to come down this way."

"I'll tell him."

"I'd appreciate it. Take care of yourself, Doc." Lamotte turned and hobbled out. A moment later David heard his pickup truck roar to life and rumble out of the yard.

As the truck's sound faded, David glanced around the room, taking stock. A shambles. Books were scattered everywhere, ripped from their shelves by gunfire. It was a miracle he was alive. With a little help from a cedar savage.

Still, he couldn't just let Lamotte run away like this. He'd killed two men and fleeing was against the law. Abetting it might make him an accessory. He kept a cellular phone packed in the boot of his Jeep for emergencies. He could give Wolinski a call and the sheriff could have Lamotte in custody before he got out of the county.

Lamotte. He called himself a cedar savage and most of the town would probably agree. Living out here alone, half crazy. Half a man, really. One arm, one leg, one eye. But he hadn't always been like that.

For a moment David tried to picture him whole, as he must have been in that sunny summer of '67, when all of these books had been plans for a life, instead of a substitute for it.

Maybe executing these two thugs wasn't legal, or even right.

But Jack had done a wrong thing once before. He'd gone to a foreign land to make war on people he'd never met because his country asked him to. And he'd paid a terrible price for it.

Did that justify what he'd done here? Of course not. Still . . .

A breeze from the open door riffled a book near David's foot. He bent stiffly and picked it up. *Meditations*, by Marcus Aurelius. Hadn't read it since college. Always meant to, never seemed to have the time. And yet how much time could it take? An hour? Two at the most.

He carried the pint of bourbon and the book outside, and eased down with his back against the cabin wall in a patch of waning sunlight.

"From my grandfather Verus I learned good morals and the government of my temper." A sharp guy, old Marcus. The world would be a better place if a few more folks would follow his example. David twisted off the cap of the whiskey bottle and tossed it aside. He took a deep pull, coughing as the smoky liquid seared a fiery path down the back of his throat.

God, it was good. So was being alive. He tilted the book to catch more of the sunlight.

"From the reputation and memory of my father, I learned modesty and . . ."

Crippen, Landru, and Carlos Palomino

As a small town veterinarian, I meet a marvelous variety of critters, from canaries to cattle. I've never met a pet I disliked. I can't say the same for their owners.

In an average year, I get clawed by cats, kicked by colts and bitten by bulldogs. A map turtle once clamped onto my ring finger so fiercely she dislocated it. That hurt. A lot.

Still, I didn't dislike her for it. Turtles are shy by nature and the lady was rightfully annoyed at being poked and prodded by a stranger. I understood how she felt. I was every bit as annoyed each time I patched up one of Leonard Rasche's dogs. Because I had to do it far too often.

Leonard shouldn't have owned pets at all, let alone four pedigreed dogs. His work as a television news analyst kept him so busy that much of the time he either boarded his dogs in our kennels or left them with friends. When he was at home, he was the worst kind of pet owner. He let his dogs run free.

Algoma's a small northern Michigan town and Leonard lived in a quiet residential neighborhood so none of the dogs had been run over in traffic, so far, but it was a slow month when I didn't sew one of them up after they'd tangled with a feral cat or a barbed wire fence.

His dogs were a mixed lot: two bright-eyed little six-pound Pomeranians called Lanny and Crip, a seventy-pound fawn-colored Boxer named Okie, and a small, golden Pug called Pal. Most often, it was the Pomeranians' curiosity that got them clawed up or bitten. Pal the Pug was a born garbage raider which occasionally got him poisoned and once I had to take a BB pellet out of his rump. Okie, the Boxer, was the least trouble, an older dog who just tagged along with the others.

The last time I saw Leonard, he brought Pal the Pug in to have a cut on his muzzle stitched up. It was a nasty gash, deeper than it was long, and any cut near a dog's mouth has a serious risk of infection.

"Any idea how he got this?" I asked.

"I imagine he dinged himself rooting through a neighbor's garbage," Leonard said with a shrug. "God knows they bitch about him enough." He was holding Pal's collar, keeping him calm while I cleaned the wound. Leonard was a small man, but solidly built and vain as a bluejay. He stayed trim, his complexion was always a uniform sunlamp tan and even his golf shirts were tailored.

"Why do you bother to have dogs?" I tried to keep my irritation under control as I stitched. "You're not at home enough to really enjoy them."

"To be honest, I like having somebody raise a row when I walk in the door. It's no fun coming home to an empty house."

"Then why not keep one dog or two? You could keep better track of them and you wouldn't have to keep paying me to patch them up."

"Ah, but then I'd miss the pleasure of your company, Doc. Besides, which one could I get rid of? The two Pomeranians were my ex-wife's dearest pals, so naturally I went after them in our divorce settlement. I keep the other two around for appearance sake. A bachelor living alone with two fluffy little dogs? Whatever would people think?"

"If you really cared what they thought you wouldn't let Pal here run loose to raid their garbage."

"I'm a great believer in personal freedom," he said with a sly grin. "If you ever watched my TV show you'd know that."

"I do watch your show, when I can squeeze it into my schedule."

"I'm surprised, Doc. I'd always pegged you as a bleeding heart liberal."

"Compared to you, Attila the Hun was a liberal. Actually, I like your show, especially the investigations you've done on corruption in state government."

"Thank you."

"One thing I don't understand, though. Considering how tough you are when you interview your guests, how on earth do you get anyone to appear on your show?"

"It's easier than you'd think. Most politicians are media junkies. They'd auction off their kids on *The Price Is Right* for five minutes of free airtime. Some guests are tougher to land, though. I usually have to blackmail them."

I couldn't tell whether he was kidding or not. That was part of Leonard's appeal, his sense of mischief. Leonard Rasche was a class cutup with his own TV talk show. He and his pet Pal the Pug had a lot in common. They both loved rooting through garbage.

Not everyone found Leonard charming, though. My next patient had words with him as they passed in the corridor. Amanda McKean was a retired high school math teacher, a tiny brown wren of a woman in a flowered dress and sensible shoes who reminds me of the maiden aunt I never had.

"He's still a smart aleck," she said, wobbling beneath the weight of her hugely overweight tomcat as she carried him into the examination room. "He was a snot-nosed little know-it-all when I taught him in high school and he hasn't changed a bit."

"Leonard's not so bad," I said, taking the cat from her. "Compared to some of the politicians he interviews he's a prince."

"You wouldn't think so if you had to live down the block from him. His dogs traipse all over the neighborhood, tip over my trash and dump their nasty little piles in my flower beds. They've no more manners than Mr. Rasche."

"What seems to be the trouble with Thomas à Bigcat today?" I asked, hoping to cool her off.

"He's has some bites, here, on his hip. He must have had a dispute with a stray cat who wandered into our yard. Thomas is very protective of our home. He never wanders off, unlike some people's pets."

I doubted the big tom could waddle a city block. He was around thirteen but his obesity concerned me more than his age. I didn't like the look of the four puncture wounds, either. The subcutaneous fat around them had a pale, soapy look, like liquid detergent. Infection had already set in and a cat's body fat is a perfect medium for spreading it.

"When did this happen?"

"Yesterday evening, I think. Is it bad?"

"It shouldn't be anything Thomas can't handle," I said cautiously, not wanting to worry her. It wouldn't help Thomas to have his mistress fret herself to death. When it came to caring about animals,

Amanda was Leonard's diametric opposite.

After cleaning and debriding the wounds to help them drain, I flushed them thoroughly with a Betadine solution, then gave Thomas an intramuscular injection of Amoxicillin and gave Miss McKean a packet of antibiotic pills.

"Give him one of these every six hours with a smear of butter on it to make it easier to swallow. I'll want to see him again in three days, but if the wounds fester or develop a foul odor, bring him in immediately or call me at home, okay? Day or night."

"Are you sure he'll be all right?" she asked uncertainly, gathering the big tom in her arms. "Please don't be offended but you seem awfully young to be a doctor, David. Most of my former students are older than you are."

"I'm a little older than I look, Ms. McKean, and some days I feel a lot older. Don't worry too much about Thomas. He's a strong, healthy fella. He should shake this off with no trouble."

I held the door for her and she carried Thomas à Bigcat through the waiting room out to her old Buick. She murmured softly to him all the way, telling him what a good cat he was and that everything would be all right. A few people glanced up as she passed and several said hello. She never noticed.

I couldn't help comparing her love for Thomas to Leonard's disregard for his dogs' safety. For all his guff about freedom, if he really cared about his pets he wouldn't just turn them loose. Dogs that roam the streets eventually end up as a tangle of bloody fur by the side of the road.

But not always. Sometimes things turn out quite differently.

Later that week, I was stitching up a cat who'd tangled with a fan belt when the phone rang in my surgery. Stan Wolinski, the Algoma County sheriff, was on the line. Leonard Rasche had been clobbered by a hit and run driver. He was dead and Stan needed my help. Now.

✳ ✳ ✳

Two county sheriff's cars and a state police cruiser were parked in front of Leonard Rasche's brick bungalow. I parked behind the State cop prowlie and clambered out as Stan Wolinski hurried over. Square and solid as a cinder block in his gray summer uniform, Stan's normally as cool as a slab of concrete. He looked worried, which worried me.

"What happened?" I asked.

"Somebody ran Rasche down a few blocks away from his house. He was jogging along the shoulder and from the skid marks it looks like the driver deliberately swerved to hit him. It's a neighborhood street, not much traffic, so we're assuming the driver either followed him or waited for him to show. He ran the same route almost every day."

"Waited for him? You think he was murdered?"

"That's the assumption we're operating under and frankly the idea scares the hell out of me. Leonard was a controversial guy. Twenty minutes after I got the call, two State Police detectives showed up to volunteer their help. It's not their jurisdiction but we're all taking heat from Lansing to solve this thing."

"What do you need me for?"

"We have to get into his house but he's got a pack of dogs loose in there raising a helluva row. We could mace 'em and haul 'em out but I don't want to risk disturbing any evidence."

"What evidence? I thought he was run down on the road."

"He was, but a couple of neighbors said they've spotted a strange car near Leonard's home the past week or so, a gray sedan. If the guy was setting Leonard up, maybe he took him out so he could burglarize his place. We just don't know. Can you get the dogs out of the way?"

"Shouldn't be a problem. I've seen a lot of them so they know me pretty well. What should I do with them?"

"Can you keep them at your kennels for now? We're trying to contact his family. I'll ask what they want done with the dogs."

"Sounds like a plan. Give me five minutes and I'll have them out of your hair."

It took less than that. Stan walked me through the police cordon and the dogs started barking frantically as soon as they heard us on the porch. The door wasn't locked, but that wasn't unusual; people seldom lock up in Algoma. I eased it open and edged inside.

The two Pomeranians, Crip and Lanny, promptly started ragging on my pants cuffs, while Pal the Pug held back, cowering. With new stitches in his muzzle, he wasn't all that glad to see me. Okie the Boxer woofed at me but he was no real threat. Some people think large dogs are more aggressive, but it's not so. Dogs have no sense of their own size. Aggression's a matter of personality with them. And with us.

Fortunately, this bunch was all noise. I scooped up Lanny and Crip and carried them out to my Jeep. Okie tagged dutifully along while Pal brought up the rear, unwilling to be left behind. Stan gave us a grateful wave as I pulled away.

⁕ ⁕ ⁕

Stan stopped by my office late that afternoon just before closing. "You look beat," I said. "How did it go?"

"Terrific," he sighed, tossing a manila file folder on my desk. "I brought you the dogs' pedigree papers, thought you might need 'em. Didn't turn up anything useful in the house. It's a back street and most of the neighbors were at work so nobody saw doodley. Several people mentioned spotting the gray sedan in the area but couldn't say anything specific about it except that the driver looked odd."

"Odd?"

"Something about his face, a mask maybe. Meanwhile I've had at least a half dozen calls from politicians in Lansing who want me to keep them informed of our progress."

"I didn't realize Leonard was that popular."

"Popularity hasn't got squat to do with it," Stan said grimly. "Most of the calls started out politely but the nice wore off quick. They want this thing solved with as little fuss as possible. I won't mention names, but I'm talking about powerful people here. I have to run for election in this county and a lot of campaign money comes from Lansing. They can complicate my life and they're used to having people jump when they say so."

"And which way do they want you to jump?"

"I'm honestly not sure. Ordinarily, when a pol tries to muscle you they have an aide call. A mind game. It shows how important they are and gives them a cutout to blame if anything goes wrong. But these calls were all personal, senators and congressmen from both sides of the aisle, even a few lobbyists."

"About what?"

"Damned if I know. They all seemed nervous about getting specific. When I tried to pump them, they'd say they were depending on my discretion, which in pol-speak means keep your mouth shut about any politically sensitive dirt that turns up. The problem is, I have no idea what I'm looking for."

"I once asked Leonard how he got people to appear on his show," I mused. "He said some were easy and he blackmailed the others. I thought he was joking."

"Maybe he was. On the other hand, that egotistical little bastard's idea of a joke wasn't always funny."

"That sounds personal."

"It's not, exactly. Rasche never did me a bad turn but he definitely had a mean streak. Back in high school he was a major cutup. Sometimes he got laughs, but I noticed his jokes were always on someone else, never Leonard. He liked hurting other people and not just with wisecracks. Sometimes he got physical."

"How do you mean?"

"Leonard may not have looked the type but he was one helluva fighter in high school, a Golden Gloves champ. Liked to fight outside the ring too. He'd con bigger guys into a situation where they either had to challenge him or back down. He wouldn't start the fight, he was too clever for that, but he'd damn sure finish it. He'd clean their clocks and make it look like he was only defending himself. Like Gary Cooper in *High Noon*. He picked his targets pretty carefully, though. They were always hicks, big, but a little slow. Pushovers for a guy with Leonard's skills."

"Small Man's Rage," I said.

"What?"

"In a psych course in college, a prof said that smaller men tend to be more aggressive, either because they resent their size or because they learn to make their moves first to gain an edge. It's called Small Man's Rage Syndrome."

"Maybe that was it. He definitely liked roughing people up. He was the same way on TV. He acted like he was dishing the dirt as a public service, but you could tell he enjoyed it. He was a bully, plain and simple. I'm not surprised somebody finally did him in; I'm just sorry they hunted him down in my town."

"You think that's what happened?"

"Looks like it. He got hit on a back street that only serves his neighborhood which pretty much rules out an accident. The driver either knew his jogging route or tailed him."

"The gray sedan you mentioned?"

"Maybe. So far, it's our only lead. None of the usual motives for murder apply, his ex-wife's happily remarried and his nearest relative is a cousin out in Albuquerque. She asked if we could place the dogs in good homes. Can you handle that for me?"

"No problem. His ex may want the Poms, Lanny and Crip, and the other two will be better off with someone who cares about them. Leonard never really did."

"I don't think he ever cared for anyone but himself," Stan said, rising. "I'd better get back to work. Looks like I'm in for a long week."

And he wasn't the only one.

✳ ✳ ✳

I took Leonard's dogs home with me after work. We have cages at the clinic but the boarding kennels at our farm have outdoor runs and Leonard's dogs were used to them. They'd spent a lot of time there.

My wife, Yvonne, had heard about Len's death, of course; news travels fast in a small town. I've only lived here a few years but Yvonne grew up in Algoma so she's usually my primary source of local lore. Not this time, though.

When I mentioned Leonard's death at supper, she pointedly changed the subject. I let it pass, but afterward, when we were relaxing on the back deck watching the sunset, "You're holding out on me," I said.

"How do you mean?"

"Come on, Stan told me he went to high school with Leonard so you must have too. Why don't you want to talk about him? Were you two sweethearts or something?"

"With Leonard? Hardly. I wasn't his type."

"I find that hard to believe."

"Why?"

"Because I think you're everyone's type. So what was the problem between you and Leonard?"

"He beat up a boyfriend of mine once," she said, looking away and taking a deep breath. "Jimmy Delage."

"You've never mentioned him."

"That's because he . . . died. He was in the army during the invasion of Panama, Operation Just Cause. Remember that one? Jimmy was killed there. I always blamed Leonard for it."

"How so?"

"He goaded Jimmy into a fistfight. He made it seem as though they were fighting over me, but they weren't. Leonard never gave a damn about me; it was all about him. Jimmy was bigger than Len, but it was no contest. Leonard kicked his butt. Totally embarrassed him. A month later Jimmy quit school and joined the army. I think he may have gotten himself killed trying to salvage his so-called honor."

"I'm sorry."

"So am I," she said, "but not about Leonard. Is that a terrible thing to say?"

I hesitated, realizing there was more going on here than a high school scuffle. In the game of husbands and wives, there generally is.

"No," I said carefully. "Where you're concerned, I'll take honesty over a polite fib any day. Besides, we have a chance to make up for your ill will. Stan asked me to find a good home for his dogs. Any suggestions?"

"Not offhand. Are they pedigreed?"

"Yep, I even have the papers here." I riffled through the file Stan had left at my office. "Ouch. Only Leonard would have picked names like these for dogs. The Pomeranians' names are Henri Désiré Landru and Hawley Harvey Crippen. Lanny and Crip. Okie's real name is Cameron Wilson McGraw. How did he get Okie out of that? He was born in a Saginaw kennel."

"Nickname," Yvonne said, frowning. "I think the real Cameron 'Okie' McGraw is an actor. Usually plays tough guys."

"Then Leonard shouldn't have named his dog after him. Okie the Boxer's a pussycat. Pal the garbage raiding pug's full name is Carlos Palomino."

"Sounds like a horse from Mexico."

"Pal's blonde and so are palomino horses. Maybe that's the connection."

"With Leonard it's hard to say," she said. "I'll ask my friends at the humane society if they know anyone who's looking to adopt a dog or two, but beyond that, I'd really rather not talk about this, okay?"

"Fine by me, from this moment on, the subject of Leonard

Rasche is officially closed, off-limits, taboo."

Well, not quite. The next day I spotted a gray Chevrolet sedan parked across the street from my clinic. There was nothing special about it except that the driver was behind the wheel reading a newspaper that obscured his face. Probably just waiting for someone. I'd never have noticed it if Stan hadn't mentioned a gray car hanging around Leonard's place.

I checked from time to time and after he'd been there over an hour without moving I got curious. I edged out the back door of the clinic intending to come up behind the Chevy but as I rounded the corner he was already pulling away into traffic. I only glimpsed his face, but there was something odd about it, though maybe that was only the power of suggestion. I couldn't make out his license plate numbers but I could tell it wasn't a standard Michigan plate or a designer plate. I couldn't be positive at that distance, but I was fairly sure it was a government plate, the kind used on official state vehicles. A cop? A politician's aide?

I intended to call Stan about it later, but we got busy at the clinic and I forgot about it. Until that night. When I saw it again.

The dogs woke me. We'd kept Lanny and Crip, the two Pomeranians, in the house rather than in the kennels. Ordinarily, they curled up together near the foot of our four-poster and didn't move again until morning. Sometime in the night, though, I was awakened by a thump. One of the Poms was jumping against the bed while the other danced anxiously in circles, whining.

Damn. If they wanted out, there was a dog door in the kitchen that opened into our fenced back yard . . . but they knew that. They'd been here many times before. I sat up, bleary-eyed, only half awake.

"What is it?" Yvonne mumbled.

"I don't know. The Poms are wired up about something. Go back to sleep." I grabbed my robe off the bedpost, and started downstairs to re-educate the dogs about their door but halfway down the stairs I realized why they'd roused me. Muffled barking was coming from the kennels.

Our kennels are soundproofed out of consideration for our neighbors. If I could hear the barking in the house, it was a lot louder out there. Something was definitely wrong.

I started out the back door, then hesitated. Soundproofing works both ways. The dogs in the kennels couldn't hear much from outside the building, so if they were raising a fuss, something or someone might be inside the building with them.

Fully awake now, I wheeled and trotted through the house, pulled back a corner of the drapes and peered out the front window. A gray sedan was parked on the street, a two-year old Chevy. No driver was behind the wheel this time, but I had an idea where he might be.

I quickly dialed 911, asked the operator to get Sheriff Wolinski out here, but to come quietly, no lights or sirens. I thought a minute, then against my better judgement I went into the den, unlocked the gun case and took a shotgun out of the rack.

The gun had belonged to Yvonne's father. I don't hunt; I spend too much time patching up animals to want to shoot any, but in the dead of night with an intruder on the grounds, the weight of the old Remington twelve-gauge felt damned comforting.

I met Yvonne coming down the stairs as I padded through the living room.

"My God, David, what are you doing?"

"I think someone's broken into the kennel building. I've called Stan, he's on his way, but this is the second time I've seen this guy and I don't want to lose him again. Lock the house and—"

I didn't have to bother with the rest. Gravel crunched in the driveway as a county sheriff's car pulled up and Stan Wolinski piled out. I hurried out to meet him.

"What's up, David?"

"I think someone's in the kennel and a gray sedan's parked on the street."

"The kennel? What the hell would anyone be doing in there?"

"I've no idea. Maybe we should find out."

"Right," Stan nodded, eyeing the shotgun doubtfully. "Do you actually know how to use that thing?"

"I'm no Wyatt Earp but I know one end from the other."

"Good, it'll save waiting for backup. You'd better go around back and cover the rear door on the building. I'll give you a minute to get set then go in the front. Don't come in until I call you and for God's sake don't shoot anybody, okay? Especially not me."

I was trotting around the building before he'd finished. I waited in the dark for what seemed a lifetime before it dawned on me that Stan couldn't ask for help if he wanted to. Between the muffled barking coming from inside and the building's soundproofing, I'd never hear him.

Enough. I eased open the back door and sidled in. Stan had a heavyset biker-type in a black leather jacket backed against the wall with his hands raised. He wasn't wearing a mask but his face could have passed for one. It was severely scarred on the left side, deep abrasions that gave him a demonic look. My hand instinctively tightened on the shotgun.

"Meet your burglar, Doc. His name's Axton, and according to his ID, he's a private investigator out of Detroit. You can point that shotgun the other way, he's not armed."

"Look, I'm sorry about this," Axton said calmly. "I didn't damage anything and didn't intend any harm. I'll be happy to pay for your trouble, Dr. Westbrook. You two seem like reasonable guys; can't we work something out?"

"That depends," Stan said. "What were you doing out here?"

"I'm sorry, I'm not at liberty to say."

"Liberty?" Stan chuckled. "Buddy, you're not at liberty, period. I spotted the state plates on your car when I pulled in. Maybe you've got some juice back in Lansing but that won't cut you any slack here. You've just become a prime suspect in a homicide case."

"Homicide? You mean Rasche? I don't know a thing about it."

"No? Several witnesses placed your car in his neighborhood."

"Sure, I've been tailing him off and on for the past few weeks," Axton admitted. "I wasn't subtle about it, I wanted him to see me."

"You wanted to be seen?" I interjected.

"That's right. Leonard's been muscling half the pols in the legislature. He'd pick up a rumor here, an innuendo there then threaten to smear some poor bastard on TV unless he gave him more dirt on somebody else. He used the info to punch up his TV ratings at first, but lately he's been hitting some of his victims up for money. So a few of them got together and hired me to . . . discourage him."

"Discourage him how?" Stan asked. "By putting tire tracks up the middle of his back?"

"No way. Take a look at my mug, Sheriff. It got rearranged when I dumped a motorcycle six years ago. I was too broke for plastic surgery at the time and now I'm not sure I'd fix it if I could. It's my money face. I scare people just by lookin' at 'em. If they owe a debt, they pay up on the spot and if I ask 'em something, they generally tell me what I want to know. I never lay a finger on them. Don't have to. Check my record; it's squeaky clean. Besides, the day Rasche got popped I was in court in Detroit testifying in a re-possession case. All day."

"That's a fair alibi if it holds up," Stan admitted. "It doesn't mean you didn't send somebody else."

"Sure it does," Axton countered. "If I was involved I wouldn't be within fifty miles of this town. I'd be home counting my thank-you notes."

"Why are you here?" I asked. "I mean, what did you expect to find in a kennel?" Axton glanced at me with that gargoyle face and I instantly realized why he was so effective at getting what he wanted from people.

"Sorry," he said. "I'm afraid I can't tell you that."

"Wrong," Stan said, "that's exactly what you're going to do. You want a deal? Here it is: I won't ask who your clients are, you wouldn't tell me and they'd deny it anyway. But if you want to walk away from this, you'll tell me what you were looking for. If you don't, you and your money face are going to take a fall for burglary and you can kiss your license goodbye. So how about it? Deal?"

Axton chewed the corner of his ruined lip a moment, then nodded. "I can't tell you much. I'm looking for Rasche's files, the information he had on my clients."

"But why come here?" I asked. "Why not check Leonard's place?"

"Because the sheriff already searched it and came up empty. I thought the stuff might be here."

"How did you know I didn't find anything?" Stan asked.

Axton arched an eyebrow without replying.

"The two helpful state cops," Stan said, answering his own question. "They told you, or told your clients. I'm impressed. You must be working for some major players."

"They pay on time," Axton admitted. "But not enough to get me to whack Leonard Rasche."

"I don't understand," I said. "What made you think the files might be here?"

Axton eyed me a moment, then shrugged. "All I can tell you is that in the middle of an argument once, Rasche threatened to throw my client to the dogs if he didn't cooperate. Then he laughed and said that in a way, he'd already done so."

"Thrown him to the dogs?" Stan echoed. "What was that supposed to mean?"

"I don't know. I know you took some paperwork concerning the dogs to the doc the other day. I thought there might be something in them."

"There wasn't," I said. "They're only pedigrees, plain and simple." Stan nodded, backing me up.

"Then I apologize for kicking up a fuss over nothing. That really is all I can tell you, Sheriff. So, do we have a deal?"

"You can go," Stan nodded. "I'll hang onto your license for now. If your story checks out I'll mail it to you."

"That's fair enough. Sorry for rousting you in the middle of the night, Doc, but you really shouldn't leave your doors unlocked. There are some weird folks wandering around nowadays." He sauntered out without looking back. It was just as well. I'd already seen more of his money face than I cared to.

"Interesting fella," Stan said. "The hell of it is, I think he was telling us the truth. His story's too easy to check out."

"Maybe, but I think he fudged one small point. Axton's no fool. He knows damned well you would have looked those pedigrees over before giving them to me. He knew there was nothing in them."

"Then why was he here?"

"The dogs," I said simply. "Whatever he was after had something to do with Rasche's dogs."

"Like what?"

"I don't know," I said. "Why don't we ask them?"

* * *

The key to our little mystery turned out to be . . . a key. It was almost in plain sight, hanging on Okie the Boxer's collar, between his license tag and rabies shot tag. You'd never notice it if you weren't looking and I doubt anyone but Leonard or myself could have retrieved it without losing an arm. Okie snarled at me when I reached for it and it took a solid twenty minutes of coaxing and a half dozen doggie treats before he finally let me unbuckle his collar.

"Whew," Stan whistled. "I thought we'd have to zap him with a stunner to get that thing off. Is he always that surly?"

"Not at all. The few times I've treated Okie he's been a sweetheart. Leonard must have trained him to react if anyone fiddled with his collar." I tossed him the key and he held it up to the light.

"Looks like a safety deposit box key from the National Bank of Detroit, Algoma branch. With any luck, this little baby might just unlock a motive for murder."

And it did. But not quite the way Stan expected.

✳ ✳ ✳

"The list is a gold mine," he said. We were in my office, sharing a lunch bag of burgers he'd brought from Tubby's, our local greasy-spoon café. "Rasche had files on at least sixty people in that box, complete with dates and places for everything from office romances to kickback schemes, plus a serious stash of cash, nearly a hundred and seventy grand."

I whistled. "That's serious in my neighborhood."

"Mine too. Axton was apparently right about Leonard padding his income with blackmail. We found a list of people who'd paid and how much. The problem is, all the names are in some kind of private code. Nicknames. He obviously knew who they were but I can't tell who's guilty of what." He bit a savage chunk out of his cheeseburger.

"The list is useless then?"

"Not all of it. A few are entries fairly obvious, like Thunderjugs, and Satan's Little Helper."

"Thunderjugs? That's a strip joint, isn't it?"

"Exactly. We're running a background check on the club's owner against the material in the files, to see if we can match any crimes to him. Satan's Little Helper may be a nightclub owner in Lansing who owns a dump called Dante's Inferno. He's had some police trouble but not the kind Rasche mentions in his file. But even if we can positively identify these two mopes, there are fifty others and all of them had cause to do Rasche in. But you know what the worst of it is?"

"What's that?"

"I can almost hear Leonard laughing at me. The small-town cop blowing the big political case. Even dead, that smug little bastard's still jerking people around."

✳ ✳ ✳

"That's him," Yvonne said.

"That's who?" We were in bed, reading. The bedroom TV was flickering in the corner with the volume turned down. Neither of us was really watching.

"The guy in that movie is Cameron 'Okie' McGraw. See that group of soldiers in the helicopter? McGraw's the one in the blue headband."

"The big guy? With the moustache?"

"Right. That's him."

I watched for a minute. Apparently it was some kind of Vietnam war movie. McGraw was struggling with two or three men in a chopper, and for a moment his face filled the screen. "I've seen him before."

"Probably. He's done a lot of movies."

"No, not in the movies. Somewhere else." I chewed my lip, trying to remember. "In college, maybe."

"You were in college with Okie McGraw?"

"No, but I remember . . . rats. I can't recall. But I remember seeing him somewhere."

"He certainly has a memorable face," Yvonne said.

"That he does. Maybe it'll come to me." McGraw? College? I had a sudden flash of being in the rec room of my dorm, screaming at the TV with twenty other guys. Watching Cameron 'Okie' McGraw fight for his life.

"He was a prizefighter," I said slowly.

"In one of the 'Rocky' movies, you mean?"

"No, in real life. I saw him fight once . . . but there was something odd about it."

"How do you mean, odd?"

"I don't know," I groaned as I got up and slipped on my robe. "But I'd better find out if I expect to get any sleep tonight."

I found it in a sports encyclopedia. Cameron 'Okie' McGraw really was a boxer. Well, sort of. He'd parlayed a tough-guy reputation earned as a nightclub bouncer and some big wins in martial arts bouts into a fight for the heavyweight championship of the world. I remembered that fight now.

Nobody thought he'd survive the first round. Nobody. But he did. In fact, he fought the champ like a lion for fifteen rounds. He lost the fight on points, but it was a victory all the same, of courage and will over skill. It was like watching a Rocky movie in real life. Somebody in the dorm had switched on the TV out of morbid curiosity, but by the end of that fight we were all cheering him.

Okay, Rasche was a boxer himself and he'd named his boxer dog after a real fighter, Cameron 'Okie' McGraw. Curious now, I looked up the Pug's name, Carlos Palomino. Palomino was a prizefighter too, a former welterweight champion with a great record.

I couldn't find any listing for either Crippen or Landru. If they were sports figures, they were too obscure to rate an entry in my encyclopedia. Partially satisfied, I padded back upstairs. Yvonne had already fallen asleep, so I switched off the TV and the lights and crawled carefully back into bed.

But not to sleep. Each time I'd doze off, Cameron 'Okie' McGraw would pop up in my dreams. He was dancing around a boxing ring with his arms upraised, wearing the headband and the ratty army uniform he'd worn in the movie. His face was battered from his fifteen-round slugfest with the champ but his grin was pure, triumphant glee. He'd survived. In a way, he'd won.

There was something wrong with his uniform though, something out of place. I couldn't put my finger on what it was, yet even half asleep I knew it meant something, that it was important.

And sometime in the early hours of the morning, it came to me. His collar was facing the wrong way. In my dream, Okie was wearing his shirt backwards. And that was it. His uniform was backwards, and so was everything else.

I was out of bed at first light. In the den, I fired up our home computer, logged onto the Internet, and confirmed what I'd already learned from the sports encyclopedia about Okie McGraw and Carlos Palomino. Plus a bit more.

There was a reason I hadn't found Crippen and Landru in the record book. Hawley Harvey Crippen and Henri Désiré Landru weren't sports figures at all. They were murderers.

∗ ∗ ∗

I mulled it over as I drove into Algoma, but instead of stopping at my clinic, I continued into the village and pulled up in front of

Tubby's restaurant.

Tubby's is an Algoma institution. Built at the turn of the century, its atmosphere is north-country chic: hardwood floors, knotty pine walls and massive oaken tables and chairs that look like they were hand carved with broadaxes.

Stan Wolinski was at his usual corner booth, polishing off the wreckage of a huge breakfast of bacon, eggs and kielbasa. Enough cholesterol to fuel an ocean liner.

"Good morning, Doc; you look like hell."

"I had a bad night," I said, easing in across from him and stealing a piece of his toast. "Have you had any luck identifying the people on Rasche's list?"

"Not a damned bit, why? Did you come up with something?"

"Maybe." I took a deep breath. "Look, I could be way off base here, but if Leonard identified the people on his list the way he named his dogs, then they may be backward."

"How do you mean, backward?"

"It's a bit complicated. He named his pug after a famous boxer, his boxer is named for a guy who only fought a few times in his life, and the Pomeranians are named for two killers, Crippen and Landru."

"Who?"

"Hawley Harvey Crippen and Henri Désiré Landru were famous murderers in the early 1900s. They were both cold-blooded killers, which the two Poms definitely aren't. The dogs' names are all sarcastic, which is a fair description of Leonard's sense of humor."

"So you're saying that if he picked the code names on the list the same way . . . ?"

"Then they'll be the opposite of what they seem. You said Thunderjugs was one?"

"That's right."

"Then forget about the strip joint. You're probably looking for a straitlaced woman with a beanpole figure."

"And Satan's Little Helper could be an overweight archbishop," Stan said, nodding. "My God, I think I may know who he is already. I've got to get back to the office. Order yourself a breakfast, Doc, best in the house, and put it on my tab. You've earned it."

He hustled off to his prowl car, but I didn't order anything.

Maybe it was due to my restless night, but I still felt uneasy about this business. Stan had a long list of blackmail victims, any one of whom might have killed Leonard. They all had motives, and in a way, that's what was troubling me.

The people on Stan's list had been paying Leonard big bucks to keep their secrets. Why would one of them risk killing him, knowing his death might bring those secrets into the open?

Axton was hired to find Leonard's files, but surely if the killing was planned, they would have gone after the files first.

He'd been killed on a back street with very little traffic and no witnesses. Stan thought the killer chose the spot to avoid being identified. But perhaps not.

With half an hour to kill before I had to be at the office, I turned right at the light and began retracing the route Leonard had followed that day. There wasn't much to see. It was a quiet residential street, mostly older middle class homes of brick or clapboard with postage stamp lawns.

The yellow police tape was still taut across Leonard Rasche's driveway so I parked on the street and sat there awhile, thinking. Then I climbed out and walked around to his back yard. A low fieldstone fence divided his property from his neighbor's, but it would have been no barrier for his dogs. They could have jumped it easily, and doubtless had, many times.

I stepped over the fence into the adjoining yard, crossed the neatly trimmed lawn and rapped on the back door, glancing around as I waited. A lovely yard. The flower beds were filled with blooms and the crab apple trees were in full blossom. There was a fresh mound of earth at the foot of one of them.

I rapped again. The door opened slowly.

"Hello, Ms. McKean," I said. "How are you?"

She didn't reply. She didn't have to. She looked like death, haggard and drawn as though she hadn't slept in days.

"What do you want, David?"

"I've been concerned about Thomas à Bigcat. I expected to see him yesterday. How is he coming along?"

"He's not. He . . . died." Her voice was flat, no inflection.

"I'm very sorry, but I don't understand. The wound wasn't that serious. Did it turn septic or—"

"It wasn't the wound," she snapped, showing a flash of her usual firmness. "Those damned dogs killed him."

"Leonard's dogs, you mean? What happened?"

"We were puttering in the back yard, enjoying the sun. I went inside for a moment to get Thomas his medicine. I only left him a minute, I swear. While I was gone Leonard's dogs came boiling into my yard and chased Thomas up the tree. He would have been safe there, but he was weak and . . . he fell. I chased the dogs away and yelled at Mr. Rasche to come and get them. Then I carried Thomas to my car and started for your clinic."

"But you never got there."

"No. I was holding Thomas on my lap, driving like a madwoman, when I felt him . . . pass away. He groaned and burrowed his face in my chest. And then he was gone. I pulled over and tried to revive him, but it was too late. Too late. I sat there holding him for a long time. And then I turned around and started home. But . . . somewhere on the way, I saw Leonard Rasche, jogging along in his natty little running suit—"

She swallowed hard, shaken by a gust of emotion, grief or rage, I couldn't tell. Perhaps both.

"It seemed so unfair," she said after a time. "That Thomas was gone while Leonard . . . I'm not sure about what happened. I can't seem to remember it clearly. I believe I swerved the car and hit him. Then I drove Thomas home. I buried him under the crab apple tree. He likes the morning sun there . . ." Her voiced trailed off, as though she'd lost her train of thought.

"The police came by later but I didn't answer the door and they went away. I should tell them, I suppose. Will you . . . go with me, Doctor? I don't think I ought to drive myself."

I didn't answer for a moment. Couldn't. She'd taught generations of kids in this town, gave her life to them for forty years, and when she couldn't care for children anymore she'd transferred that love to her best friend, who happened to be a cat. And what she'd said rang absolutely true. It just wasn't fair.

"Of course I'll take you, Ms. McKean, but before we go, we'd better clear one thing up. I think you're mistaken about what happened."

"How do you mean?"

"As a veterinarian I've seen this kind of thing many times before. People who truly care for their pets are so upset when one dies that their memory can play tricks on them. You said you couldn't remember the incident very clearly, is that right?"

She nodded.

"I thought so. It's a false memory, Ms. McKean. I doubt that you swerved your car deliberately to hit Mr. Rasche. More likely you were terribly upset by Thomas's death, you were probably crying, and you . . . just didn't see him. Isn't that what really happened? You were crying, and you just didn't see him?"

She raised her eyes to mine for what seemed like a very long time, and then she swallowed. "Yes, perhaps you're right. I was crying. And I didn't see him."

"Good. That's much better. Have you eaten anything today?"

"No, I—"

"I haven't either. I wonder if I could trouble you for a cup of coffee? It's liable to be a long day. We'll have coffee, and talk a little more. Then we'll go in together. Doctor's orders."

She hesitated a moment, then shook her head slowly. "I'm sorry but . . . you really do seem very young to be a doctor."

"Thank you, ma'am," I said. "Thanks very much."

Doug Allyn: A Checklist

NOVELS:

The Cheerio Killings. St. Martin's Press, 1989
Motown Underground. St. Martin's Press, 1993
Icewater Mansions. St. Martin's Press, 1995; and as a "Dead Letter" paperback
Black Water. St. Martin's Press,1996; and as a "Dead Letter" paperback
A Dance in Deep Water. St. Martin's Press, 1997

SHORT STORY COLLECTION:

All Creatures Dark and Dangerous: The Dr. David Westbrook Stories. Crippen & Landru, Publishers, 1999

SHORT STORIES:

Those starred have been anthologized in hardcover, here and abroad.

"Final Rites," *Alfred Hitchcock's Mystery Magazine* (hereafter *AHMM*), December 1985 (Robert L. Fish Award Winner for best first short story from the Mystery Writers of America)
"Firebomb," *AHMM*, May1986
*"Wolf Country," *AHMM*, September 1986
*"The Puddle Diver," *AHMM*, October 1986 (Nominated for an Edgar Award for best short story by the Mystery Writers of America)
"Homecoming," *AHMM*, December 1986
"Death of a Poet," *AHMM*, April 1987
"Witch," *AHMM*, January 1987
"Supersport," *AHMM*, December 1987
*"The Ching Lady," *AHMM*, March 1988

"Bloodlines" *AHMM*, February 1988

*"Deja Vu," *AHMM*, January 1988 (Nominated for an Edgar Award)

"Night of the Grave Dancer," *AHMM*, September 1988

"Lancaster's Ghost," *AHMM*, Mid December 1988

"A Death in Heaven," *Ellery Queen's Mystery Magazine* (hereafter *EQMM*), December 1988 (Sold to movies)

"Evil Spirits," *AHMM*, January 1989

"Debt of Honor," *EQMM*, January 1989

"The Last Reunion," *EQMM*, June 1989

"Cannibal," *AHMM*, November 1989

*"Star Pupil," *EQMM*, October 1989 (2nd place *EQMM* Readers Award)

"Mojo Man," *AHMM*, October 1990

*"Sleeper," *EQMM*, May 1991 (Nominated for an Edgar Award)

"Speed Demon," *EQMM*, October 1991

*"Icewater Mansions," *EQMM*, January 1992 (3rd place *EQMM* Readers Award)

"Ten Pound Parrott," *EQMM*, February 1992

*"Candles in the Rain," *EQMM*, November 1992 (1st place *EQMM* Readers Award; won American Mystery Award for best short story; nominated for Edgar and Anthony Awards)

"The Sultans of Soul," *EQMM*, March 1993 (Nominated for a Shamus Award; Hardboiled 10 Best List)

"The Meistersinger," *AHMM*, September 1993

"Dancing on the Centerline," *EQMM*, October 1993

*"The Ghost Show," *EQMM*, December 1993 (Nominated for an Edgar Award)

"Pageant," *EQMM*, Mid December 1993

"Fire Lake," *EQMM* April 1994

*"The Dancing Bear," *AHMM*, March 1994 (Winner of the Edgar Award for best short story)

"Black Water," *EQMM*, August 1994 (2nd place *EQMM* Readers Award)

"Wrecker," *EQMM*, November 1994

"The Bearded Lady," *EQMM*, December 1994

"The Cross Wolf," *EQMM*, Mid December 1994 (3rd place *EQMM* Readers Award)

"Demons," *EQMM*, February 1996

"Franken Kat," *EQMM*, Mid-December 1995   (1st place *EQMM* Readers Award; included in *All Creatures Dark and Dangerous*)

"Blind Lemon," *AHMM*, May 1996

"Roadkill," *EQMM*, May 1996 (1st place *EQMM* Readers Award; included in *All Creatures Dark and Dangerous*)

"Animal Rites," *EQMM*, July 1996 (Included in *All Creatures Dark and Dangerous*)

"Puppyland," *EQMM*, September/October 1996 (2nd place *EQMM* Readers Award; included in *All Creatures Dark and Dangerous*)

"Green as Grass," *EQMM*, November 1996

"Money Face," *EQMM*, December 1996

"The Beaches of Paraguay," *EQMM*, May 1997 (Included in *All Creatures Dark and Dangerous*)

"Bush Leaguer," *AHMM* April 1997

"Copperhead Run," *EQMM*, June 1997 (2nd place *EQMM* Readers Award)

"Cedar Savage," *EQMM*, March 1998 (Included in *All Creatures Dark and Dangerous*)

"Crippen, Landru, and Carlos Palomino," *EQMM*, August 1998 (Included in *All Creatures Dark and Dangerous*)

"The Taxi Dancer," *AHMM* , October 1998

"St. Margaret's Kitten," *Cat Crimes Through Time*, 1999 (Also included as a separate pamphlet with the limited edition of *All Creatures Dark and Dangerous*)

"Saint Bobby," *EQMM*, April 1999

All Creatures Dark and Dangerous

All Creature Dark and Dangerous by Doug Allyn is printed on 60-pound Glatfelter Supple Opaque recycled acid-free paper, from 12-point Baskerville. The cover painting is by Barbara Mitchell and the cover design is by Deborah Miller. The first edition comprises two hundred copies sewn in cloth, signed and numbered by the author, and approximately one thousand copies in trade softcover. Each clothbound copy includes a separate pamphlet, *Saint Margaret's Kitten*, by Doug Allyn. *All Creatures Dark and Dangerous* was printed and bound by Thomson-Shore, Inc., Dexter, Michigan, and published in May 1999 by Crippen & Landru Publishers, Norfolk, Virginia.

CRIPPEN & LANDRU, PUBLISHERS

P. O. Box 9315
Norfolk, VA 23505

Crippen & Landru publishes first editions of important works by detective and mystery writers, specializing in short-story collections. Most books are published both in trade softcover and in signed, limited clothbound with either a typescript page from the author's files or an additional story in a separate pamphlet. The following books have been published:

Speak of the Devil by John Dickson Carr. Eight-part impossible crime mystery broadcast on BBC radio. Introduction by Tony Medawar; cover design by Deborah Miller.   Out of Print

The McCone Files by Marcia Muller. Fifteen Sharon McCone short stories by the creator of the modern female private eye, including two written especially for the collection. Winner of the Anthony Award for Best Short Story collection. Introduction by the author; cover painting by Carol Heyer.

Signed, limited edition, Out of Print
Softcover, fourth printing, $15.00

The Darings of the Red Rose by Margery Allingham. Eight crook stories about a female Robin Hood, written in 1930 by the creator of the classic sleuth, Albert Campion. Introduction by B. A. Pike; cover design by Deborah Miller.   Softcover, Out of Print

Diagnosis: Impossible, The Problems of Dr. Sam Hawthorne by Edward D. Hoch. Twelve stories about the country doctor who solves "miracle problems," written by the greatest current expert on the challenge-to-the-reader story. Introduction by the author; chronology by Marvin Lachman; cover painting by Carol Heyer.

Signed, limited edition, Out of Print
Softcover, Out of Stock

Spadework: A Collection of "Nameless Detective" Stories by Bill Pronzini. Fifteen stories, including two written for the collection, by a Grandmaster of the Private Eye tale. Introduction by Marcia Muller; afterword by the author; cover painting by Carol Heyer.

Signed, limited edition, $40.00
Softcover, $16.00

Who Killed Father Christmas? And Other Unseasonable Demises by Patricia Moyes. Twenty-one stories ranging from holiday homicides to village villainies to Caribbean crimes. Introduction by the author; cover design by Deborah Miller.

> Signed, limited edition, $40.00
> Softcover, $16.00

My Mother, The Detective: The Complete "Mom" Short Stories, by James Yaffe. Eight stories about the Bronx armchair maven who solves crimes between the chicken soup and the *schnecken*. Introduction by the author; cover painting by Carol Heyer.

> Signed, limited edition, Out of Print
> Softcover, $15.00

In Kensington Gardens Once . . . by H. R. F. Keating. Ten crime and mystery stories taking place in London's famous park, including two written for this collection, by the recipient of the Cartier Diamond Dagger for Lifetime Achievement. Illustrations and cover by Gwen Mandley.

> Signed, limited edition, $35.00
> Softcover, $12.00

Shoveling Smoke: Selected Mystery Stories by Margaret Maron. Twenty-two stories by the Edgar-award winning author, including all the short cases of Sigrid Harald and Deborah Knott, including a new Knott story. Introduction and prefaces to each story by the author; cover painting by Victoria Russell.

> Signed, limited edition, Out of Print
> Softcover, second printing, $16.00

The Man Who Hated Banks and Other Mysteries by Michael Gilbert. Eighteen stories by the recipient of the Mystery Writers of America's Grandmaster Award, including mysteries featuring Inspectors Petrella and Hazlerigg, rogue cop Bill Mercer, and solicitor Henry Bohun. Introduction by the author; cover painting by Deborah Miller.

> Signed, limited edition, Out of Print
> Softcover, second printing, $16.00

The Ripper of Storyville and Other Ben Snow Tales by Edward D. Hoch. The first fourteen historical detective stories about Ben Snow, the wandering gunslinger who is often confused with Billy the Kid. Introduction by the author; Ben Snow chronology by Marvin Lachman; cover painting by Barbara Mitchell.

> Signed, limited edition, Out of Print
> Softcover, $16.00

Do Not Exceed the Stated Dose by Peter Lovesey. Fifteen crime and mystery stories, including two featuring Peter Diamond and two featuring Bertie, Prince of Wales. Preface by the author; cover painting by Carol Heyer.
Signed, limited edition, Out of Print
Softcover, $16.00

Renowned Be Thy Grave; Or, The Murderous Miss Mooney by P. M. Carlson. Ten stories about Bridget Mooney, the Victorian actress who becomes involved in important historical events. Introduction by the author; cover design by Deborah Miller.
Signed, limited edition, $40.00
Softcover, $16.00

Carpenter and Quincannon, Professional Detective Services by Bill Pronzini. Nine detective stories, including one written for this volume, set in San Francisco during the 1890's. Introduction by the author; cover painting by Carol Heyer.
Signed, limited edition, Out of Print
Softcover, second printing, $16.00

Not Safe After Dark and Other Stories by Peter Robinson. Thirteen stories about Inspector Banks and others, including one written for this volume. Introduction and prefaces to each story by the author; cover painting by Victoria Russell.
Signed, limited edition, Out of Print
Softcover, second printing, $16.00

The Concise Cuddy, A Collection of John Francis Cuddy Stories by Jeremiah Healy. Seventeen stories about the Boston private eye by the Shamus Award winner. Introduction by the author; cover painting by Carol Heyer.
Signed, limited edition, Out of Print
Softcover, $17.00

One Night Stands by Lawrence Block. Twenty-four early tough crime stories from the legendary digest magazines—*Manhunt, Keyhole, Offbeat, Two-Fisted, Trapped, Guilty*, and others—by a Grandmaster of the Mystery Writers of America. Introduction by the author; cover painting by Deborah Miller. Published only in a signed, limited edition.
Out of Print

All Creatures Dark and Dangerous by Doug Allyn. Seven long stories about the veterinarian detective Dr. David Westbrook by the Edgar and (multiple) Ellery Queen Readers Award winner. Introduction by the author; cover painting by Barbara Mitchell.
Signed, limited edition, $40.00
Trade softcover, $16.00